SIMON TEMPLAR faced the customs officer with an easy smile. "Yes," he said, "I'm carrying large quantities of silks, perfumes, wines, tobacco, watches, and explosives. I also have some opium and a couple of howitzers. . ." "You don't have to be funny about it, anyway," grunted the official, and scrawled the cryptic hieroglyphics that passed him through with his two guns into England . . .

Simon Templar—alias the Saint—pursues his battle with Chief Inspector Teal of Scotland Yard; always on the side of justice, seldom the law!

He might have been the greatest detective in England; he chose to be the Saint!

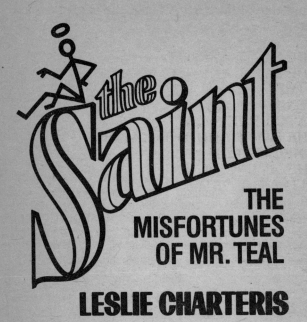

the Saint

THE MISFORTUNES OF MR. TEAL

LESLIE CHARTERIS

CHARTER
NEW YORK

A DIVISION OF CHARTER COMMUNICATIONS INC.
A GROSSET & DUNLAP COMPANY
51 Madison Avenue
New York, New York 10010

THE MISFORTUNES OF MR. TEAL
Copyright © 1934 by Leslie Charteris

An Ace Charter Book
by arrangement with Doubleday & Co.

TO
TOOTS AND JOANNE
who have been helping
for years

First Ace Charter Printing: April 1982
Published simultaneously in Canada

2 4 6 8 0 9 7 5 3 1

Printed in U.S.A.

CONTENTS

I

The Simon Templar Foundation.   P. 3

II

The Higher Finance   P. 109

III

The Art of Alibi   P. 215

I

THE SIMON TEMPLAR FOUNDATION

I

THERE was nothing unusual about the fact that when Simon Templar landed in England he was expecting trouble. Trouble was his chosen vocation: the last ten years of his life had held enough of it to satisfy a couple of dozen ordinary men for three or four lifetimes, and it would have been surprising if after so many hectic events he had contemplated a future of rustic quietude, enlivened by nothing more thrilling than wild gambles on the laying abilities of Leghorns. But it was perhaps more unusual that the particular trouble which he was expecting on this occasion could not be blamed on any fault of his.

He came down the gangway of the *Transylvania* with a light step in the summer sunlight, with a soft grey hat canted rakishly over one eye and a raincoat slung carelessly over his shoulder. There was death in his pocket and peril of an even deadlier kind under his arm; but he faced the customs officer across his well-labelled luggage with an easy smile and ran a humorous glance down the list of dutiable and prohibited articles presented for his inspection.

"Yes," he said, "I'm carrying large quantities of

silk, perfume, wines, spirits, tobacco, cut flowers, watches, embroidery, eggs, typewriters, and explosives. I also have some opium and a couple of howitzers——"

"You don't have to be funny about it, anyway," grunted the official and scrawled the cryptic hieroglyphics that passed him through with his two guns into England.

He sauntered on through the bleak echoing shed, waving casual adieus to his acquaintances of the voyage. An American banker from Ohio, who had lost three thousand dollars to him over the poker table, buttonholed him without malice.

"See you look me up next time you're in Wapakoneta," he said.

"I won't forget," Simon answered gravely.

There was a girl with raven hair and deep grey eyes. She was very good to look upon, and Simon had sat out with her on the boat deck under the moon.

"Perhaps you'll be coming to Sacramento one day," she said.

"Maybe I will," he said with a quick smile; and the deep grey eyes followed him rather wistfully out of sight.

Other eyes followed the tall lean figure as it swung by, and carried their own pictures of the brown fighting face and the smile that touched the strong reckless mouth and the gay blue eyes. They belonged to a Miss Gertrude Tinwiddle, who had been seasick all the way over, and who would never have been taken onto the boat deck anyhow.

"Who is that man?" she asked.

"His name is Templar," said her neighbour, who knew everything. "And you mark my words, there's something queer about him. I shouldn't be surprised if he was a sort of gangster."

"He looks like a—a sort of cavalier," said Miss Tinwiddle timidly.

"Pish!" said her companion testily and returned to the grim task of trying to convince a cynical customs officer that twenty-four silk dresses would have been a beggarly allowance even for a week-end traveller.

At the end of the shed Detective Sergeant Harry Jepson, of the Southampton C. I. D., said to Police Constable Ernest Potts:

"You see the tall fellow in the grey tweeds coming this way? Handsome devil, isn't he? Well, you'd better remember that face."

"Who is he?" asked Police Constable Potts.

"That," said Sergeant Jepson, "is Mr. Simon Templar, alias the Saint; and you aren't likely to see a smarter crook than him in your time. At least, I hope not. He's committed every blooming crime there is from murder downwards, and he'll tell you so himself, but nobody's ever been able to hang a thing on him. And to look at him you'd think he had a conscience like a new-born babe."

In which utterance Detective Sergeant Harry Jepson was as close to eternal truth as he was ever likely to get; for the Saint had never been sure that he had a conscience at all, but if he had one there was certainly nothing on it. He looked the two officers shamelessly in the eye as he approached, and as he strolled past them his right hand waved a quizzical salute that had no regard whatever for the affronted majesty of the Law.

"D'you ever hear of such blooming sauce?" demanded Mr. Jepson indignantly.

But Simon Templar, who was called the Saint, neither heard nor cared. He stood on the railroad platform, tapping a cigarette on a thin platinum case, and panned a thoughtful and quietly vigilant eye along the whole length of the train. He was expecting somebody to meet him, but he knew that it would not be anyone whose welcome would be friendly; and he had the additional disadvantage of not even being able to guess what the welcomer might look like. The Saint's vocation was trouble, but he had contrived to stay alive for thirty-two years only because of an unceasing devotion to the business of divining where the trouble would come from and meeting it on his toes.

"Wantcher luggidge in the van, sir?" asked the porter who was wheeling his barrow.

The Saint's gaze travelled round to measure up two suitcases and a wardrobe trunk.

"I think so, George," he murmured. "I shouldn't be able to run very far with that load, should I?"

He took over his small overnight bag and saw the rest of his impedimenta registered through to his apartment on Piccadilly. He was still carrying the black book under his arm, and it occurred to him that there were more convenient forms of camouflage for it than the slung raincoat by which it was temporarily hidden. He paused at the book-stall and glanced over the volumes of fiction offered for the entertainment of the traveller. In the circumstances, his choice had to be dictated by size rather than subject matter.

"I'll take this," he said brazenly; and the assistant's eyes bulged slightly as he paid over three half-crowns for a copy of an opus entitled *Her Wedding Secret*.

A signpost adjoining the bookstall invited Gentlemen to enter and make themselves at home, and the Saint drifted through with his purchase. No other Gentlemen were availing themselves of the Southern Railway's hospitality at the time, and it was the work of a moment to slip the intriguing jacket from the volume he had just bought and transfer it to the black book from under his arm, where it fitted quite comfortably. He pitched the unknown lady's wedding secret dexterously through the skylight and went out again with the newly jacketed black book conspicuously flaunted in his hand—no one who had been watching him would have had any reason to suspect that there had been any change in the contents of that artis-tically suggestive wrapper.

There were several minutes left before the train was due to leave, and the Saint strolled unhur-riedly along the platform with his bag, as though selecting a carriage. If the welcomer or welcomers that he expected were there, he wanted to help them in every possible way. He covered the whole length of the train before he turned back, and then made his choice of an empty smoker. Pushing his suitcase up onto the rack, and dumping his rain-coat and book on a corner seat, he leaned out of the window and slid another idly thoughtful glance over the scene.

A military-looking man of about forty-five, with a strongly aquiline nose and a black guardee moustache, came slowly down the platform. He passed the window without looking round, walked on a little way, and turned. He stood there for a while, teetering toe to heel and gazing vacantly over the gallery of posters plastered on the opposite wall; then he came back, past the Saint's window again, circumnavigated a farewell party congre-gated outside the next carriage, and did the same thing on the other side.

The Saint's cool blue eyes never once looked directly at him; his brown keen-cut face never changed its expression from one of languid pa-tience; but he had seen every movement of the military-looking man's manœuvres. And Simon Templar knew, beyond a shadow of doubt, that this was at least one of the welcomers whom he had been expecting.

Along the train came a bustle of belated activity, the banging of doors, the scream of the guard's whistle. Simon remained in his window, finishing his cigarette, and saw the military-looking man climb into an adjoining compartment. The engine let out a hiss of steam, and the platform began to slip back under his eyes.

Simon dropped his cigarette and settled back into his corner. He turned the pages of the black book in its new wrapper, refreshing his memory. The action was more automatic than deliberate, only different in degree from a nervous person's gesture in twiddling his thumbs while waiting on tenterhooks for some anticipated event to happen. The Saint already knew almost every line of that amazing volume by heart—he had had plenty of time to study it from cover to cover on the voyage over. The odds were about fifty to one that the military-looking man was mentioned somewhere in its pages; but it was rather difficult to decide, out of the available names, which one he was most likely to bear.

The conductor came round and collected tickets; and then fifteen minutes passed before the door of the Saint's compartment slid back again. Simon closed his book and looked up with exactly the conventional nuance of irritated curiosity which darkens the distinguished features of the railroad passenger who has contrived to secure a compartment to himself and who finds his privary illegitimately invaded at the last moment; but the military-looking man put his back to the door and stared at him with a grimness that was by no means conventional.

"Come on," he said grimly. "Give me that book!"

"What, this?" said the Saint in innocent surprise, raising *Her Wedding Secret*. "You're welcome to it when I've finished, brother, but I hardly think it's in your line. I've only got to the part where she discovers that the man she has married is a Barbarian Lover——"

The intruder pushed the unoffending volume roughly aside.

"I don't mean that," he said shortly. "You know perfectly well what book I mean."

"I'm afraid I don't," said the Saint.

"And you know perfectly well," continued the intruder, "what I'm going to do to you if I don't get it."

Simon shook his head.

"I can't guess that one, either," he remarked mildly. "What is it—slap my wrist and tell me to stand in the corner?"

The man's mouth was working under his moustache. He came further into the compartment, past the Saint, and jerked a small automatic from his pocket. It was an almost pathetically amateurish movement—Simon could have forestalled it easily, but he wanted to see how far the other would go.

"Very well," grated the man. "I'll have to take it myself. Put 'em up!"

"Up what?" asked the Saint, doing his best to understand.

"Put your hands up. And don't think of any more of that funny stuff, or you'll be sorry for it."

Simon put his hands up lazily. His bag was on the rack directly over his head, and the handle was within an inch of his fingers.

"I suppose the keepers will be along to collect you in a minute, old fruit," he drawled. "Or do you fancy yourself as a sort of highwayman?"

"Now listen, you bastard," came the snarling answer. "I'm going to allow you five seconds to give me that book. If I haven't got it in that time, I'm going to shoot. I'll start counting now. One . . . two . . ."

There was a crazy red glare in the intruder's eyes, and although the gun was shaking unsteadily something told Simon that he had permitted the melodrama to go far enough.

"You know all the rules, don't you, brother?" he said gently; and his fingers grasped the handle of his bag and hurled it full into the other's face.

The man reeled back with the force of the impact and went crashing against the outside door. It flew open under his weight; and the Saint's blue eyes turned to sudden ice as he realized that it could not have been properly latched when he got in. For one awful instant the man's fingers clawed at the frame; and then with a choking gasp he was gone, and there was only the drab streaked wall of the cutting roaring by the door. . . .

Simon's hand reached up instinctively towards the communication cord. And then it drew back.

The intruder, whoever he was, had asked for it: he had taken his own chances. And although Simon Templar had only done what was justified in self-defense, he knew his own reputation at Scotland Yard too well to believe for a moment that it would be a brief and simple task to impress that fact upon the suspicious hostility of the C. I. D. To stop the train would achieve nothing more helpful than his own immediate arrest; and of all the things which might happen to him while he had that black book in his possession, an interlude behind bars in Brixton Prison was the least exhilarating.

He caught the swinging door and closed it again and then restored his suitcase to the rack. The unknown casualty's gun had gone out with him—there was no other evidence that he had ever entered the compartment.

The Saint lighted a cigarette and sat down again, listening to the rhythmic thrum and rattle of the wheels pounding over the metals towards London. There was nothing unusual about the fact that he was expecting trouble when he returned to Europe, or even about the fact that a fair sample of that trouble should have greeted him within such a short time of setting foot in England.

But it was perhaps more unusual that the particular trouble he was expecting could not be blamed on any fault of his. And the queerest thing of all was that everything should hinge around the black book on his knee which was the legacy of

Rayt Marius—the strangest and deadliest gift that any man ever received.

II

HE WAS one of the first passengers to alight from the train at Waterloo, with his raincoat slung over his shoulder and the book in his hand; but he did not take the first available taxi. He allowed six to go by him, and boarded the seventh after taking a good look at it.

"Hyde Park Corner," he directed it clearly and watched the traffic out of the rear window as they drove away.

Another taxi swung in behind them, and he noted the number. Five minutes later he looked back again, and it was still there. Simon pressed the button of the telephone.

"Turn right round at Hyde Park Corner and go back the way we've come," he said.

He waited a short time after his instructions had been carried out, and looked back for the third time. The other taxi was plugging patiently along three yards behind, and the Saint's teeth gleamed in a thin smile. Coincidence of destination was one thing, but coincidence of such a radical change of direction as he had ordered his driver to carry out was quite another matter.

"Now we'll go through the Green Park and up St. James's Street," he said through the telephone.

The driver was so moved that he opened the door an inch and performed incredible contortions to yell back through it.

"Wot is this?" he demanded. "A game of 'ide and seek?"

"You have no idea," said the Saint.

The apartment he was heading for was on the north side of Piccadilly, overlooking the Green Park. It was only one of many addresses that he had had at various times, to several of which he still owned the keys; but it was the one which had been prepared for his return, and he had no intention of being prevented from going there. The only question was how the shadowing party was to be shaken off.

As they ran up St. James's Street he looked at the meter and counted off the necessary change to pay the fare with a substantial tip. When the next traffic light reddened against them he stretched a long arm through the window and thrust the money into the driver's hand.

"I shall be leaving you any minute now, Alphonse," he said. "But don't let that stop you. Keep right on your way, and don't look back till you get to Hyde Park Corner. And have a bob on Samovar for the Derby."

He had the door on the latch as they passed the Ritz, and his steel-blue eyes were watching the traffic intently. Three buses were taking on passengers at the stop just west of the hotel, and as they went past the leader was edging out into

the stream. Simon looked back and saw it cut out
close behind him, baulking the following taxi; and
that was his chance. In a flash he was out of his
cab, dropping nimbly to the road, and the red side
of the bus thundered by a couple of inches from
his shoulder. It hid him perfectly from whoever
was trailing him in the other cab, which was trying
to pass the obstruction and catch up again; and he
stood on the sidewalk and watched the whole
futile procession trundling away westwards with
a relentless zeal which brought an irresponsible
twinkle of sheer urchin mischief into his eyes.

A few minutes later he was sauntering into his
apartment building and nodding cheerily to the
janitor.

"Anybody called while I've been away, Sam?"
he asked, as if he had only been away for a week-
end.

Sam Outrell's beam of delight gave way to a
troubled gravity. He looked furtively about him.

"There was two detectives here the other day,
sir," he said.

The Saint frowned at him thoughtfully for a
moment. Although Sam Outrell was nominally
employed by the management of the building, he
was on Simon Templar's private payroll as well;
but no stipend could have bought the look of
almost doglike devotion with which he waited anxiously for the Saint's reaction. Simon looked up at
him again and smiled.

"I expect they were the birds I hired to try and

find a collar stud that went down the waste pipe," he said and went whistling on his way to the lift.

He let himself into his apartment noiselessly. There were sounds of someone moving about in the living room, and he only stopped to throw his hat and coat onto a chair before he went through and opened the second door.

"Hullo, Pat," he said softly. "I thought you'd be here."

Across the room, a tall slender girl with fair golden hair gazed at him with eyes as blue as his own. There was the grace of a pagan goddess in the way she stood, caught in surprise as she was by the sound of his voice, and the reward of all journeys in the quiver of her red lips.

"So you have come back," she said.

"After many adventures," said the Saint and took her into his arms.

She turned away presently, keeping his arm round her, and showed him the table.

"I got in a bottle of your favourite sherry," she said rather breathlessly, "in case you came."

"In case?" said the Saint.

"Well, after you wired me not to meet you at Southampton——"

He laughed, a quiet lilt of laughter that had rung in her memory for many weeks.

"Darling, that was because I was expecting another deputation of welcome at the same time, and it might have spoilt the fun for both of us. The deputation was there, too—but you shall hear about that presently."

He filled the two glasses which stood beside the bottle and carried one of them over to an armchair. Over the rim of his glass he regarded her, freshening the portrait which he had carried with him ever since he went away. So much had happened to him, so many things had touched him and passed on into the illimitable emptiness of time, but not one line of her had changed. She was the same as she had been on the day when he first met her, the same as she had been through all the lawless adventures that they had shared since she threw in her lot irrevocably with his. She looked at him in the same way.

"You're older," she said quietly.

He smiled.

"I haven't been on a picnic."

"And there's something about you that tells me you aren't on a picnic even now."

He sipped the golden nectar from his glass and delved for a cigarette. When she said that he was older she could not have pointed to a grey hair or a new line on his face to prove her statement. And at that moment she felt that the clock might well have been put back five years. The fine sunburnt devil-may-care face, the face of a born outlaw, was in some subtle way more keenly etched than ever by the indefinable inward light that came to it when trouble loomed up in his buccaneering path. She knew him so well that the lazy quirk of the unscrupulous freebooter's mouth told a story of its own, and even the whimsical smile that lurked on in his eyes could not deceive her.

"It isn't my fault if you develop these psychic powers, old sweetheart," he said.

"It's your fault if you can't even stay out of trouble for a week now and again," she said and sat on the arm of his chair.

He shook his head and took one of her hands.

"I tried to, Pat, but it just wasn't meant to happen. A wicked ogre with a black guardee moustache hopped through a window and said 'Boo!' and my halo blew off. If I wanted to, I could blame it all on you."

"How?"

"For just managing to catch me in Boston before I sailed, with that parcel you forwarded!"

Patricia Holm puckered her sweet brow.

"Parcel? . . . Oh, I think I remember it. A thing about the size of a book—it came from Monte Carlo, didn't it?"

"It came from Monte Carlo," said the Saint carefully, "and it was certainly about the size of a book. In fact, it was a book. It was the most amazing book I've ever read—maybe the most amazing book that was ever written. There it is!"

He pointed to the volume which he had put down on the table, and she stared at it and then back at him in utter perplexity.

"*Her Wedding Secret?*" she said. "Have you gone mad or have I?"

"Neither of us," said the Saint. "But you wouldn't believe how many other people are mad about it."

She looked at him in bewildered exasperation. He was standing up again, a debonair wide-shouldered figure against the sunlight that streamed in through the big windows and lengthened the evening shadows of the trees in the Green Park. She felt the spell of his daredevil delight as irresistible as it had always been, the absurd glamour which could even take half the sting from his moments of infuriating mysteriousness. He smiled, and his hands went to her shoulders.

"Listen, Pat," he said. "That book is a present from an old friend, and he knew what he was doing when he sent it to me. When I show it to you, you'll see that it's the most devilishly clever revenge that ever came out of a human brain. But before we go any further, I want you to know that there's more power in that book for the man who's got it than anyone else in England has today, and for that very reason——"

The sharp trill of the telephone bell cut him off. He looked at the instrument for a moment and then lifted the receiver.

"Hullo," he said.

"This is Outrell, sir," said an agitated voice. "Those two detectives I told you about—they've just bin here again. They're on their way up to you now, sir."

Simon gazed dreamily at the ceiling for a

second or two, and his fingertips played a gently syncopated tattoo on the side table.

"Okay, Sam," he said. "I'll give them your love."

He replaced the instrument and stood with his hand on it, looking at Patricia. His level blue eyes were mocking and enigmatic, but this time at least she knew enough of his system to read beyond them.

"Hadn't you better hide the book?" she said.

"It is hidden," he answered, touching the gaudy wrapper. "And we may as well have a look at these sleuths."

The ringing of another bell put a short stop to further discussion, and with a last smile at her he went out to open the door. The trouble was coming thick and fast, and there were tiny chisellings at the corners of his mouth to offset the quiet amusement in his eyes. But he only stopped long enough in the little hall to transfer the automatic from his hip pocket to a pocket in his raincoat, and then he opened the door wide with a face of seraphic tranquillity.

Two men in dark suits stood on the mat outside. Both of them wore bowler hats; neither of them carried sticks or gloves.

"Mr. Simon Templar?" queried one of them, in a voice of astounding refinement.

Simon nodded, and they moved determinedly through the door with a concerted solidity which

would certainly have obstructed any attempt he
might have made to slam it in their faces.

"I am Inspector Nassen," said the genteel
spokesman, "and I have a warrant to search your
flat."

"Bless my soul!" ejaculated the Saint, with his
juiciest lisp. "So you're one of our new public-
school policemen. How perfectly sweet!"

The other's lips tightened.

"We'll start with searching you," he said shortly.

His hands ran over the Saint's pockets in a few
efficient movements which were sufficient to assure
him that Simon had no lethal weapon on his person. The Saint restrained a natural impulse to
smack him on the nose and smiled instead.

"This is a great game, Snowdrop, isn't it?" he
said. "Personally I'm broad-minded, but if you did
these things to a lady she might misunderstand
you."

Nassen's pale face flushed wrathfully, and an
unholy gleam came into the Saint's eye. Of all the
detectives who ought never to have called upon
him, one who was so easily baited was booked for
a rough passage before he ever set out.

"We'll go over the flat now," he said.

Simon led them into the living room and calmly
set about refilling his sherry glass.

"Pat," he explained casually, "these are two
little fairies who just popped through the keyhole.
They seem to want to search the place and see if

it's all cleany-weeny. Shall we let them get on with it?"

"I suppose so," said Patricia tolerantly. "Did they wipe their tootsy-wootsies before they came in?"

"I'm afraid not," said the Saint. "You see, they aren't very well-bred little fairies. But when you have a beautiful Oxford accent you aren't supposed to need manners as well. You should just hear Snowdrop talking. Sounds as if all his teeth were loose. . . ."

He went on in the same vein throughout the search, with an inexhaustible resource of wicked glee, and it was two very red and spluttering men who faced him after they had ransacked every room under the running commentary with which he enlivened their tour.

"Get your hat," Nassen said. "You're coming along with us."

Simon put down his glass—they were back in the living room then.

"On what charge, Snowdrop?" he inquired.

"The charge is being in possession of information contrary to the Official Secrets Act."

"It sounds a mouthful," Simon admitted. "Shall I pack my powder puff as well, or will you be able to lend me one?"

"Get your hat!" Nassen choked out in a shaking voice.

The Saint put a cigarette between his lips and stroked a thumb over the cog of his lighter. He looked at Patricia through the first feather of smoke, returning the lighter to his pocket, and the careless twinkle in his eyes might or might not have been an integral part of the smile that flitted across his brown face.

"It looks as if we shall have to finish our talk later, old darling," he murmured. "Snowdrop is in a hurry. Save some sherry for me, will you?—I shan't be long."

Almost incredulously, but with a sudden leap of uncomprehending fear, she watched him saunter serenely from the room, and through the open door she saw him pick up his raincoat from the hall chair and pause to adjust his soft hat to its correct piratical angle before he went out. Long after he had gone, she was still trying to make herself believe that she had seen Simon Templar, the man who had tantalized all the forces of law and order in the world for more years than any of them liked to be reminded of, arrested as easily as that.

III

RIDING in a taxi between the two detectives, the Saint looked at his watch and saw that he had been in England less than four hours, and he had to admit that the pace was fairly rapid even by his exacting standards. One whiskered hold-up merchant, an unidentified shadower in a taxi, and two public-school detectives worked out at a reasonably hectic average for the time involved; but Simon knew that that was only a preliminary sample of the kind of attention he could expect while he remained the holder of *Her Wedding Secret*.

On either side of him, Nassen and the other sleuth licked their sores in silence. Whether they were completely satisfied with the course of events so far is not known, nor does the chronicler feel that posterity will greatly care. Simon thought kindly of other possible ways of adding to their martyrdom; but before he had made his final choice of the various forms of torment at his disposal the taxi was stopped by a traffic light at the corner of St. James's Street, and the Saint looked through the window from a range of less than two yards full into the chubby red face and sleepy eyes of the man without whom none of his adventures were really complete.

Before either of the other two could stop him, he had slung himself forward and loosed a delighted yell through the open window.

"Claud Eustace, by the bed socks of Dr. Barnardo!" cried the Saint joyfully.

The man's drowsy optics revolved towards the source of the sound, and, having located it, widened with indescribable eloquence. For a second or two he actually stopped chewing on his gum. His jaws seized up, and his portly bowler-hatted figure halted statuesquely.

There were cogent and fundamental reasons for

the tableau—reasons which were carved in imper-
ishable letters across the sluggish coagulation of
emotions which Chief Inspector Claud Eustace
Teal himself would have been much too diffident
to call his soul. They were reasons which went
'way back through the detective's life to those
almost unimaginably distant blissful days before
anyone in England had ever heard of the Saint—
the days when a policeman's lot had been a reasonably happy one, moving through well-ordered
grooves to a stolid and methodical percentage of
success, and there had been no such incalculable
filibuster sweeping at intervals into the peaceful
scene to tie all averages in knots and ride such
rings round the wrath and vengeance of Scotland
Yard as had never been ridden before. They were
reasons which could have been counted one by one
on Mr. Teal's grey hairs; and all of them surged
out of his memory in a solid phalanx at such moments as that, when the Saint returned to England
after an all-too-brief absence, and Mr. Teal saw
him in London again and knew that the tale was
no nearer its end than it had ever been.

All these things came back to burden Mr. Teal's
overloaded heart in that moment's motionless
stare; and then with a sigh he stepped to the window of the taxicab and faced his future stoically.

"Hullo," he said.

The Saint's eyebrows went up in a rising slant
of mockery.

"Claud!" he protested. "Is that kind? I ask you,

is that a brotherly welcome? Anyone might think you weren't pleased to see me."

"I'm not," said Mr. Teal dourly. "But I shall have to see you."

The Saint smiled.

"Hop in," he invited hospitably. "We're going your way."

Teal shook his head—that is the simplest way of describing the movement, but it was such a perfunctory gesture that it simply looked as if he had thought of making it and had subsequently decided that he was too tired.

"Thanks," he said. "I've got another job to do just now. And you seem to be in good company." His baby-blue eyes, restored to their habitual affectation of sleepiness, moved over the two embarrassed men who flanked the Saint. "You know who you're with, boys," he told them. "Watch him."

"Pardon me," said the Saint hastily. "I forgot to do the honours. This specimen on my left is Snowdrop, the Rose of Peckham——"

"All right," said Teal grimly. "I know them. And I'll bet they're going to wish they'd never known you—if they haven't begun wishing it already." The traffic light was at green again, and the hooting of impatient drivers held up behind made the detective step back from the window. "I'll see you later," he said and waved the taxi on.

The Saint grinned and settled back again, as the cab turned south towards the Park. That chance encounter had set the triumphal capstone on his homecoming: it was the last familiar chord of the old opening chorus, his guarantee that the old days had finally come back in all their glory. The one jarring note was in the sinister implications of Teal's parting speech. Ever frank and open, the Saint sought to compare opinions on the subject.

"It sounds," he murmured, "almost as if Claud Eustace had something on his mind. Didn't it sound that way to you, Snowdrop?"

Nassen was wiping his forehead with a large white handkerchief; and he seemed deaf to the advance. His genteel sensitive soul had been bruised, and he had lost the spirit of such candid camaraderie. He put his handkerchief away and slipped an automatic from his pocket. Simon felt the muzzle probe into his ribs, and glanced down at it with one satirical eyebrow raised.

"You know, you could kill someone with that," he said reprovingly.

"I wish it could be you," said the Rose of Peckham in a tone of passionate earnestness, and relapsed into morbid silence.

Simon chuckled and lighted another cigarette. The gun in his own raincoat pocket rested comfortingly across his thigh, but he saw no need to advertise his own armoury. He watched their route with patient interest—they emerged at Parliament Square, but instead of turning down to the Embankment they circled the square and went back up Victoria Street.

"I suppose you know this isn't the way to Scotland Yard, Snowdrop?" he remarked helpfully.

"This is the way you're going first," Nassen told him.

The Saint shrugged. They turned quickly off Victoria Street, and pulled up shortly afterwards outside a house in one of those almost stupefyingly sombre and respectable squares in the district known to its residents as Belgravia but to the vulgar public, less pretentiously, as Pimlico. Nassen's colleague got out and went up the steps to ring the bell, and the Saint followed under the unnecessarily aggressive propulsion of Nassen's gun.

The door was opened by one of the most magnificently majestic butlers that the Saint had ever seen. He seemed to be expecting them, for he stood aside immediately, and the Saint was led quickly through the hall into a spacious library on the ground floor.

"I will inform his lordship of your arrival," said the butler and left them there.

Simon Templar, who had been taking in his surroundings with untroubled interest, turned round as the door closed.

"You ought to have told me we were going to visit a Lord, Snowdrop," he said reproachfully. "I'd have put on my Old Etonian suspenders and washed my neck. I know you washed your neck to-day, because I can see the line where you left off."

Nassen tugged at his lower lip and simmered audibly, but his woes had passed beyond the remedy of repartee. And he was still smouldering pinkly when Lord Iveldown came in.

Lord Iveldown's name will not go down to history in the company of Gladstone, Disraeli, or the Earl of Chatham. Probably it will not go down to history at all. He was a minor statesman whose work had never been done in the public eye, which was at least a negative blessing for a public eye which has far too much to put up with already. In plain language, which tradition forbids any statesman to use, he was one of those permanent government officials who do actually run the country while the more publicized politicians are talking about it. He was a big man inclined to paunchiness, with thin grey hair and pince-nez and the aura of stupendous pomposity by which the permanent government official may instantly be recognized anywhere; and the Saint, whose portrait gallery of excrescences left very little ground uncovered, recognized him at once.

He came in polishing his pince-nez and took up a position with his back to the fireplace.

"Sit down, Mr. Templar," he said brusquely and turned to Nassen. "I take it that you failed to find what you were looking for?"

The detective nodded.

"We turned the place inside out, your Lordship, but there wasn't a sign of it. He might have sewn it up inside a matttress or in the upholstery of a chair, but I don't think he would have had time."

"Quite," muttered Lord Iveldown. "Quite." He

took off his pince-nez, polished them again, and looked at the Saint. "This is a serious matter, Mr. Templar," he said. "Very serious."

"Apparently," agreed the Saint blandly. "Apparently."

Lord Iveldown cleared his throat and wagged his head once or twice.

"That is why I have been obliged to adopt extraordinary measures to deal with it," he said.

"Such as sending along a couple of fake detectives to turn my rooms inside out?" suggested the Saint languidly.

Lord Iveldown started, peered down at him, and coughed.

"Ah-hum," he said. "You knew they were—ah —fakes?"

"My good ass," said the Saint, lounging more snugly in his armchair, "I knew that the Metropolitan Police had lowered itself a lot by enlisting Public School men and what not, but I couldn't quite believe that it had sunk so low as to make inspectors out of herbaceous borders like Snowdrop over there. Besides, I'm never arrested by ordinary inspectors—Chief Inspector Teal himself always comes to see me."

"Then why did you allow Nassen to bring you here?"

"Because I figured I might as well take a gander at you and hear what you had to say. The gander," Simon admitted frankly, "is not quite the greatest thrill I've had since I met Dietrich."

Lord Iveldown cleared his throat again and expanded his stomach, clasping his hands behind his back under his coat tails and rocking slightly in the manner of a schoolmaster preparing to deal with a grave breach of the Public School Code.

"Mr. Templar," he said heavily, "this is a serious matter. A very serious matter. A matter, I might say, of the utmost gravity. You have in your possession a volume which contains certain—ah—statements and—ah—suggestions concerning me—statements and suggestions which, I need scarcely add, are wholly without foundation——"

"As, for instance," said the Saint gently, "the statement or suggestion that when you were Under-Secretary of State for War you placed an order for thirty thousand Lewis guns with a firm whose tender was sixty per cent. higher than any other, and enlarged your own bank balance immediately afterwards."

"Gross and damnable falsehoods," persisted Lord Iveldown more loudly.

"As, for instance," said the Saint, even more gently, "the gross and damnable falsehood that you accepted on behalf of the government a consignment of one million gas masks which technical experts had already condemned in the strongest language as worse than useless——"

"Foul and calumnious imputations," boomed Lord Iveldown in a trembling voice, "which can easily be refuted, but which if published would nevertheless to some degree smirch a name which hitherto has not been without honour in the annals of this nation. It was only for that reason, and not because I feared that my public and private life could not stand the light of any inquiry whatever that might be directed into it, that I consented to —ah—grant you this interview."

Simon nodded.

"Since your synthetic detectives had failed to steal that book from me," he murmured, "it was— ah—remarkably gracious of you."

His sardonic blue eyes, levelled over the shaft of a cigarette that slanted from between his lips like the barrel of a gun, bored into Lord Iveldown with a light of cold appraisal which made the nobleman shift his feet awkwardly.

"It was an extraordinary situation," repeated his lordship in a resonant voice, "which necessitated extraordinary measures." He cleared his throat, adjusted his pince-nez, and rocked on his heels again. "Mr. Templar," he said, "let us not beat about the bush any longer. For purely personal reasons—merely, you understand, because I desire to keep my name free from common gossip—I desire to suppress these base insinuations which happen to have come into your possession; and for that reason I have accorded you this personal interview in order to ascertain what—ah—value you would place on this volume."

"That's rather nice of you," said the Saint guardedly.

"If, for example," said Lord Iveldown throatily,

"a settlement of, shall we say—ah—two thousand pounds——"

He broke off at that point because suddenly the Saint had begun to laugh. It was a very quiet, very self-contained laugh—a laugh that somehow made the blood in Lord Iveldown's hardened arteries run colder as he heard it. If there was any humour in the laugh, it did not reach the Saint's eyes.

"If you'd mentioned two hundred thousand," said the Saint coolly, "you would have been right on my figure."

There was a long terrific silence in which the mere rustle of a coat sleeve would have sounded like the crash of doom. Many seconds went by before Lord Iveldown's dry cough broke the stillness like a rattle of musketry.

"How much did you say?" he articulated hoarsely.

"I said two hundred thousand pounds."

Those arctic blue eyes had never shifted from Lord Iveldown's faintly empurpled face. Their glacial gaze seemed to go through him with the cold sting of a rapier blade—seemed to strip away all his bulwarks of pomposity like tissue, and hold the naked soul of the man quivering on the point like a grub on a pin.

"But that," said Lord Iveldown tremblingly, "—that's impossible! That's blackmail!"

"I'm afraid it is," said the Saint.

"You sit there, before witnesses——"

"Before all the witnesses you like to bring in. I

don't want you to miss the idea, your Lordship. Witnesses don't make any difference. In any ordinary case—yes. If I were only threatening to advertise your illicit love affairs, or anything like that, you could bring me to justice and your own name would quite rightly be suppressed. But in a case like this even the chief commissioner couldn't guarantee you immunity. This isn't just ordinary naughtiness. This is high treason."

Simon tapped the ash from his cigarette and blew a smoke ring towards the ceiling; and once again his relentless eyes went back to Lord Iveldown's face. Nassen and the other detective, staring at the Saint in sullen silence, felt as if an icy wind blew through the room and goosefleshed their skin in spite of the warmth of the evening. The bantering buffoon who had goaded them to the verge of apoplexy had vanished as though he had never existed, and another man spoke with the same voice.

"The book you're talking about," said the Saint, in the same level dispassionate tones, "is a legacy to me, as you know, from Rayt Marius. And you know what made him a millionaire. His money was made from war and the instruments of war. All those amazing millions—the millions out of which you and others like you were paid, Lord Iveldown—were the wages of death and destruction and wholesale murder. They were coined out of blood and dishonour and famine and the agony of peaceful nations. Men—and women and chil-

dren, too—were killed and tortured and maimed
to find that money—the money out of which you
were paid, Lord Iveldown."

Lord Iveldown licked his lips and opened his
mouth to speak. But that clear ruthless voice went
on, cleaving like a sword through his futile attempt at expostulation:

"Since I have that book, I had to find a use for
it. And I think my idea is a good one. I am organizing the Simon Templar Foundation, which will
be started with a capital of one million pounds—
of which your contribution will be a fifth. The
foundation will be devoted to the care and comfort
of men maimed and crippled in war, to helping
the wives and children of men killed in war, and
to the endowment of any cause which has a chance
of doing something to promote peace in the future.
You must agree that the retribution is just."

Iveldown's bluff had gone. He seemed to have
shrunk, and he was not teetering pompously on the
hearth any more. His blotched face was working,
and his small eyes had lost all their dominance—
they were the mean shifty eyes of a man who was
horribly afraid.

"You're mad!" he said, and his voice cracked.
"I can't listen to anything like that. I won't listen
to it! You'll change your tune before you leave
here, by God! Nassen——"

The two detectives started forward, roused abruptly from their trance; and in the eyes of the
Rose of Peckham particularly Simon saw the

dawn of a sudden vengeful joy. He smiled and moved his raincoat a little to uncover the gun in his hand.

"Not just now, Snowdrop," he said smoothly, and the two men stopped. "I have a date, and you've kept me too long already. A little later, I think, you'll get your chance." His gaze roved back to Lord Iveldown's sickly features, on which the fear was curdling to a terrible impotent malevolence; and the Saintly smile touched his lips again for a moment. "I shall expect that two hundred thousand pounds by Saturday midnight," he said. "I haven't the least doubt that you'll do your best to kill me before then, but I'm equally sure that you won't succeed. And I think you will pay your share. . . ."

IV

SIMON TEMPLAR was not a light sleeper, by the ordinary definition. Neither was he a heavy one. He slept like a cat, with the complete and perfect relaxation of a wild animal, but with the same wild animal's gift of rousing into instant wakefulness at the slightest sound which might require investigation. A howling thunderstorm would not have made him stir, but the stealthy slither of a cautiously opened drawer brought him out of a dreamless untroubled slumber into tingling consciousness.

The first outward sign of awakening touched nothing more than his eyelids—it was a trick he had learned many years ago, and it had saved his life more than once. His body remained still and passive, and even a man standing close beside his bed could have detected no change in the regular rate of his breathing. He lay staring into the dark, with his ears strained to pick up and locate the next infinitesimal repetition of the noise which had awaked him.

After a few seconds he heard it again, a sound of the identical quality but from a different source —the faint scuff of a rubber sole moving over the carpet in his living room. The actual volume of sound was hardly greater than a mouse might have made, but it brought him out of bed in a swift writhing movement that made no sound in response.

And thereafter the blackness of the bedroom swallowed him up like a ghost. His bare feet crossed the floor without the faintest whisper of disturbance, and his fingers closed on the door-knob as surely as if he could have seen it. He turned the knob without a rattle and moved noiselessly across the hall.

The door of the living room was ajar—he could see the blackness ahead of him broken by a vague nimbus of light that glowed from the gap and shifted its position erratically. He came up to the door softly and looked in.

The silhouette of a man showed against the

darkened beam of an electric torch with the aid of which he was silently and systematically going through the contents of the desk; and the Saint showed his teeth for a moment as he sidled through the doorway and closed the door soundlessly behind him. His fingers found the switch beside the door, and he spoke at the same time.

"Good-morrow, Algernon," he murmured.

The man swung round in the sudden blaze of light. At the very moment when he started to turn, Simon saw the gun in his hand, and thanked his immoral deities that he had not removed his fingers too promptly from the switch. In a split second he had clicked the lever up again, and the darkness fell again with blinding intensity after that one dazzling instant of luminance.

The Saint's voice floated once more out of the blackness.

"So you pack a rod, do you, Algernon? You must know that rods aren't allowed in this respectable city. I shall have to speak to you severely about that presently, Algernon—really I shall."

The beam of the intruder's torch stabbed out again, printing a white circle of light on the door; but Simon was not inside the circle. The Saint had no rooted fear of being cold-bloodedly shot down in that apartment—the chances of a clean getaway for the shooter were too remote—but he had a very sound knowledge of what a startled burglar, amateur or professional, may do in a moment of panic; and what had been visible of the intruder's masked

face as he spun round had not been tender or sentimental.

Simon heard the man's heavy breathing as the
ray of the flashlight moved to left and right of the
door and then began with a wilder haste to dance
over the other quarters of the room. For the space
of about half a minute it was a game of deadly
hide-and-seek: the door appeared to be unguarded,
but something told the intruder that he would be
walking into a trap if he attempted to make a dash
for liberty that way. At the end of that time his
nerve broke and he plunged desperately for the
only visible path of escape, and in so doing found
that his suspicions had been almost clairvoyantly
accurate.

A weight of teaklike bone and muscle landed on
his back with a catlike spring; steel fingers fastened on his gun hand, and another equally strong
hand closed round his throat, driving him re-
morselessly to the floor. They wrestled voicelessly
on the carpet, but not for long. Simon got the gun
away without a single shot being fired and flung
himself clear of his opponent with an acrobatic
twist of his body. Then he found his way to the
switch and turned on the lights again.

The burglar looked up at him from the floor,
breathing painfully; and Simon permitted the
muzzle of the captured gun to settle into a steady
aim on the centre of the man's tightly tailored
torso.

"You look miserable, Algernon," he remarked

affably. "But you couldn't expect to have all the fun to yourself, could you? Come on, my lad—take that old sock off your head and let's see how your face is put together."

The man did not answer or obey, and Simon stepped forward and whipped off the mask with a deft flick of his hand.

Having done which, he remained absolutely motionless for several ticks of the clock.

And then, softly, helplessly, he started to laugh.

"Suffering snakes," he wailed. "If it isn't good old Hoppy Uniatz!"

"For cryin' out loud," gasped Mr. Uniatz. "If it ain't de Saint!"

"You haven't forgotten that time when you took a dive through the window of Rudy's joint on Mott Street?"

"Say, an' dat night you shot up Angie Paletta an' Russ Kovari on Amsterdam Avenue."

"And you got crowned with a chair and locked in the attic—you remember that?"

Mr. Uniatz fingered his neck gingerly, as though the aches in it brought back memories.

"Say," he protested aggrievedly, "whaddaya t'ink I got for a memory—a sieve?" He beamed again, reminiscently; and then another thought overcast his homely features with a shadow of retrospective alarm. "An' I might of killed you!" he said in an awed voice.

The Saint smiled.

"If I'd known it was you, I mightn't have thought this gun was quite so funny," he admitted. "Well, well, well, Hoppy—this is a long way from little old New York. What brings you here?"

Mr. Uniatz scrambled up from the floor and scratched his head.

"Well, boss," he said, "t'ings never were de same after prohibition went out, over dere. I bummed around fer a while, but I couldn't get in de money. Den I hoid dey was room fer guys like me to start up in London, so I come over. But hell, boss, dese Limeys dunno what it's all about, fer God's sake. Why, I asks one mob over here what about gettin' a coupla typewriters, an' dey t'ink I'm nuts." Mr. Uniatz frowned for a moment, as if the incapability of the English criminal to appreciate the sovereign uses of machine guns was still preying on his mind. "I guess I must of been given a bum steer," he said.

Simon nodded sympathetically and strolled across to the table for a cigarette. He had known Hoppy Uniatz many years ago as a seventh-rate gunman of the classical Bowery breed and had never been able to regard him with the same distaste as he viewed other hoodlums of the same species. Hoppy's outstanding charm was a skull of almost phenomenal thickness, which, while it had protected his brain from fatal injury on several occasions, had by its disproportionate density of bone left so little space for the development of grey matter that he had been doomed from the beginning to linger in the very lowest ranks even of that unintellectual profession; but at the same time it lent to Hoppy's character a magnificent simplicity which the Saint found irresistible. Simon could understand that Hoppy might easily have been lured across the Atlantic by exaggerated rumours of an outbreak of armed banditry in London; but that was not all he wanted to know.

"My heart bleeds for you, Hoppy," he murmured. "But what made you think I had anything worth stealing?"

"Well, boss," explained Mr. Uniatz apologetically, "it's like dis. I get interdooced to a guy who knows annudder guy who's bein' blackmailed, an' dis guy wants me to get back whatever it is he's bein' blackmailed wit' an' maybe bump off de guy who's got it. So I'm told to rent an apartment here, an' I got de one next door to you—it's a swell apartment, wit' a bathroom an' everyt'ing. Dat's how I'm able to come in de building wit'out de janitor stoppin' me an' askin' who I wanna see."

Simon blew out a thoughtful streamer of smoke —he had overlooked that method of slipping through his defenses.

"Didn't they tell you my name?" he asked.

"Sure. But all dey tell me is it's a Mr. Templar. When I hear it, I feel somehow I oughta remember de name," said Mr. Uniatz, generously forgetting the indignation with which he had received a recent aspersion on his memory, "but I never knew it was you. Honest, Saint, if I'd of known it was you, it'd of been ixnay on de job, for mine. Ya wouldn't believe anyt'ing else, woujja, boss?"

The Saint shook his head.

"You know, Hoppy," he said slowly, "I don't think I would."

An idea was germinating in his mind—one of those sublimely fantastic ideas that sometimes came to him, an idea whose gorgeous simplicity, even in embryo, brought the ghost of a truly Saintly smile back to his lips. He forgot his interrupted beauty sleep.

"Could you do with a drink, old man?" he asked.

Hoppy Uniatz allowed the breath to hiss between his teeth, and a light of childlike beatitude irradiated his face.

"Boss," he replied, "what couldn't I do with a drink?"

Simon refrained from suggesting any answers to the conundrum. He poured out a liberal measure and saved his soda water. Mr. Uniatz took the glass, sniffed it, and sucked his saliva for a moment of disciplined anticipation.

"Don't get me wrong, boss," he said earnestly. "Dose t'ings I said about Limeys wasn't meant poisonal. I ain't never t'ought about you as a Limey. You been in New York, an' you know what it's all about. I know we had some arguments over dere, but over on dis side it don't seem de same. Say, I been so lonesome here it makes me feel kinda mushy just to have a little fight like we had just now wit' a guy like you, who knows what a Roscoe's for. I wish you an' me could of teamed up before, boss."

The Saint had helped himself to a more modest dose of whisky. He stretched himself out on the davenport and waved Mr. Uniatz to an armchair.

"Maybe it's not too late even now, Hoppy," he said; and he had much more to talk about, which kept him out of bed for another two hours.

V

CHIEF INSPECTOR TEAL arrived while the Saint was finishing a belated breakfast. Simon Templar's breakfasts were usually belated, for he had never been able to appreciate the spiritual rewards of early rising; but on this particular morning the lateness was not entirely his fault. He had already been interrupted twice during the meal, and the bell which heralded the third interruption made him finally abandon a cup of coffee which had abandoned all pretension to being even lukewarm.

"Mr. Teal is here, sir," said Sam Outrell's voice on the telephone; and the Saint sighed.

"Okay, Sam. Send him up." He replaced the microphone and turned back to Mr. Uniatz, who was engulfing quantities of toast with concentrated gusto. "I'm afraid you've got to blow again, Hoppy," he said. "I'll see you later."

Mr. Uniatz rose wearily. He had been shot out of the Saint's apartment to make room for other visitors so often that morning that he had grave fears for his digestion. There was one slice of toast left for which even his Gargantuan mouth was temporarily unable to find room. In order to eliminate any further risks of having his meal disturbed, he put the slice in his pocket and went out obediently; and he was the first thing that Teal saw when Simon opened the door.

"Hi, Claud," said Mr. Uniatz amiably and drifted on towards the sanctity of his own quarters.

"Who the deuce is that?" demanded the startled detective, staring after Hoppy's retreating rear.

The Saint smiled.

"A friend of mine," he said. "Come along in, Claud, and make yourself uncomfortable. This is just like old times."

Mr. Teal turned round slowly and advanced into the apartment. The momentary human surprise which Hoppy's greeting had given him faded rather quickly out of his rubicund features. The poise of his plump body as he came to rest in the living room, the phlegmatic dourness of his round pink face under its unfashionable bowler hat, was exactly like old times. It was Chief Inspector Teal paying an official call: Chief Inspector Teal, with the grim recollection of many such calls haunting his mind, trundling doggedly out once again to take up his hopeless duel with the smiling young freebooter before him. The sum of a score of inter-

views like that drummed through his head, the
memory of a seemingly endless sequence of failures
and the bitter presentiment of many more to come
was in his brain; but there was no hint of weakness
or evasion in the somnolent eyes that rested on the
Saint's brown face.

"Well," he said, "I told you I'd be coming to see
you."

Simon nodded pleasantly.

"It was nice of you to make it so soon, Claud,"
he murmured. "And what do you think is going to
win the Derby?"

He knew as well as the chief commissioner himself that Mr. Teal would never have called on him
to enjoy small talk and racing gossip; but it was
not his business to make the first move. A faint
smile of humorous challenge stayed on his lips, and
under the light of that smile Teal rummaged in his
pockets and pulled out a folded sheet of paper.

"Do you know anything about that?" he asked.

Simon took the sheet and flattened it out. It was
his own notehead, and there was certainly no surprise for him in the words which were written
on it; but he read the document through obligingly.

THE RT. HON. LEO FARWILL,
384, HANOVER SQUARE,
LONDON W. I.
DEAR SIR:
   *As you have probably been informed, I have in my
possession a volume of unique international interest in*

*which your own distinguished name happens to be
mentioned.*

*I have decided to sell this volume, in sections, for
the benefit of the Simon Templar Foundation, which I
am founding. This foundation will exist for the purpose of giving financial and other assistance to the
needy families of men who were killed or deprived of
their livelihood in the last war, to the care of the
incurably crippled wounded, and to the endowment of
any approved cause which is working to prevent a repetition of that outbreak of criminal insanity.*

*The price to you, of the section in which your name
appears, is £200,000; and, knowing your interest in
literature, I am sure you will decide that the price is
reasonable—particularly as the Simon Templar Foundation will in its small way work towards the promise
of "a land fit for heroes to live in" with which you
once urged men to military service, death, and disable-
ment, and which circumstances (always, of course,
beyond your control) have since made you unable to
fulfil.*

*In expecting your check to reach me before next
Saturday midnight, I am, I feel sure, my dear honourable Leo, only anticipating your own natural urgent
desire to benefit such a deserving charity.*

Yours faithfully,
SIMON TEMPLAR.

"Very lucid and attractive, I think," said the
Saint politely. "What about it?"

Teal took the letter back from him.

"It's signed with your name, isn't it?" he asked.

"Certainly," said the Saint.

"And it's in your handwriting."

"Beyond a doubt."

"So that it looks very much as if you wrote it."

Simon nodded.

"That Sherlock Holmes brain of yours goes straight to the point, Claud," he said. "Faced with such keen deductive evidence, I can't deceive you. I did write it."

Teal folded the letter again and put it back in his pocket. His mouth settled into a relentless line. With any other man than the one who faced him, he would have reckoned the interview practically over; but he had crossed swords with the Saint too often ever to believe that of any interview— had seen too many deadly thrusts picked up like the clumsy lunges of an amateur on the rapierlike brilliance of the Saint's brain, and tossed aside with a smile that was more deadly than any riposte. But the thrust had to be made.

"I suppose you know that's blackmail," Teal said flatly.

The Saint frowned slightly.

"Demanding money with menaces?" he asked.

"If you want the technical charge," Teal said stubbornly, "yes."

And it came—the cool flick of the rapier that carried his point wide and aimless.

"Where," asked the Saint puzzledly, "are the menaces?"

Teal swallowed an obstruction in his throat. The game was beginning all over again—the futile hammering of his best blades on a stone wall that was as impalpable as ether, the foredoomed pursuit of the brigand who was easier to locate than any other lawbreaker in London, and who was more elusive than a will-o'-the-wisp even when he was most visible in the flesh. All the wrath that curdled his milk of human kindness was back in the detective at that moment, all the righteous anger against the injustice of his fate; but he had to keep it bottled up in his straining chest.

"The menaces are in the letter," he said bluntly.

Simon stroked his chin in a rendering of ingenuous perplexity that acted on Teal's blood pressure like a dose of strychnine.

"I may be prejudiced," he remarked, "but I didn't see them. It seemed a very respectable appeal to me, except for a certain unconventional familiarity at the end, where Leo's Christian name was used—but these are free-and-easy days. Otherwise I thought it was a model of restrained and touching eloquence. I have a book, of which it occurs to me that Leo might like to buy the section in which his name appears—you know what publicity hounds most of these politicians are. Therefore I offer to sell it to him, which I'm sure must be strictly legal."

"Mr. Farwill's statement," retorted Teal, "is that the part of the book you're referring to is nothing but a collection of libellous lies."

Simon raised his eyebrows.

"He must have a guilty conscience," he murmured. "But you can't put me in jail for that. I didn't say anything in my letter to give him that impression. I defy you to find one threat, one word of abuse, one questionable insinuation. The whole epistle," Simon said modestly, "is couched in the most flattering and even obsequious terms. In expecting his check to reach me before next Saturday midnight, I am, I feel sure, only anticipating his own natural urgent desire to benefit such a deserving charity. Leo may have turned out to be not quite the eager philanthropist I took him for," said the Saint regretfully, "but I still hope he'll see the light of godliness in the end; and I don't see what you've got to do with it, Claud."

Mr. Teal gulped in a breath that hurt him as it went down his windpipe.

"Oh, you don't, don't you?" he bit out.

"I'm afraid I don't, Claud," said the Saint. "Leo may have been caught in a hysterical moment, but other blokes have had the identical letter without feeling that way about it. Look at this."

He picked up a slip of tinted paper from beside the coffee pot and held it out so that the detective could read the words. It was a check on the City & Continental Bank, dated that day, and it was made out for two hundred thousand pounds.

"Sir Barclay Edingham came here at half-past nine to give me that—he was in such a hurry to do his share. Major General Sir Humboldt Quipp blew in at half-past ten—he grumbled and thundered a bit about the price, but he's gone away again to think it over, and I'm sure he'll pay it in the end. The other contributors will be coming through in the next day or two, and I wouldn't mind betting that Leo will be one of them as soon as he comes out of his tantrum. You ought to have another talk with him, Claud—it might help him to see the path of duty."

"Never you mind what I ought to do," Teal said hotly. His baby-blue eyes, with all the sleepiness knocked out of them, were goggling like young balloons at the check which Simon was dangling under his nose, as if his brain had flatly refused to believe their message and they had swollen to twice their normal size with proper indignation at the insult. With a genuine physical effort he averted them from the astounding figures. "Sir Barclay Edingham gave you that?" he repeated incredulously.

Simon inclined his head.

"And he was glad to. Sir Barclay Edingham has a very keen appreciation of literature. The pages I sold him are now his most treasured possession, and you couldn't buy them off him for twice as much as he gave me."

He folded the check carefully and put it away in his wallet; and the detective straightened up.

"Where is this book?" he demanded.

The Saint's eyebrows shifted again fractionally. It was a gesture that Teal knew better than any other of the Saint's bar one, and that almost imperceptible change of alignment carried more meaning than a thousand words of description could convey.

"It's in England," he answered.

"That's good," said Teal grimly, "because I want to see it."

The Saint picked up a cigarette, spun it into the air, and caught it in his mouth without moving his head. He snapped a flame from his lighter and blew out a long feather of smoke.

"Do you?" he murmured interestedly.

"Yes, I do!" barked the detective. "And I mean to see it before I go. I mayn't be much of a critic, but I'll soon find out whether this literary work is worth two hundred thousand pounds a chapter. I'll get my own ideas about whether it's libellous. Now are you going to show me that book or am I going to look for it?"

"Where's your search warrant?" inquired Simon imperturbably.

Teal gritted his teeth.

"I don't need a search warrant. You're a suspected person——"

"Only in your wicked suspicious mind, Claud. And I'm telling you that you do need a search warrant. Or, if you're going to take my home apart without one, you need three or four strong men with you. Because if you try to do it yourself, I shall pick you up by the scruff of your neck and the seat of your pants and throw you over the Ritz, and there's no magistrate in England who could give you a comeback!"

The Saint was smiling; but Mr. Teal had no illusions about that smile. It was not a smile of simple-hearted bonhomie and good will towards policemen. It was a smile that could have been worn by no one but that lean dangerous privateer who was never more dangerous than when he smiled.

And Mr. Teal knew that he hadn't a leg to stand on. The Saint had tied him in a knot again. There were no menaces, no threats of any kind, in the letter with which the Honourable Leo Farwill had gone to Scotland Yard—it was a pleasant polite epistle with no unlawful insinuations whatsoever, and any fairly clever advocate could have convinced a normally half-witted jury that the suspicions attached to it arose from nothing but the notorious Simon Templar's signature at the end. And without a definite charge of blackmail, there were no grounds at all for demanding an inspection of the literary work on which the whole case hinged.

Mr. Teal knew all these things as well as anyone —and knew also that in spite of the strictly legal appearances no man had ever given the Saint two hundred thousand pounds except as the reward of some devilish and unlawful cunning that had been born in that gay unscrupulous brain. He knew all these things as well as he knew his own birthday; but they did not cheer him. And Simon Templar's forefinger went out and tapped him on the stomach in the Saintly gesture that Mr. Teal knew and hated best of all.

"You're too full of naughty ideas and uncharitable thoughts these days," said the Saint. "I was hoping that after I'd been away for a bit you might have got over them; but it seems as if you haven't. You're having one of your relapses into detectivosis, Claud; and it offends me. You stand there with your great stomach wobbling——"

"It doesn't wobble!" yapped the detective furiously.

"It wobbles when I poke it with my finger," said the Saint coldly and proceeded to demonstrate.

Teal struck his hand aside.

"Now listen," he brayed. "You may be able to twist the law around to suit yourself for a while——"

"I can twist the law around to suit myself as long as I like," said the Saint cheerfully; "and when I fall down on it will be soon enough for you to come and see me again. Now you've completely spoiled my breakfast; and I've got an important appointment in ten minutes, so I can't stop to play with you any more. Drop in again next time you wake up, and I'll have some more to say to you."

Chief Inspector Teal settled his bowler hat. The wrath and righteous indignation were steaming together under his waistcoat; but with a terrific effort he recovered his pose of torpid weariness.

"I'll have some more to say to you," he replied

curtly, "and it'll keep you out of trouble for several years."

"Let me know when you're ready," murmured the Saint and opened the door for him with Old World courtesy.

A couple of minutes later, with his wide-brimmed felt hat tipped challengingly over his right eye, he was knocking at the door of the adjoining apartment.

"Come along, Hoppy," he said. "We've left it late enough already—and I can't afford to miss this date."

Mr. Uniatz put down a bottle of whisky regretfully and took up his hat. They left the building by the entrance in Stratton Street; and as they came out onto the pavement a shabby and ancient touring car pulled away from the curb and went past. Simon felt as if a gust of wind plucked at his swashbuckling headgear and carried it spinning: the crack that went with the gust of wind might have been only one of the many backfires that a big city hears every hour.

VI

SIMON collected his hat and dusted it thoughtfully. The bullet hole made a neat puncture in the centre of the crown—the only mistake in the aim had been the elevation.

The attack surprised him seriously. He had allowed himself to believe that during his possession of *Her Wedding Secret* his life at least was safer than it had ever been—that while the opposition would go to any lengths to obtain that classic work, they would be extraordinarily solicitous about his own bodily health. He turned to Mr. Uniatz, and had a sudden spasm of alarm when he saw that enterprising warrior standing out on the edge of the sidewalk with an automatic waving towards the retreating car. Simon made a grab at the gun and whipped it under his coat.

"You everlasting fathead!" he said. "Where the blazes d'you think you are?"

Mr. Uniatz scratched his head and looked around him.

"I t'ink we're in Stratton Street, boss," he said anxiously. "Ain't dat right? I can't seem to find my way around dis town. Why ja grab de Betsy off of me? I could of plugged dat guy easy."

The Saint sighed. By some miracle the street had been practically deserted, and no one appeared to have noticed the brief flourish of gangland armaments.

"Because if you'd plugged that guy you'd have had us both in the hoosegow before you knew what had happened, you poor sap," he said tersely and slipped the lethal weapon cautiously back into its owner's pocket. "Now keep that Betsy of yours buttoned up until I tell you to let it out—and try to remember which side of the Atlantic you're on, will you?"

They walked round to the garage where Simon kept his car, with Mr. Uniatz preserving a silence of injured perplexity. The ways of the Old World were strange to him; and his brain had never been geared to lightning adaptability. If one guy could take a shot at another guy and get away with it, but the other guy couldn't take a shot back at the first guy without being clapped in the hoosegow, what the hell sort of a country was this England, for God's sake? There was just no percentage in trying to hold down a racket in those parts, reflected Hoppy Uniatz, and laboured over the subtleties of this sociological observation for twenty minutes, while Simon Templar whisked the huge purring Hirondel through the traffic to the southwest.

Simon had a difficult problem to ponder, and he was inclined to share it.

"Tell me, Hoppy," he said. "Suppose a bloke had some papers that he was blackmailing you with—papers that would be the end of you if they ever came out. Suppose he'd got your signed confession to a murder, or something like that. What would you do about it?"

Mr. Uniatz rubbed his nose.

"Dat's easy, boss. I'd bump de guy off, sure."

"I'm afraid you would," said the Saint. "But suppose you did bump him off—those papers would still be around somewhere, and you wouldn't know who was going to get hold of them next."

This had not occurred to Mr. Uniatz. He frowned gloomily for a while; and then he brightened again as the solution struck him like a ray of sunshine.

"Why, boss," he said, "I know what I'd do. After I'd bumped him off, I'd look for de papers."

"And where would you look for them?" asked the Saint.

"In de guy's pocket," said Mr. Uniatz promptly.

"And suppose they weren't there?"

Hoppy sighed. The corrugations of worried thought returned to his brow. Thinking had never been his greatest talent—it was one of the very few things that were capable of hurting his head.

Simon shot the Hirondel between a lorry and an omnibus with the breadth of a finger to spare on either side and tried to assist.

"I mean, Hoppy," he said, "you might have thought: 'Suppose I bump this guy off. Suppose he isn't carrying the papers in his pocket. Well, when a guy's bumped off, one of the first things the cops want to know is who did it. And one of the ways of finding that out is to find out who might have had a reason to do it. And one of the ways of finding that out is to go through his letters and everything else like that that you can get hold of.' So if you'd thought all that out, Hoppy, you might have decided that if you bumped him off, the cops might get hold of the papers, and that wouldn't be too healthy for you."

Mr. Uniatz ruminated over this point for two or three miles, and finally he shrugged.

"I dunno," he said. "It looks like we better not bump off dis guy, at dat. Whadda you t'ink, boss?"

Simon realized that he would have to be content with his own surmises, which were somewhat disturbing. He had been prepared to bank heavily on his immunity from death, if not from organized discomfort, so long as the ungodly were in doubt about the concurrent fate of *Her Wedding Secret;* but the recent episode was a considerable discouragement to his faith. Leaving aside the possibility that Lord Iveldown had gone completely and recklessly berserk, it meant that the ungodly were developing either a satanic cunning or a denseness of cranium equalled only by that of Hoppy Uniatz.

He made a rough summary of the opposition. They had been five in number originally, and it was only to be expected that out of those five a solid percentage would have been nonresisters; Sir Barclay Edingham had paid. Major General Sir Humbolt Quipp would pay. The active dissenters consisted of Lord Iveldown, who had already declared his hand, a certain Mr. Neville Yorkland, M.P., with whom the Saint was going to have an interview, and perhaps the Honourable Leo Farwill, who might jump either way. But none of these three gentlemen, undesirable citizens though they might be, could lightly be accused of excessive denseness of cranium. Neither, as a matter of fact, had the Saint been prepared to credit them with talents of satanic cunning; but on that score it was dawning on him that he might do well to maintain an open mind.

The inevitable triangle possessed a third corner —if anything so nearly spherical could be described as a corner—in the rotund shape of Chief Inspector Claud Eustace Teal. Whatever his other errors may have been, Simon Templar was not guilty of kidding himself that he had finally and eternally disposed of that menace in the brief *tête-à-tête* they had enjoyed that morning.

The Saint, it must be confessed, had sometimes been guilty of deceiving Chief Inspector Teal. He had not always unbosomed all his secrets as Mr. Teal had liked him to. At times, even, he had deliberately and grievously misled that persistent enforcer of the law—a breach of the Public School Code which all English Gentlemen will undoubtedly deplore.

He had misled Mr. Teal that morning, when telling him that he had an appointment in ten minutes. As a matter of fact, the Saint's appointment was not until that evening, and he had merely been promising himself an idle day in the country on the way, with which he did not propose to allow Scotland Yard to interfere. It was a casual and almost pointless untruth; but he might have thought more about it if he had foreseen its results.

Mr. Teal brooded all day over his problem. In the course of the afternoon he had a second interview with the Honourable Leo Farwill; and that estimable politician's reaction to his report, far from consoling him, made him still more uneasy.

Later that evening he saw the assistant commissioner.

"There's something darned funny going on, sir," he summarized his conclusions tentatively.

The assistant commissioner sniffed. He had a sniff which annoyed Mr. Teal almost as much as Simon Templar's irreverently prodding forefinger.

"I, in my humble way, had reached the same conclusion," said the commissioner sarcastically. "Has Farwill said any more?"

"He was just wooden," said Teal. "That's what I don't like about it. If he'd gone off the deep end and ranted about the inefficiency of the police and the questions he was going to ask in Parliament— all the usual stuff, you know—I'd have felt happier about it. That was what I was expecting him to do, but he didn't do it. He seemed to go back into a sort of shell."

"You mean you got the impression that he was rather regretting having gone to the police with that letter?"

Teal nodded.

"It did seem like that. I've seen it happen before, when the Saint's on a job. The fellow may kick up a fuss at first, but pretty soon he shuts down like a clam. Either he pays, or he tries to deal with the Saint on his own. He doesn't ask us to interfere again."

"And yet you haven't the faintest idea why solid and respectable people—public men like Farwill, for instance—crumple up like frightened babies just because this man writes them a letter," remarked the assistant commissioner acidly.

The detective twiddled a button on his coat.

"I have got the faintest idea, sir," he said redly. "I've got more than a faint idea. I *know* why they do it. I know why they're doing it now. It's blackmail."

"Do you know, I really believe you've solved the mystery," said the commissioner, with a mildness that singed the air.

"If I've done that, I've done more than anyone else in this building," retorted Teal heatedly. "But there are plenty of people sitting in their offices criticizing me who couldn't have got half as far as I have, even if that isn't saying much." He glared at his chief stubbornly, while all the accumulated wrath and resentment of a score of such conferences rose up recklessly in his breast and strangled his voice for a moment. "Everybody knows that it's some kind of blackmail, but that doesn't help. We can't prove it. When I produced that letter, Templar simply laughed at me. And he was right. There wasn't a line of blackmail in it—except to anyone who knew what was in that book he mentions."

"Which you failed to find out," said the commissioner.

"Which I failed to find out," agreed Teal feverishly, "because I'm not a miracle worker, and I never said I was."

The assistant commissioner picked up his pen.

"Do you want a search warrant—is that what all these hysterics are about?" he inquired icily.

Teal gulped.

"Yes, I want a search warrant!" he exploded defiantly. "I know what it means. The Saint'll probably get around that somehow. When I get there, the book will have disappeared, or it'll turn out to be a copy of *Fairy Tales for Little Children,* or something. And Edingham and Quipp will get up and swear it was never anything else." Goaded beyond endurance though he was, the detective checked for an instant at the horrific potentialities of his prophecy; but he plunged on blindly: "I've seen things like that happen before, too. I've seen the Saint turn a cast-iron conviction into a cast-iron alibi in ten seconds. I'm ready to see it happen again. I'm ready to see him give the newspapers a story that'll make them laugh themselves sick for two months at my expense. But I'll take that search warrant!"

"I'll see that you have it in half an hour," said the assistant commissioner coldly. "We will discuss your other remarks on the basis of what you do with it."

"Thank you, sir," said Chief Inspector Teal

and left the room with the comfortless knowledge
that the last word on that subject was a long way
from having been said.

VII

"GENTS," announced Mr. Uniatz, from a chest
swelling with proper pride, "dis here is my pal
Mr. Orconi. Dey calls him Pete de Blood. He's
de guy youse guys is lookin' for. He'll fix
t'ings. . . ."

From that moment, with those classic words, the
immortal gorgeousness of the situation was established for all time. Simon Templar had been in
many queer spots before, had cheerfully allowed
his destiny to be spun giddy in almost every conceivable whirlpool of adventure; but never before
had he entered such a portentous conclave to discuss solemnly the manner in which he should
assassinate himself; and the sheer ecstatic pulchri-
tude of the idea was prancing balmily through his
insides in a hare-brained saraband which only a
delirious sense of humour like the Saint's could
have appreciated to the full.

He stood with his hands in his pockets, survey-
ing the two other members of the conference with
very clear blue eyes and allowing the beatific
fruitiness of scheme which Mr. Uniatz had made
possible to squirm rapturously through his system.

"Pleased to meet ya," he drawled, with a perfect gangster intonation that had been learned in more perilous and unsavoury surroundings than a fireproof air-conditioned movie theatre.

Mr. Neville Yorkland, M.P., fidgeted with his tie and looked vaguely about the room. He was a broad tubby little man, who looked something like a cross between a gentleman farmer and a dilettante artist—an incongruous soufflé of opposites, with a mane of long untidy hair crowning a vintage-port complexion.

"Well," he said jerkily, "let's sit down. Get to business. Don't want to waste any time."

The Honourable Leo Farwill nodded. He was as broad as Yorkland, but longer; and he was not fussy. His black brows and heavy moustache were of almost identical shape and dimensions, so that his face had a curiously unfinished symmetry, as if its other features had been fitted quite carelessly into the decisive framework of those three arcs of hair.

"An excellent idea," he boomed. "Excellent. Perhaps we might have a drink as well. Mr.—ah —Orconi——"

"Call me Pete," suggested the Saint affably, "and let's see your liquor."

They sat, rather symbolically, on opposite sides of the long table in Farwill's library. Hoppy Uniatz gravitated naturally to the Saint's elbow, while Yorkland pulled up a chair beside Farwill.

The Honourable Leo poured sherry into four glasses from a crystal decanter.

"Mr.—er—Uniatz gives us to understand that you are what is known as a—ah—gunman, Mr. Orconi."

"Pete," said the Saint, sipping his drink.

"Ah—Pete," Farwill corrected himself, with visible distaste.

Simon nodded gently.

"I guess that's right," he said. "If there's anyone horning in on your racket, you've come to the guy who can stop him."

"Sure," echoed Hoppy Uniatz, grasping his opportunity and swallowing it in one gulp. "We'll fix him."

Farwill beamed laboriously and produced a box of cigars.

"I presume that Mr. Uniatz has already acquainted you with the basic motives of our proposition," he said.

"Hoppy told me what you wanted—if that's what you mean," said the Saint succinctly, stripping the band from his selected Corona. "This guy Templar has something on you, an' you want him taken off."

"That—ah—might be a crude method of expressing it," rumbled the Honourable Leo. "However, it is unnecessary to go into the diplomatic niceties of the dilemma. I will content myself with suggesting to you that the situation is one of, I might almost say, national moment."

"Tremendous issues involved," muttered Mr.

Neville Yorkland helpfully. "World-wide catastrophe. The greatest caution is called for. Tact. Secrecy. Emergency measures."

"Exactly," concluded Farwill. "Emergency measures. The ordinary avenues are closed to us by the exigencies of the crisis. You would, in fact, find yourself in the position of an unofficial secret service agent—taking your own risks, fighting your own battles, knowing that in the event of failure you will be disowned by your employers. The situation, in short, calls for a man who is able to take care of himself, who is prepared to endanger his life for a reasonable reward, who— who——"

"I get it," said the Saint blandly. "This guy Templar has something on you, an' you want him taken off."

Farwill compressed his lips.

"At this stage of developments, I feel called upon neither to confirm that statement nor repudiate it," he said with the fluency of many years in Parliament. "The points at issue are, first, whether you are a suitable man for the mission——"

"Nuts," said the Saint tersely. "You want a guy like me, an' I'm the guy you want. When do you cut the cackle an' come to the hosses?"

The Honourable Leo glanced despairing at Yorkland, as if appealing to the Speaker on a point of order. Yorkland twiddled his thumbs.

"Should be all right," he mumbled. "Looks the type. Vouched for by Mr. Uniatz. Been to

America myself. Can't pick and choose. Got to decide."

"Ah, yes," admitted Farwill despondently, as if the very idea violated all his dearest principles. "We have got to decide." He inflated his chest again for the only outlet of oratory that was left to him. "Well, Mr. Orconi—ah—Pete, you are doubtless familiar with the general outline of the engagement. This book, of which Mr. Uniatz must have told you, must be recovered—whether by guile or force is immaterial. Nothing must be permitted to obstruct a successful consummation of the undertaking. If, in the course of your work, it should prove necessary to effect physical injuries upon this man Templar, or even to—er—expedite his decease, humanitarian considerations must not influence our firmness. Now I would suggest that a fee of two hundred pounds——"

Simon straightened up in his chair and laughed rudely.

"Say, whaddaya think I'm lookin' for?" he demanded. "Chicken feed?"

The Honourable Leo drew further breath for eloquence, and the argument was on. It would scarcely be profitable to record it in detail. It went on for a long time, conducted on the Parliamentary side in rounded periods which strayed abstractly to every other subject on earth except the one in hand and nearly sent the Saint to sleep. But Simon Templar had a serene determination of his own which could even survive the soporific

flatulence of Farwill's long-winded verbiage; he
was in no hurry, and he was still enjoying himself
hugely. Hoppy Uniatz, endowed with a less vivid
appreciation of the simple jests of life, did actually
fall into a doze.

At long last a fee of two thousand pounds was
agreed on; and the Saint helped himself to a fifth
glass of sherry.

"Okay, boys," he murmured. "We'll get that
guy."

"Sure," echoed Mr. Uniatz, rousing with a
snort. "We'll get him."

Yorkland shuffled about on the edge of his seat,
buttoned and unbuttoned his coat, and got up.

"Very well," he stuttered. "That's settled. Glad
it's all fixed up. Now I must get back to town.
Late already. Important meetings." His restless
eyes glanced at the other member of his side.
"Count on me for my share, Farwill."

The Honourable Leo nodded.

"Certainly," he reverberated. "Certainly. You
may leave it to me to arrange the details." He
drew the sherry decanter towards him and replaced the stopper unobtrusively but firmly. "I
think we owe a vote of thanks to Mr. Uniatz for
the—er—introduction."

Simon Templar surveyed him dispassionately
over a second Corona.

"You owe more than that, fella," he said.

Farwill coughed.

"I thought the—er—honorarium was payable

when the commission had been—ah—executed."

"Half of it is," agreed the Saint pleasantly. "The first half is payable now. I done business with politicians before. You make so many promises in your job, you can't expect to remember 'em all."

"Sure," seconded Hoppy Uniatz heartily. "Cash wit' order is de rule in dis foim."

Farwill drew out his wallet grudgingly; but it was stocked with a supply of currency which indicated that some such demand had not been unforeseen. He counted out a number of banknotes with reluctant deliberation; and Yorkland watched the proceeding with a hint of hollowness in his round face.

"Well," he said with a sigh, "that's done. Send you a check tonight, Farwill. Thanks. Really must be off now. Excuse me. Good-bye."

He shook hands all round, with the limp perfunctory grip of the professional handshaker, and puttered out of the room; and they heard his car scrunching away down the drive.

The Saint smiled to himself and raked in the money. He counted it into two piles, pushed one towards Hoppy Uniatz, and folded the other into his pocket. There were five hundred pounds in his own share—it was a small enough sum as the Saint rated boodle, but there were circumstances in which he could take a fiver with just as much pleasure as he would have taken five thousand. It was not always the amount of the swag, it was the twists of the game by which it was collected; and beyond all doubt the twist by which that five hundred had been pulled in ranked high in the scale of pure imponderable delights. On such an occasion even a nominal allowance of loot was its own reward; but still the Saint had not achieved everything that had been in his mind when he set out on that soul-satisfying jag.

One other riddle had been working in his brain ever since he left his apartment that morning, and he led up to it with studied casualness.

"The job's as good as done, Leo," he said.

"Sure," echoed the faithful Mr. Uniatz. "De guy is dead an' buried."

"Excellent," responded Farwill formally. "Ah —excellent."

He had almost got the decanter away when Simon reached it with a long arm. Farwill winced and averted his eyes.

"This ain't such bad stuff, Leo," the Saint commented kindly, emptying his glass and refilling it rapidly. He spilt an inch of ash from his cigar onto the carpet and cocked one foot on to the polished table with a callous disregard for his host's feeling which he felt would go well with the imaginary character of Pete de Blood, and which soothed his own sleepless sense of mischief at the same time. "About this guy Templar," he said. "Suppose I do have to rub him out?"

"Rub him out?" repeated Farwill dubiously. "Ah—yes, yes. Suppose you have to kill him." His eyes shifted for a moment with the hunted look of the politician who scents an attempt to commit him to a definite statement. "Well, naturally it is understood that you will look after yourself."

"Aw, shucks," said the Saint scornfully. "I can look after myself. That ain't what I mean. I mean, suppose he was rubbed out, then there wouldn't be any way to find out where the book was, an' the cops might get it."

Farwill finally collared the decanter and transported it in an absent-minded way to the cellaret, which he locked with the same preoccupied air. He turned round and clasped his hands under his coattails.

"From our point of view, the problem might be simplified," he said.

The Saint rolled his cigar steadily between his finger and thumb. The question with which he had taxed the imagination of Mr. Uniatz had been propounded again where it might find a more positive reply; but the Saint's face showed no trace of his eagerness for a solution. He tipped the dialogue over the brink of elucidation with a single impassive monosyllable:

"How?"

"The Saint has a—ah—confederate," said Farwill, looking at the ceiling. "A young lady. We understand that she shares his confidence in all his —ah—enterprises. We may therefore assume that she is cognizant of the whereabouts of the volume in question. If the Saint were—ah—removed, therefore," Farwill suggested impersonally, "one would probably have a more—ah—tractable person with whom to deal."

A flake of ash broke from the Saint's cigar and trickled a dusty trail down his coat; but his eyes did not waver.

"I get you," he said.

The simplicity of the argument hit him between the eyes with a force that almost staggered him. Now that it had been put forward, he couldn't understand how he had failed to see it himself from the beginning. It was so completely and brutally logical. The Saint was tough: everyone knew it, everyone admitted it. And he held the whip hand. But he could be—ah—removed; and the whip would pass into the hands of one lone girl. Undoubtedly the problem might be simplified. It would be reduced to an elementary variant of an old game of which the grim potentialities were still capable of sending a cold trickle down his spine. He should have seen it at once. His hat hung in the hall with a bullet-punched ventilation through the crown which was an enduring testimony that the opposition had neither gone berserk nor sunk into the depths of imbecility; without even charting the pinnacles of satanic cunning, they had merely grasped at the elusive obvious— which he himself had been too wooden-headed to see.

"That's a great idea," said the Saint softly. "So after we've rubbed out this guy Templar, we go after his moll."

"Ah—yes," assented Farwill, staring into the opposite corner as if he were not answering the question at all. "If that should prove necessary— ah—yes."

"Sure," chirped Mr. Uniatz brightly, forestalling his cue. "We'll fix de goil."

The Saint silenced him with a sudden lift of ice-blue eyes. His voice became even softer, but the change was too subtle for Farwill to notice it.

"Who thought of that great idea?" he asked.

"It was jointly agreed," said the Honourable Leo evasively. "In such a crisis, with such issues at stake, one cannot be sentimental. The proposition was received with unanimous approval. As a matter of fact, I understand that an abortive attempt has already been made in that direction—I should perhaps have explained that there is another member of our—er—coalition who was unfortunately unable to be present at our recent discussion. I expect him to arrive at any moment, as he is anxious to make your acquaintance. He is a gentleman who has already done valuable independent work towards this—ah—consummation which we all desire."

The Saint's eyebrows dropped one slow and gentle quarter-inch over his steady eyes.

"Who is he?"

Farwill's mouth opened for another elaborate

paragraph; but before he had voiced his preliminary "Ah" the headlights of a car swept across
the drawn blinds, and the gravel scraped again
outside the windows. Footsteps and voices sounded
in the hall, and the library door opened to admit
the form of the Honourable Leo's butler.

"Lord Iveldown," he announced.

VIII

SIMON TEMPLAR'S cigar had gone out. He put it
down carefully in an ashtray and took out his
cigarette case. It stands as a matter of record that
at that moment he did not bat an eyelid, though
he knew that the showdown had arrived.

"Delighted to see you, Iveldown," the Honourable Leo was exclaiming. "Yorkland was unfortunately unable to stay. However, you are not too
late to make the acquaintance of our new—ah—
agents. Mr. Orconi . . ."

Farwill's voice trailed hesitantly away. It began
to dawn on him that his full-throated flow of
oratory was not carrying his audience with him.
Something, it seemed, was remarkably wrong.

Standing in front of the door which had closed
behind the retiring butler, Lord Iveldown and
Mr. Nassen were staring open-mouthed at the
Saint with the aspect of a comedy unison dance
team arrested in midflight. The rigidity of their

postures, the sag of their lower jaws, the glazed
bulging of their eyes, and the suffusion of red in
their complexions were so ludicrously identical
that they might have been reflections of each other.
They looked like two peas who had fallen out of
their pod and were still trying to realize what
had hit them; and the Honourable Leo looked
from them to the Saint and back again with a
frown of utter bewilderment.

"Whatever is the matter?" he demanded, startled into uttering one of the shortest sentences of
his life; and at the sound of his question Lord
Iveldown came slowly and painfully out of his
paralysis.

He turned, blinking through his pince-nez.

"Is that—that—the American gunman you told
me about?" he queried awfully.

"That is what I have been—ah—given to understand," said Farwill, recovering himself. "We are
indebted to Mr. Uniatz for the introduction. I
am informed that he has had an extensive career
in the underworld of—ah—Pittsburgh. Do you
imply that you are already acquainted?"

His lordship swallowed.

"You bumptious blathering ass!" he said.

Simon Templar uncoiled himself from his chair
with a genial smile. The spectacle of two politicians preparing to speak their minds candidly to
one another was so rare and beautiful that it
grieved him to interrupt; but he had his own part
to play. It had been no great effort to deny him-

self the batting of an eyelid up to that point—the
impulse to bat eyelids simply had not arisen to
require suppressing. Coming immediately on the
heels of Leo Farwill's revelation, he was not sorry
to see Lord Iveldown.

"What ho, Snowdrop," he murmured cordially.
"Greetings, your noble Lordship."

Farwill gathered himself together.

"So you are already acquainted!" he rumbled
with an effort of heartiness. "I thought——"

"Do you know who that is?" Iveldown asked
dreadfully.

Some appalling intuition made Farwill shake
his head; and the Saint smiled encouragingly.

"You tell him, Ivelswivel," he urged. "Relieve
the suspense."

"That's the Saint himself!" exploded Iveldown.

There are times when even this talented chronicler's genius stalls before the task of describing
adequately the reactions of Simon Templar's vic-
tims. Farwill's knees drooped, and his face took
on a greenish tinge; but in amplification of those
simple facts a whole volume might be written in
which bombshells, earthquakes, dynamite, mule-
kicks, and other symbols of devastating violence
would reel through a kaleidoscope of similes that
would still amount to nothing but an anæmic ghost
of the sight which rejoiced Simon Templar's eyes.
And the Saint smiled again and lighted his cigarette.

"Of course we know each other," he said. "Leo

and I were just talking about you, your Lordship. I gather that you're not only the bird who suggested bumping me off so that you'd only have Patricia Holm to deal with, but your little pal Snowdrop was the bloke who tried it on this morning and wrecked a perfectly good hat with his rotten shooting. I shall have to add a fiver onto your account for that, brother; but the other part of your brilliant idea isn't so easily dealt with."

Farwill's face was turning from green to grey.

"I seem to have made a mistake," he said flabbily.

"A pardonable error," said the Saint generously. "After all, Hoppy Uniatz didn't exactly give you an even break. But you didn't make half such a big mistake as Comrade Iveldown over there——"

Out of the corner of his eye he saw Nassen make a slight movement, and his hand had flashed to his pocket before he remembered that he had set out to enjoy his joke with so much confidence that he had not even gone heeled. But even if there had been a gun there, he would have reached it too late. Nassen had a hand in his coat pocket already; and there was a protuberance under the cloth whose shape Simon knew only too well.

He looked round and saw the reason for it. The ponderous thought processes of Hoppy Uniatz had at last reduced the situation to terms which he could understand. In his slow but methodical way, Mr. Uniatz had sifted through the dialogue and action and arrived at the conclu-

sion that something had gone amiss. Instinct had
made him go for his gun; but the armchair in
which he was ensconced had impeded his agility
on the draw, and Nassen had forestalled him. He
sat with his right hand still tangled in his pocket,
glaring at the lanky stillness of Iveldown's private
detective with self-disgust written all over his
face.

"I'm sorry, boss," he growled plaintively. "De
guy beat me to it."

"Never mind," said the Saint. "It's my fault."

Iveldown came forward, with his mouth twitching.

"The mistake could have been worse," he said.
"At least we have the Saint. Where is Yorkland?"

Farwill chewed his lower lip.

"I believe he could be intercepted. When he
first arrived, he told me that he had meant to call
on Lady Bredon at Camberley on his way down,
but he had not had time. He intimated that he
would do so on his way back——"

"Telephone there," snapped Iveldown.

He strode about the room, rubbing his hands
together under his coattails, while Farwill made
the call. He looked at the Saint frequently, but
not once did he meet Simon's eyes. Simon Templar
never made the mistake of attributing that avoid-
ance of his gaze to fear; at that moment, Iveldown
had less to fear than he had ever had before.
Watching him with inscrutable blue eyes, the
Saint knew that he was looking at a weak pompous

egotistical man whom fear had turned into jackal
at bay.

"What message shall I leave?" asked Farwill,
with his hand over the transmitter.

"Tell them to tell him—we've caught our man,"
said Iveldown.

The Saint blew a smoke ring.

"You seem very sure about that, brother," he
remarked. "But Snowdrop doesn't look too happy
about that gun. He looks as if he were afraid
it might go off—and do you realize, Snowdrop,
that if it did go off it'd burn a hole in your beautiful Sunday suit, and Daddy would have to smack
you?"

Nassen looked at him whitely.

"Leave him to me," he said. "I'll make him
talk."

Simon laughed shortly.

"You might do it if you're a ventriloquist," he
said contemptuously. "Otherwise you'd be doing
good business if you took a tin cent for your
chance. Get wise to yourself, Snowdrop. You've
lost your place in the campaign. You aren't dealing with a girl yet. You're talking to a man—if
you've any idea what that means."

Lord Iveldown stood aside, with his head
bowed in thought, as if he scarcely heard what
was going on. And then suddenly he raised his
eyes and looked at the Saint again for the first time
in a long while; and, meeting his gaze, Simon
Templar read there the confirmation of his

thoughts. His fate lay in the hands of a creature more ruthless, more vindictive, more incalculable than any professional killer—a weak man, shorn of his armour of pomposity, fighting under the spur of fear.

"The mistake could have been worse," Iveldown repeated.

"You ought to be thinking about other things," said the Saint quietly. "This is Friday evening; and the sun isn't standing still. By midnight tomorrow I have to receive your contribution to the Simon Templar Foundation—and yours also, Leo. And I'm telling you again that whatever you do and whatever Snowdrop threatens, wherever I am myself and whether I'm alive or dead, unless I've received your checks by that time Chief Inspector Teal will get something that at this moment he wants more than anything else you could offer him. He'll get a chance to read the book which I wouldn't let him see this morning."

"But meanwhile we still have you here," said Lord Iveldown, with an equal quietness that contrasted strangely with the nervous flickers that jerked across his mottled face. He turned to his host. "Farwill, we must go to London at once. Miss Holm will be—ah—concerned to hear the news."

"She has a great sense of humour," said the Saint metallically, but his voice sounded odd in his own ears.

Iveldown shrugged.

"That remains to be seen. I believe that it will be comparatively easy to induce her to listen to reason," he said thoughtfully; and the Saint's blood went cold.

"She wouldn't even listen to you," he said and knew that he lied.

Lord Iveldown must have known it, too, for he paid no attention. He turned away without answering, gathering his party like a schoolmaster rallying a flock of boys.

"Nassen, you will remain here and guard these two. When Mr. Yorkland arrives, explain the developments to him, and let him do what he thinks best. . . . Farwill, you must find some pretext to dismiss your servants for the night. It will avoid difficulties if Nassen is compelled to exercise force. We will leave the front door open so that Yorkland can walk in. . . ."

"Mind you don't catch cold," said the Saint in farewell.

He smoked his cigarette through and listened to the hum of Lord Iveldown's car going down the drive and fading away into the early night.

Not for a moment since Iveldown walked into the room had he minimized his danger. Admittedly it is easier to be distantly responsible for the deaths of ten thousand unknown men than to order directly the killing of one; yet Simon knew that Lord Iveldown, who had done the first many years ago, had in the last two days slipped over a borderline of desperation to the place where he would be capable of the second. The fussiness, the pretentious speech, the tatters of pomposity which still clung to him and made him outwardly ridiculous made no difference. He would kill like a sentious ass; but still he would kill. And something told the Saint that the Rose of Peckham would not be unwilling to do the job at his orders.

He lighted another cigarette and paced the room with the smooth nerveless silence of a cat. It was queer, he thought, how quickly and easily, with so little melodrama, an adventurer's jest could fall under the shadow of death; and he knew how utterly false to human psychology were the ranting bullying villains who committed the murders in fiction and films. Murder was so rarely done like that. It was done by heavy, grandiose, flabby, frightened men—like Lord Iveldown or the Honourable Leo Farwill or Mr. Neville Yorkland, M.P. And it made no difference that Simon Templar, who had often visualized himself being murdered, had a futile angry objection to being murdered by pettifogging excrescences of that type.

They would have no more compunction in dealing with Patricia. Perhaps less.

That was the thought which gnawed endlessly at his mind, infinitely more than any consideration of his own danger. The smooth nerveless silence of his own walking was achieved only by a grim effort of will. His muscles strained against it; a savage helplessness tore at his nerves while the minutes went by. Farwill and Iveldown had seventy-five miles to go; and with every minute his hope of overtaking them, even with his car and brilliant driving, was becoming more and more forlorn.

He glanced at Hoppy Uniatz. Mr. Uniatz was sitting hunched in his chair, his fists clenched, glowering at Nassen with steady unblinking malevolence. In Hoppy's philosophy there could be only one outcome to what had happened and his own failure on the draw. There was no point in revolving schemes of escape: the chance to put them into practice was never given. The only question to be answered was—how long? His wooden nerves warping under the strain of the long silence, he asked it.

"Well," he growled, "when do we go for dis ride?"

"I'll tell you when the time comes," said Nassen.

The Saint pitched away his cigarette and lighted yet another. Nassen was alone. There were two of them; and nobody had thought to take Hoppy's gun away. If Hoppy could only get a second chance to draw—if Nassen's nerves could be played on, skilfully and relentlessly, until it became a question of which side could outlast the other . . .

"What does it feel like to be monarch of all you survey, Snowdrop?" he asked. "Doesn't it make your little heart go pit-a-pat? I mean, suppose

Hoppy and I suddenly decided we didn't love you any more, and we both jumped up together and slapped you?"

"You'd better try," said Nassen. "I'd be glad of the excuse."

He spoke with a cold stolidity that made the Saint stop breathing for a moment. Not until then, perhaps, had he admitted to himself how hopeless was the idea which had crossed his mind—hopeless, at least, to achieve any results in time for it to be worth the effort.

He halted in front of Nassen, gazing at him over the gun between them. So there was only one way left. Nassen could not possibly miss him; but he might be held long enough to give Hoppy Uniatz a chance. And after that, Hoppy would have to carry the flag. . . .

"You know that would be murder, don't you, Snowdrop?" he said slowly, without a flinch of fear in his bleak watchful eyes.

"Would it?" said Nassen mincingly. "For all anyone would ever know, you're a couple of armed burglars caught red-handed. Your record at Scotland Yard will do the rest. Don't forget whose house this is——"

He broke off.

Another pair of headlights had flashed across the windows; and a car, frantically braked, skidded on the gravel outside. A bell rang in the depths of the house; the knocker hammered impatiently; then came the slight creak of the front door opening. Every movement of the man outside could be pictured from the sounds. The unlatched door moved when he plied the knocker: he looked at it for a moment in indecision—took the first hesitant step into the hall—hurried on. . . .

Nassen was listening, too. And suddenly the Saint realized that the chance he had never looked for, the chance he had never thought of, had been given him. Nassen's attention was distracted—he, too, had been momentarily fascinated by the imaginary picture that could be deduced from the sequence of sounds. But he recovered less quickly than the Saint. And Simon's fist had already been clenched for a desperate blow when the interruption came.

The Saint launched it.

Snowdrop, the Rose of Peckham, was never very clear in his mind about what happened. He was not by nature addicted to physical violence of the cruder sort; and no experience of that kind had ever come his way before to give him a standard of comparison. He saw a bony fist a few inches from his face, travelling towards him with appalling speed; and his mouth opened. The fist shut it again for him, impacting on the point of his chin with a crack that seemed to jar his brain against the roof of his skull. And beyond that there was nothing but a great darkness filled with the hum of many dynamos. . . .

Simon caught him by the coat lapels and eased

him silently to the floor, gathering up the automatic as he did so. As he did so, the door burst open and the rounded rabbit features of Mr. Neville Yorkland looked into the room.

"Hullo," he stuttered. "What's happened? Got Lord Iveldown's message. Said he'd caught our man." His weak blinking eyes travelled all over the room and came to rest on the prostrate form of the slumbering Nassen. He pursed his lips. "Oh. I see. Is this——"

The Saint straightened up; and a slow godless gleam came into his blue gaze.

"That's the guy," he said, in the accents of Pete the Blood. "Hoppy an' me was just waitin' to see ya before we scram. We gotta get on to London— Lord Iveldown wants us there!"

IX

PATRICIA HOLM was waiting for the Saint when the telephone bell rang to announce the penultimate round of that adventure.

"It's that detective again, miss," said Sam Outrell hoarsely. "Mr. Teal. An' he's got another detective with him. They wouldn't wait for me to ask if they could go up."

The girl's heart missed a beat; and then she answered quite quietly:

"All right, Sam. Thanks. Tell Mr. Templar as soon as you see him—if they haven't gone before he comes in."

She put down the receiver and picked up the cigarette which she had been about to light. She looked about the room while she put a match to it —her hand was steady, but her breath was coming a little faster. She had walked with Simon Templar in the ways of lawlessness too long to be flung into panic; but she knew that she was on trial. The Saint had not come back, and he had sent no message: his habits had always been too erratic for a thing like that to frighten her, but this time she was left to hold the fort alone, with no idea of what he had done or was doing or what his plans might be. The only thing she could be sure of was that Chief Inspector Teal had not arrived for the second time that day, bringing another detective with him, on a purely social call.

The book, *Her Wedding Secret,* lay on the table. Patricia picked it up. She had to think—to think quickly and calmly, building up deduction and prophecy and action, as the Saint himself would have done. Simon had left the book there. He had not troubled to move it when Nassen came. But Teal—Teal and another man. . . . The bell of the apartment rang while she was still trying to reach a conclusion. There was an open bookcase beside the fireplace, and with a sudden tightening of her lips she thrust the book in among the row of novels on the bottom shelf. She had no time to do anything more; but she was desperately conscious of the inadequacy of what she had done.

Chief Inspector Teal did not know it. He looked across the threshold with affectedly weary eyes at the slim startling beauty of the girl who even to his phlegmatic unimpressionable mind was more like a legendary princess than any other woman he had ever seen, who for reasons not utterly beyond his understanding had chosen to give up the whole world that she might have queened to become the companion in outlawry of a prince of buccaneers; and he saw in her blue eyes, so amazingly like the Saint's own, the same light of flickering steel with which Simon Templar had greeted him so many times.

"Good-evening, Miss Holm," he said sleepily. "I think you know me; and this is Sergeant Barrow. We have a warrant to search this apartment."

He held out the paper; and she glanced at it and handed it back.

"Mr. Templar isn't in," she said coolly. "Hadn't you better call back later?"

"I don't think so," said Mr. Teal and walked past her into the hall.

She closed the door and followed the two detectives into the living room. Mr. Teal took off his bowler hat and put it on the table—it was the only concession he made to her presence.

"We may as well start here," he said to Barrow. "Go over the usual places first."

"Would you like to borrow the vacuum cleaner," inquired Patricia sweetly, "or will you just use your heads?"

"We'll manage," said Teal dourly.

He was more keyed up than he would have cared to admit. The assistant commissioner's parting speech still rang in his ears; the resentment of many other similar interviews rang carillons through his brain. He was a man of whom Fate had demanded many martyrdoms. In doing his duty he had to expose himself to the stinging shafts of Saintly irreverence; and afterwards he had to listen to the acidulated comments of the assistant commissioner; and there were days when he wondered whether it was worth it. Sometimes he wished that he had never been a policeman.

Patricia stood around and watched the progress of the search with a triphammer working under her ribs and a sinking sensation in her stomach. And in a frightful hopeless way she realized that it was not going to fail. It was not a hurried haphazard ransacking of drawers and cupboards such as Nassen and his colleague had conducted. It was thorough, systematic, scientific, ordered along the rigid lines of a training that had reduced hiding places to a tabulated catalogue. It would not glance at the cover of a book and pass on. . . .

She knew that even before Barrow came to the bookcase and began to pull out the books one by one, opening them and flicking over the pages without looking at the titles. . . .

What would the Saint have done?

Patricia didn't know. Her face was calm, almost unnaturally calm; but the triphammer under her ribs was driving her into the clutches of a maddening helplessness that had to be fought off with all her willpower. There was an automatic in the bedroom: if she could only put over some excuse to reach it . . . But the Saint would never have done that. Teal had his warrant. He was within his rights. Violence of any kind would achieve nothing—nothing except to aggravate the crash when it came.

Barrow had reached the second row of books. He was halfway through it. He had finished it. The first two shelves were stripped, and the books were heaped up untidily on the floor. He was going on to the third.

What would the Saint have done?

If only he could arrive! If only the door would open, and she could see him again, smiling and unaccountable and debonair, grasping the situation with one sweep of lazy blue eyes and finding the riposte at once! It would be something wild and unexpected, something swift and dancing like sunlight on open water, that would turn everything upside down in a flash and leave him mocking in command with his forefinger driving gaily and unanswerably into Teal's swelling waistcoat; she knew that, but she could not think what it would be. She only knew that he had never been at a loss—that somehow, madly magnificently, he could always retrieve the lost battle and snatch victory from under the very scythe of defeat.

Barrow was down to the third shelf.

On the table were the bottle of beer and the glass which she had set out ready for him—the glass over which the Saint's eyes should have been twinkling while he harried the two detectives with his remorseless wit. Her hands went out and took up the bottle and the opener, as she would have done for the Saint if he had walked in.

"Would you care for a drink?" she asked huskily.

"No, thank you, Miss Holm," said Teal politely, without looking at her.

She had the opener fitted on the crown cap. The bottle opened with a soft hiss before she fully realized that she had done it. She tried to picture the Saint standing on the other side of the table—to make herself play the scene as he would have played it.

"Excuse me if I have one," she said.

The full glass was in her hand. She sipped it. She had never cared for beer, and involuntarily she grimaced. . . .

Teal heard a gasp and a crash behind him and whirled round. He saw the glass in splinters on the table, the beer flowing across the top and pattering down onto the carpet, the girl clutching her throat and swaying where she stood, with wide horrified eyes.

"What's the matter?" he snapped.

She shook her head and swallowed painfully before she spoke.

"It . . . burns," she got out in a whisper. "Inside. . . . Must have been something in it. . . . Meant for . . . Simon. . . ."

Then her knees crumpled and she went down.

Teal went to her with surprising speed. She was writhing horribly, and her breath hissed sobbingly through her clenched teeth. She tried to speak again, but she could not form the words.

Teal picked her up and laid her on the chesterfield.

"Get on the phone," he snarled at Barrow with unnatural harshness. "Don't stand there gaping. Get an ambulance."

He looked about him awkwardly. Water—that was the first thing. Dilute the poison—whatever it was. With a sudden setting of his lips he lumbered out of the room.

Patricia saw him go.

Sergeant Barrow was at the telephone, his back towards her. And the bookcase was within a yard of her. Writhing as she was, the sound of one movement more or less would not be noticed. There was no need for stealth—only for speed.

She rolled over and snatched *Her Wedding Secret* from its place in the bottom shelf. Barrow had been too practical—too methodical. He had not looked at titles. With a swift movement she lifted the first three volumes of one of the inspected piles which he had stacked on the floor, and thrust the book underneath. . . .

"Thank you," said Teal's drowsy voice.

He was standing in the doorway with a grim gleam of triumph in his eyes; and he had not even got a glass of water in his hand. She realized that he had never gone for one. He had thought too fast.

Barrow was gaping at him stupidly.

"You can cancel that call," said Teal shortly.

Patricia sat up and watched him cross the room and pick the book out of the pile. The trip hammer under her ribs had stopped work abruptly; and she knew the fatalistic quiet of ultimate defeat. She had played and lost. There was no more to do.

Mr. Teal opened the book with hands that were not quite steady. The realization of success made him fumble nervously—it was a symptom which amazed himself. He learned then that he had never really hoped to succeed; that the memory of infinite failures had instilled a subconscious presentiment that he never could succeed. Even with the book in his hands, he could not quite believe that the miracle had happened.

It was in manuscript—he saw that in a moment. Manuscript written in a minute pinched hand that crowded an astonishing mass of words onto the page. Methodically he turned to the beginning.

The first page was in the form of a letter:

Villa Philomène,
Nice,
A. M.

My dear Mr. Templar:

It is some time now since we last met, but I have no fear that you will have forgotten the encounter. Lest it should have slipped my mind at the time, let me immediately pay you the tribute of saying that you are the only man in the world who has successfully frustrated my major plans on two occasions, and who has successfully circumvented my best efforts to exterminate him.

It is for this reason that, being advised that I have not many more months to live, I am sending you this small token of esteem in the shape of the first volume of my memoirs.

In my vocation of controller of munition factories, and consequently as the natural creator of a demand for their products, I have had occasion to deal with other Englishmen, fortunately in a more amicable manner than you would permit me to deal with you. In this volume, which deals with certain of my negotiations in England before and during the last World War, you will find detailed and fully documented accounts of a few notable cases in which prominent countrymen of yours failed to view my activities with that violent and unbusinesslike distaste which you yourself have more than once expressed to me.

The gift has, of course, a further object than that of diminishing any insular prejudices you may have.

At the same time as this book is sent to you, there will be sent, to the gentlemen most conspicuously men-

tioned in these notes, letters which will inform them into whose hands the book has fallen. After reading it yourself, you will see that this cannot fail to cause them great perturbation.

Nevertheless, while it would be simple for you to allay their alarm and assure your own safety from molestation, I cannot foresee that a man such as I recall you to be would so tamely surrender such a unique opportunity to apply moral pressure towards the righting of what you consider to be wrongs.

I therefore hope to leave behind me the makings of a most diverting contest which my experiments in international diplomacy may have excelled in dimension, but can scarcely have excelled in quality. And you will understand, I am sure, my dear Mr. Templar, that I can hardly be blamed for sincerely trusting that these gentlemen, or their agents, will succeed where I have failed.

Very truly yours,
RAYT MARIUS.

Teal read the letter through and looked up with an incredulous half-puzzled frown. Then, without speaking, he began to read it through again. Patricia stood up with a little sigh, straightened her dress, and began to comb out her hair. Sergeant Barrow shifted from one foot to the other and compared his watch with the clock on the mantelpiece—it would be the fourth consecutive night that he had been late home for dinner, and his wife could scarcely be blamed for beginning to view his explanations with suspicion.

Mr. Teal was halfway through his second reading when the telephone rang. He hesitated for a moment and then nodded to the girl.

"You can answer it," he said.

Patricia took up the instrument.

"There are two gentlemen here to see you, miss," said Sam Outrell. "Lord Iveldown and Mr. Farwill."

"Send them up," she said recklessly.

She had no idea why those two should have called to see her, but she was also beyond caring.

"Lord Iveldown and the Home Secretary are on their way," she told Teal, as she put down the telephone. "You're holding quite a gathering here, aren't you?"

The detective blinked at her dubiously. He was unable to accept her statement at its face value, and he was unable for the moment to discover either an insulting witticism or the opening of another trap in it. He returned to his reading with only half his mind on it; and he had just finished when the buzz of the doorbell took her from the room.

He closed the book and changed his position so that he could see the hall.

". . . so unceremoniously, Miss Holm," Lord Iveldown was saying, as he entered the room. "But the matter is urgent—most urgent." He stopped as he saw Teal. "And private," he added. "I did not know that you were entertaining."

"It must have been kept a secret," said the girl ironically.

She moved aside to shut the door; and as she did so, Mr. Teal and the Honourable Leo Farwill saw each other at the same time. There was a moment's dead silence; and then Farwill coughed.

"Ah—Inspector," he said heavily. "I hope we are not—ah—disturbing you."

"No, sir," said Teal, looking at him curiously. He added: "I think you'll be glad to know, sir, that as far as I can see we've got all the evidence we need."

Farwill's hand went to his moustache. His face had gone puffy and grey, and there was a dry hoarseness in his voice.

"Ah—evidence," he repeated. "Ah—quite. Quite. Ah—evidence. That book——"

"Have you read it?" asked Iveldown raspingly.

"Only the first page, my lord," said Teal. "The first page is a letter—it's rather involved, but I think the book will turn out to be the one we were looking for."

His heavy-lidded china-blue eyes were fixed on the Home Secretary perplexedly and with a trace of subconscious hostility. There was a kind of gritty strain in the atmosphere which he could not understand; and, not understanding it, it bothered him. His second reading of the letter had definitely been distracted, and he had not yet clearly sorted its meaning out of the elaborate and unfamiliar phrases in which it was worded. He only knew that he held triumph in his hands, and that for some unaccountable reason the Honourable Leo Farwill, who had first put him on the trail, was not sharing his elation.

"Let me see the book," said Farwill.

More or less hypnotized, Teal allowed it to be taken out of his hand; and when it was gone, a kind of wild superstitious fear that was beyond logic made him breathe faster, as if the book had actually dissolved into thin air between his fingers.

Farwill opened the book at the first page and read the letter.

"Ah—quite," he said short-windedly. "Quite. Quite."

"Mr. Farwill was going to say," put in Lord Iveldown, "that we came here for a special purpose, hoping to intercept you, Inspector. Critical international developments——"

"Exactly," boomed Farwill throatily. "The matter is vital. I might almost say—ah—vital." He tucked the book firmly under his arm. "You will permit me to take complete charge of this affair, Inspector. I shall have to ask you to accompany Lord Iveldown and myself to Scotland Yard immediately, where I shall explain to the chief commissioner the reasons of state which obviously cannot be gone into here—ah—and your own assiduous efforts, even if misdirected, will be suitably recognized——"

The gentle click of a latch behind him made everyone spin round at once; and Patricia gave a little choking cry.

"Well, well, well!" breathed the smiling man

who stood just inside the door. "That's great stuff, Leo—but how on earth do you manage to remember all those words without notes?"

It was the Saint.

X

HE STOOD with his hands in his pockets and a freshly lighted cigarette tilting between his lips, with his hair blown awry by the sixty miles an hour he had averaged and the sparkle of the wind in his eyes; and Hoppy Uniatz stood beside him. According to their different knowledge, the others stared at him with various emotions registering on their dials; and the Saint smiled on them all impartially and came on in.

"Hullo, Pat," he murmured. "I didn't know you'd asked the Y. M. C. A. to move in. Why didn't you tell me?" His keen blue eyes, missing nothing, came to rest on the gaudily covered volume that Farwill was clutching under his arm. "So you've taken up literature at last, Leo," he said. "I always thought you would."

To say that Farwill and Iveldown were looking at him as if they had seen a ghost would be a trite understatement. They were goggling at him as if he had been the consolidated incarnation of all the spooks and banshees that ever howled through a maniac's nightmare. Their prosperous paunches

were caving in like rubber balloons punctured
with a sharp instrument; and it seemed as though
all the inflation that escaped from their abdomens
was going straight into their eyeballs. There was
a sick blotchy pallor in their faces which suggested that they had been mentally spirited away
onto the deck of a ship that was wallowing
through all the screaming furies of the Horn.

It was Farwill who first found his voice. It was
not much of a voice—it was more like the croak
of a strangling frog—but it produced words.

"Inspector," it said, "arrest that man."

Teal's somnolent eyes opened a little, and there
was a gleam of tentative exhilaration in them. So,
after all, it seemed as if he had been mistaken. He
was not to be cheated of his triumph. His luck had
turned.

"I was going to," he said and started forward.

"On what charge?" asked the Saint.

"The same charge," said Teal inexorably.
"Blackmail."

The Saint nodded.

"I see," he said and shrugged his shoulders.
"Oh, well—no game can go on for ever, and
we've had lots of fun." His gaze watched the
advancing detective with a hint of wicked banter
in it that belied the rueful resignation of his features; but Teal did not see that at once. "It'll be
a sensational case," said the Saint. "Let me give
you an idea."

And without warning, with a flow of movements

too swift to follow, he took a couple of paces sideways and aimed a punch at what was left of the Honourable Leo's prosperous corporation. Farwill instinctively jerked up his hands; and with a quick smile Simon turned the feint into a deft reach of his hand that caught *Her Wedding Secret* as it fell.

Barrow and Teal plunged towards him simultaneously; and the Saint moved rapidly back— past the automatic that had appeared like magic in the hand of a Mr. Uniatz who this time had not been artificially obstructed on the draw.

"Stay back, youse guys!" barked Hoppy, in a voice quivering with exultation at his achievement; and involuntarily the two detectives checked.

The two politicians, equally involuntarily taking the lead in any popular movement, went farther. They went back as far as the confines of the room would allow them.

"You know your duty, Inspector," said the Home Secretary tremblingly. "I order you to arrest those men!"

"Don't order a good man to commit suicide," said the Saint curtly. "Nobody's going to get hurt —if you'll all behave yourselves for a few minutes. I'm the bloke who's being arrested, and I want to enjoy it. Readings by the public prosecutor of extracts from this book will be the high spot of the trial, and I want to have a rehearsal."

He turned the pages and quickly found a place.

"Now here's a juicy bit that'll whet your appetites," he remarked. "It must have something to do with those reasons of state which you were burbling about, Leo. *'On May 15th I dined again with Farwill, then Secretary of State for War. He was inclined to agree with me about the potentialities of the Aix-la-Chapelle incident for increasing the friction between France and Germany; and on my increasing my original offer to £50,000 he agreed to place before the Cabinet——"*

"Stop!" shouted Farwill shrilly. "It's a lie!"

The Saint closed his book and put it down; and very slowly the smile returned to his lips.

"I shouldn't be so melodramatic as that," he said easily. "But of course it's a joke. I suppose it's really gone a bit too far."

There was another long silence; and then Lord Iveldown cleared his throat.

"Of course," he said in a cracked voice. "A joke."

"A joke," repeated Farwill hollowly. "Ah—of course."

Simon flicked his cigarette through the open window, and a rumble of traffic went by in the sudden quiet.

"And not, I'm afraid," he murmured, "in the best of taste."

His eyes strayed back to the staring gaze of Chief Inspector Teal.

Of all those persons present, Mr. Teal did not

seem the most happy. It would be inaccurate to
say that he realized exactly what was going on.
He didn't. But something told him that there was
a catch in it. Somewhere in the undercurrents of
that scene, he knew, there was something phony—
something that was preparing to gyp him of his
triumph at the very moment of victory. He had
only the dimmest idea of how it was being
worked; but he had seen it happen too many times
before to mistake the symptoms.

"What the heck is this joke?" he demanded.

"Leo will tell you," said the Saint.

Farwill licked his lips.

"I—ah—the joke was so—ah—silly that I—ah
. . . Well, Inspector, when Mr. Templar approached us with the offer of this—ah—literary
work, and—ah—knowing his, if I may say so,
notorious—ah—character, I—ah—that is, we—
thought that it would be humorous to play a
slight—ah—practical joke on him, with your—ah
—unwitting assistance. Ah——"

"Whereas, of course, you meant to buy it all the
time," Simon prompted him gently.

"Ah—yes," said the Honourable Leo chokingly.
"Buy it. Ah—of course."

"At once," said Lord Iveldown quaveringly,
taking out his checkbook.

"Ah—naturally," moaned the Honourable Leo,
feeling for his pen. "At once."

"Two hundred thousand pounds, was it not, Mr.
Templar?" said Lord Iveldown.

The Saint shook his head.

"The price has gone up a bit," he said. "It'll cost you two hundred and fifty thousand now—I need a new hat, and the Simon Templar Foundation isn't intended to pay for that."

With his head swimming and the blood drumming in his ears, Chief Inspector Claud Eustace Teal watched the checks being made out and blotted and handed over. He would never really know how the trick was turned. He only knew that Simon Templar was back; and anything could happen. . . .

The parting words with which the Saint shepherded the gathering out of the door did nothing to enlighten him.

"By the way, Leo," said the Saint, "you must remember to tell Neville to send on his share. If you toddle straight back home you'll find him waiting for you. He's standing guard over the Rose of Peckham with a great big gun—and for some reason or other he thinks Snowdrop is me."

"Sir Humbolt Quipp came in and left a check," said Patricia Holm uncertainly.

Simon took it and added it to his collection. He fanned out the four precious scraps of paper and brought the Honourable Leo Farwill's contribution to the top. Then he removed this one from the others and gazed at it for a long time with a rather rueful frown.

"I'm afraid we let Leo off too lightly," he said.

"When I begin to think what a splendiferous orgy of Teal-baiting we could have had with the Home Secretary permanently under our thumb, I almost wonder whether the Simon Templar Foundation is worth it."

But later on he brightened.

"It would have made life damned dull," he said.

II

THE HIGHER FINANCE

I

ONE day some literary faker with more time to waste than I have may write a precious monograph about Doors. He will point out that Doors are both entrances and exits, and draw pseudo-philosophical conclusions about Life and Death. He will drag in the Door which American diplomats always insist on keeping Open, except when they are inside. He may turn aside to toy fancifully with the Door-consciousness of Wolves. He will inevitably mention some famous Doors; such as the Great Door of the cathedral of Poillissy-sur-Loire, on which Voltaire scribbled a rude epigram addressed to the Pope; the Golden Door of the temple of Pashka in Allahabad, on which are engraved 777 sacred cows; the Door of Cesare Borgia's guest house, which drove daggers into the backs of everyone who passed through it; and so forth. Probably he will unscrupulously invent all this part out of his own imagination, exactly as I have done, but nobody will be any the wiser.

It is difficult, however, to see how the Door of the Barnyard Club, in London, could find a place in any such catalogue, being made of gimcrack deal and having no history or peculiarities. And yet, when it opened in the small hours of a certain morning to let Simon Templar out into Bond Street, it was for that brief moment the Door of Adventure.

Simon Templar stood at the edge of the sidewalk and put a thin cigarette between his lips, letting the cool air of the night play on his forehead and freshen his lungs; but there was no indication that freshening was his vital need. His dark rakish face seemed to have walked straight out of the open windswept places of the earth rather than out of the strained stuffy atmosphere of a night club, and his gay blue eyes could not have been clearer and keener at any other hour of the day. His strong lawless mouth had a curve of half-amused expectancy, as if his day were just beginning and he had a long list of diverting things to do; but there was nothing on his mind. It was only that Simon Templar's days were always ready to begin, at any hour, whenever adventure offered.

At his side Mr. Hoppy Uniatz, resplendent in a tight-waisted tuxedo and a shirtfront pinned together with a diamond stud, yawned cavernously and trod on the butt of his cigar. His was a less resiliently romantic soul, and he felt healthily depressed.

"Say, boss," he remarked querulously, "is dat what dey calls a big night in dis city?"

"I'm afraid it is," said the Saint.

Mr. Uniatz had none of that ascetic nobility of

character which enables the Englishman to suffer his legislators gladly. He spat mournfully into the road.

"Chees," he said, with a gloomy emulsion of awe and disgust, "it ain't human. De last joint we're in, dey snatch off all de glasses becos it's twelve-toity. We pay two bucks each to get into dis joint, an' then we gotta pay five bucks fer a jug of lemonade wit' a spoonful of gin in it; an' all they got is a t'ree-piece band an' no floor show. An' de guys sits an' takes it! Why, if any joint had tried to gyp guys like dat in New York, even when we had prohibition, dey'd of wrecked it in two minutes." Mr. Uniatz sighed and reached for the only apparent conclusion, unaware that other philosophers had reached it long before him: "Well, maybe dem Limeys ain't human, at dat."

"You forget that this is a free country, Hoppy," murmured the Saint gently.

He lighted his cigarette and blew out a wreath of smoke at the stars. A few spots of rain were beginning to fall from a bank of cloud that was climbing up from the west, and he scanned the street for a taxi to take them home. As if it had been conjured up in answer to his wish, a cab swung round the corner of Burlington Gardens and chugged towards them; and the Saint watched its approach hopefully. It was fifteen yards away when he saw that the flag was down, and shrugged ruefully. The setback was only an apt epilogue to a consistently inauspicious evening.

"We'd better walk," he said.

They turned down towards Piccadilly; and then, as they fell into step, he heard the rattle of the taxi die down and looked back over his shoulder. It had stopped outside the entrance of the Barnyard Club.

The Saint caught Hoppy's arm.

"Hold on," he said. "The luck's changed. We stay dry after all."

They strolled back towards the spot where this minor miracle stood panting metallically while its passenger alighted. It was a girl, he saw as she stood fumbling with her bag.

"I'm afraid I haven't anything smaller," she was saying; and he heard that her voice was low and pleasant.

The driver grunted and climbed down laboriously from his box. Standing in the gutter, he unbuttoned his overcoat, his coat, his waistcoat, his cardigan, and part of his shirt, and began a slow and painful search through the various strange and inaccessible places where London taxi drivers secrete their small change. From scattered areas of his anatomy he collected over a period of time an assortment of coins and looked at them under the light.

"Sorry, miss, I can't do it," he said at length and began phlegmatically to dress himself again.

"I'll get change inside," said the girl.

But Simon Templar had other ideas. They had been growing on him while the driver disrobed, and the Saint had always been an opportunist. He liked the girl's voice and her slim figure and the way she wore her clothes; and that was enough for a beginning.

"Excuse me," he said. "Can I help?"

She looked up with a start, and for the first time he saw her face clearly. It was small and oval, with a fascinatingly tip-tilted nose and a mouth that would smile easily; her deep brown hair, smooth and straight to the curled ends, framed her face in a soft halo of darkness. But even while he saw her brown eyes regarding him hesitantly he wondered if the dim light had deceived him—or if he had really seen, as he had thought he saw, a leap of sudden fear in them when she first looked up.

"We're only trying to change a pound," she said.

He took the note from her fingers and spread out a line of silver coins on her palm in return. She paid off the driver, who proceeded to bury the money in the outlying regions of his clothing; and she would have thanked him and gone on, but the Saint's other ideas had scarcely been tapped.

"Are you determined to go in there?" he asked, waving his pound note disparagingly in the direction of the Barnyard Club. "Hoppy and I didn't think much of it. Besides, you haven't got your pillow."

"Why should I want a pillow?"

"For comfort. Everybody else in there is asleep," he explained, "but the management doesn't provide pillows. They just create the demand."

The brown eyes searched his face doubtfully, with a glimpse of hunted suspicion that need not have been there. And once again he saw what he had seen before, the glimmering light of fear that went across her gaze—or was it across his own imagination?

"Thanks so much for helping me—good-night," she said in a breath and left the Saint staring after her with a puzzled smile till the door of the club closed behind her.

Simon tilted back his hat and turned resignedly to take possession of the asthmatic cab which was left as his only consolation; and as he turned, a hand fell on his shoulder.

"Do you know that girl?" asked a sleepy voice.

"Apparently not, Claud," answered the Saint sorrowfully. "I tried to, but she didn't seem to be sold on the idea. Life has these mysteries."

Chief Inspector Claud Eustace Teal studied him with half-closed eyes whose drowsiness was nothing but an affectation. His pudgy hand came down from the Saint's shoulder and took away the pound note which he was still holding; and the Saint's brows suddenly came down an invisible fraction of an inch.

"You don't mind if I have a look at this?" he said.

It was not so much a question as an authoritative demand; and a queer tingle of supernatural expectation touched Simon Templar's spine for an instant and was gone. For the first time since the hand fell on his shoulder he looked beyond the detective's broad and portly form and saw another solid bowler-hatted figure, equally broad but a shade less portly, kicking its regulation rubber heels a few paces away, as if waiting for the conversation to conclude. The Saint's suddenly quiet and watchful eyes swerved along the sidewalk in the other direction, and saw two other men of the same unmistakable pattern engrossed in inaudible discussion in the shadow of a shop doorway on his right. All at once, without a sound that his unguarded ears had noticed, the deserted street had acquired a population. . . .

A tiny pulse began to beat in the Saint's brain, a pulse that was little more than the echo of his own heart working steadily through a moment of utter physical stillness; and then he drew a deep lungful of air through his cigarette and let the smoke trickle out in a slow feather through the sparse twinkling beads of rain. After all, the night had not failed him. It had merely been teasing. What it would have to offer eventually he still did not know; but he knew that three men out of the mould which he saw do not abruptly assemble in Bond Street, materializing like genii out of the damp paving stones at two o'clock in the morning, and bringing Chief Inspector Teal with them, for no other reason than that they have been simultaneously smitten with an urge to discover at first hand whether the night life of London is as dull as it is universally reputed to be. And wherever and whenever such a deputation of official talent was gathered together, Simon Templar had a potential interest in the proceedings.

"What's the matter with it?" he inquired thoughtfully.

Mr. Teal straightened up slowly from his examination of the banknote under one of the taxi's feeble lights. He took out his wallet and folded the bill in deliberately.

"You won't mind if I look after it for you?" he said, with the same authoritative decision.

"Help yourself," murmured the Saint lavishly. "Are you starting a collection, or something? I've got a few more of those if you'd like 'em."

The detective buttoned his coat and glanced towards the two men who were conversing in the adjacent doorway. Without appearing to interrupt their conversation, they moved out onto the pavement and came nearer.

"I'm surprised at you, Saint," he said, with what in anyone else would have been a tinge of malicious humour, "being taken in with a thing like that at your age. Is this the first time you've seen a bit of slush?"

"I like 'em that way," said the Saint slowly. "You know me, Claud. I never cared for this mass-production stuff. I've always believed in encouraging individual enterprise——"

"It's a good job I watched you encouraging it,"

said the detective grimly. "With your reputation, you wouldn't have stood much chance if you'd been caught trying to pass a counterfeit note." A wrinkle of belated regret for a lost opportunity creased his forehead as that last poignant thought entrenched itself in his mind. "Perhaps I wouldn't have been in such a hurry to take it away from you if I'd remembered that before," he added candidly.

The Saint smiled; but the smile was only on his lips.

"You have the friendliest inspirations, dear old bird," he remarked amiably. "Why not give it back? There's still time; and I see you've got lots of your old school pals around."

"I've got something else to do," said Mr. Teal. He squared his shoulders, and his mouth set in a line along which many things might have been read. "If I want to ask you anything more about this, I'll know where to find you," he said and turned brusquely away towards the door of the club.

As he did so, the other man who had been kicking his heels in the middle background roused out of his vague detachment and went after him. The second pair of detectives who had been strolling closer drifted unobtrusively into the same route. There was nothing dramatic, nothing outwardly sensational about it; but it had the mechanical precision of a manœuvre by a well-drilled squad of soldiers. For one or two brief seconds the three men who had appeared so surprisingly out of the empty night were clustered at the doorway like bees alighting at the entrance of a hive; and then they had filtered through, without fuss or ostentation, as if they had never been there. The door was closed again, and the broken lights and shadows of the street were so still that the patter of swelling raindrops on the parched pavements could be heard like a rustle of leaves in the absence of any other sound.

Simon put his cigarette to his lips, with his eyes fixed on the blank door, and drained it of the last slow inhalation. He dropped it between his fingers and shifted the toe of a polished patent-leather shoe, blotting it out. The evening had done its stuff. It had provided the wherewithal. . . . He put his hands in his trouser pockets and felt the lightness which had been left there by the twenty shillings' worth of good silver which he had paid out in exchange for that confiscated scrap of forged Bank of England paper; and he remembered a bewitching face and the shadow of fear which had come and gone in its brown eyes. But at that moment he was at a loss to know what he could do.

And then an awful noise broke the silence behind him. It was a frightful clattering consumptive hiccough which turned into a continuous sobbing rattle in which all the primeval anguish of ancient iron and steel was orchestrated into one grinding medley of discords. The taxi which had brought Adventure's offering had started up again.

Simon Templar turned. He had been mad for years, and it was much too late in life to begin striving after sanity. His face was dazzlingly seraphic as he looked up at the rehabilimented driver, who was settling stoically into his seat.

"Does this happen to be your own cab, brother?" he asked.

"Yes, guv'nor," said the man. "Jer wanter buy it?"

"That's exactly what I do want," said the Saint.

II

THE DRIVER gaped down at him with a feeble fish-like grin—handsomer men than he had been smitten in the same way when their facetious witticisms were taken literally.

"Wot?" he said weakly, expressing the ultimate essence of cosmic doubt in the one irreducible monosyllable which philosophers have sought in vain for centuries.

"I want to buy your cab," said the Saint. "I'm collecting specimens for a museum. What's the price?"

"Five 'undred quid, guv'nor, an' it's yours,"

stated the proud owner, clinging hysterically to his joke.

Simon took out his billfold and counted out five crackling banknotes. The driver crawled down from his box with glazed eyes and clutched at one rusty mudguard for support.

"You ain't arf pulling me leg, are yer?" he said.

Simon folded the notes and pushed them into his hand.

"Take those round to a bank in the morning and see how your leg feels," he advised and took out another note as an afterthought. "Will a fiver buy your coat and cap as well?"

"Blimey, guv'nor," replied the driver, unbuttoning again with sudden vigour, "you could 'ave me shirt an' trousers as well for arf that."

The Saint stood for a moment and watched the happily bereaved driver veering somewhat light-headedly out of view; and then, beside him, Hoppy Uniatz groped audibly for comprehension.

"What kinda joke is dis, boss?" he asked; and the Saint pulled himself together.

"It'll grow on you as the years go by, Hoppy," he said kindly.

He was pulling on the driver's big grubby overcoat and winding the nondescript muffler round his neck with the speed and efficiency of a quick-change artist between scenes. In the emptiness of the street there was no one to see him. His black

felt hat came off and was dumped into Hoppy's
hands; the driver's peaked cap took its place. For
a moment Hoppy saw the dark clean-cut face
blithe and buccaneering under the shade of the
cap, the white teeth glinting in a smile that had no
respect for any impossibilities.

"You won't be able to stay here and share it
with me," said the Saint. "I've got another job
for you. Get hold of this address: 26 Abbot's
Yard, Chelsea. You'd better take a taxi—but not
this one. Go straight there and make yourself at
home. There's a bottle of Scotch in the pantry;
and here's the key. We're going to throw a party!"

"Okay, boss," said Mr. Uniatz dimly.

He took the key, stowed it away in his pocket,
and without another word hoofed phlegmatically
away in the direction of Piccadilly. It would be
untrue to say that he had grasped the point with
inspired intuition; but certain nouns and verbs
had conglomerated in his mind to indicate a course
of action, and therefore he was taking it. His
brain, which was a small and loosely knit organization of nerve endings accustomed to directing
such simple activities as eating, sleeping, and
shooting off guns, was not adapted to the higher
mysteries of inductive speculation; but it had a
protective affinity for the line of least resistance.
If the Saint required him to go to Chelsea and
look for a bottle of Scotch, that was jake with
him. . . .

And, heading on his way with that plodding

single-mindedness in which Lot's wife was so unfortunately lacking, he did not see the Saint climb into the driver's seat and steer his museum specimen up the road; nor did he see any of the other enlightening things which happened in that district shortly afterwards.

Chief Inspector Teal came out of the Barnyard Club and looked up and down the street.

"You and Henderson can go home," he said to one of the men with him. "I shan't need you any more tonight."

He put up a hand to stop the ancient taxi which came crawling hopefully towards them at that moment, and as it stopped he turned to the two people who had been added to his party since he entered the club.

"Get in," he ordered briefly.

He watched his prisoners embark with stolid vigilance—the raid had not by any means been as successful as he had hoped, and he would not know how much he had got out of it until the two arrests had been questioned. The other detective followed them in, and Teal paused to direct the driver to Cannon Row police station. Then he also got in and settled his bulk on the other folding seat, facing his captives.

The taxi jolted away with a hideous clanking of gears, and Mr. Teal pulled out a large silver watch and calculated his expectation of sleep. The other detective inspected his fingernails and nibbled a peeling scrap of cuticle on his thumb. The two prisoners sat in silence—the girl whose pound note Simon Templar had changed, and a dark florid man whose shirtfront sported a large square emerald which no arbiter of fashion could have approved. Mr. Teal did not even look at them. His hands lay primly on his knees, and his plump face was torpid, inscrutable, unworried. The case might be solved that night, or it might wait a year for solution. It made no difference to him. The relentless dogged routine which he represented took little account of time, and it had very few of the sensational brilliancies and hectic pursuits beloved of writers of fiction: it was a matter of taking up one trivial clue, following it with mechanical logic until it led no further, dropping it and patiently picking up the next; and usually the net was completed some day, and a man was prosaically caught. Except when the man for whom the net was woven happened to be the Saint. . . . A slight frown crossed Teal's round red face as that unwelcome reflection obtruded itself in his train of thought; and then the taxi, which for some minutes past had been puffing more and more wearily, finally expired with a last senile wheeze and would travel no farther.

Teal looked round with a scowl of more immediate irritation; and the driver climbed down and opened the bonnet of the machine. They were in a dingy narrow street which Teal did not recognize, for he had not been paying any attention to the route. He put his head out of the window.

"What's the matter?" he asked.

"Dunno yet," grunted the driver, still groping in the bowels of his antediluvian engine.

Teal fidgeted through a few minutes of silence and then turned to his subordinate.

"See if you can find out where we are, Durham," he said. "We can't sit here all night."

The other detective opened the door on his side and got down. Seen in fuller perspective, the road in which they had stopped was even more unprepossessing than it had looked through the windows. One thing about it at least was certain—no other taxi was likely to come cruising along it in the hope of picking up a fare.

Durham walked up to the driver, who was still half buried in his machinery and seemed ready to remain in that position indefinitely, like a modern Indian fakir trying out a novel method of mortifying the flesh.

"Where's the nearest taxi rank?" he asked.

"Nearest one I know is at Victoria Station— that's abaht ten minnits' walk," said the man. "Arf a sec, guv'nor—I think p'raps she'll go now."

He went round to the front and swung the handle. The taxi did go. It went better than Sergeant Durham had ever expected.

Confronting the seething wrath of Chief Inspector Teal later, he was unable to give any satisfactory explanation of what happened to him. He knew that the driver straightened up and walked round to resume his post at the wheel; but he did

not notice that the man reached his seat quicker
than any other taxi driver in Durham's experience
had ever known to complete such a manœuvre.
And in any case, Sergeant Durham was not expecting to be left behind.

But that was what indubitably happened to
him. At one moment, a practical hard-headed detective, secure in his faith in the commonplace
facts of life, he was putting out his hand to open
the door of the cab; in the next moment, the
handle had been whisked away from under his
very fingertips, and he was staring open-mouthed
at the retreating stern of the vehicle as it faded
noisily away down the road. The only other fact
he had presence of mind enough to grasp was that
its tail light was out so that he could not read the
number—which, as Mr. Teal later pointed out to
him, was not useful.

Chief Inspector Teal, however, had not yet got
down to that unprofitable post-mortem. The jerk
with which the taxi started off flung him forward
into the arms of his captives and some distance
was travelled before he could disentangle himself.
He rapped violently on the partition window,
without securing any response. More distance was
covered before he got it open and unleashed his
voice into the din of the thumping engine.

"You fool!" he shouted. "You've left the other
man behind!"

"Wot?" said the driver, without turning his
head or slackening speed.

"You've left the other man behind, you damned idiot!" Mr. Teal bawled furiously.

"Behind wot?" yelled the driver, taking a corner on two wheels.

Mr. Teal hauled himself up from the corner into which the sudden lurch had thrown him, and thrust his face through the opening.

"Stop the cab, will you?" he bellowed at the top of his voice.

The driver shook his head and reeled round another corner.

"You'll 'ave to talk lahder, guv'nor," he said. "I'm a bit 'ard of 'earing."

Teal clung savagely to the strap, and his rubicund complexion took on a tinge of heliotrope. He put a hand through the window, grasped the man's collar, and shook him viciously.

"*Stop,* I said!" he roared past the driver's ear. "Stop, or I'll break your bloody neck!"

"Wot did you say abaht my neck?" demanded the driver.

Thousands of things which he had not said, but which he had a sudden yearning to say, combined with multitudinous other observations on the anatomy of the man and his ancestors, flooded into the detective's overheated mind; but at that moment he felt rather than heard a movement behind him and turned round quickly. The florid man had seen heaven-sent opportunity in the accident, and Teal was just in time to dodge the savage blow that was aimed at his head.

The struggle that followed was short and one-sided. Mr. Teal's temper had been considerably shortened in the last few minutes, and he had a good deal of experience in handling refractory prisoners. In about six seconds he had the man securely handcuffed to one of the hand grips inside the cab, and as an added precaution he manacled the girl in the same way. Then, with his wrath in no way relieved by those six seconds of violent exercise, he turned again to resume his vendetta with the driver.

But the taxi was already slowing down. Filling his lungs, Teal devoted one delicious instant to a rapid selection of the words in which he would blast the chauffeur off the face of the earth; and then the cab stopped, and his vocabulary stuck in his gullet. For without a word the driver bowed over the wheel and buried his face in his arms. His shoulders heaved. Mr. Teal could scarcely believe what he heard. It sounded like a sob.

"Hey," said Mr. Teal, tentatively.

The driver did not move.

Mr. Teal began to feel uncomfortable. He reviewed the things he had said during his moment of exasperation. Had he been unduly harsh? Perhaps the driver really was hard of hearing. Perhaps he had some kind of sensitive complex about his neck. Mr. Teal did not wish to be unkind.

"Hey," he said, more loudly. "What's the matter?"

Another sob answered him. Mr. Teal ran a

finger round the inside of his collar. A demonstration like that was beyond the scope of his training in first aid. He wondered what he ought to do. Hysterical women, he seemed to remember having read somewhere, were best brought to their senses by judicious firmness.

"*Hey*," shouted Teal suddenly. "*Sit up!*"

The driver did not sit up.

Mr. Teal cleared his throat awkwardly. He glanced at his two prisoners. They were safely held. The grief-stricken driver's need seemed to be greater than theirs and Mr. Teal wanted to get on to Cannon Row and finish his night's work.

He opened the door and got down into the road.

And it was then, exactly at the moment when Chief Inspector Teal's heavy boots grounded on the tarmac, that the second remarkable incident in that ride occurred. It was a thing which handicapped Mr. Teal rather unfairly in his subsequent interview with Sergeant Durham. For as soon as he had got down, the driver, obeying his last command as belatedly as he had obeyed the former ones, did sit up. He did more than that. He lifted his foot off the clutch and simultaneously trod on the accelerator; and the taxi went rattling away and left Mr. Teal gaping foolishly after it.

III

SIMON TEMPLAR drove to Lower Sloane Street before he stopped again, and then he got down and opened the door of the passenger compartment. The dark florid man glowered at him uncertainly; and Simon decided that fifty per cent. of his freight had no further romantic possibilities.

"I don't think you're going any farther with us, brother," he said.

He produced a key from his ring, unlocked one of the handcuffs, and hauled the passenger out. The man made a lunge at him, and Simon calmly tripped him across the sidewalk and clipped the loose bracelet onto a bar of the nearest area railings. Then he went back to the cab and smiled at the girl.

"I expect you'd be more comfortable without that jewelry, wouldn't you?" he murmured.

He detached her handcuffs with the same key and used them to pinion the florid man's other wrist to a second rail.

"I'm afraid you'll have to be the consolation prize, Theobald," he remarked and stooped to remove the square emerald from the cursing consolation's shirtfront. "You won't mind if I borrow this, will you? I've got a friend who likes this sort of thing."

With only one other stop, which he made in Sloane Square to rekindle the rear light from which he had thoughtfully removed the bulb some time before, he drove the creaking taxi to Abbot's Yard. The tears were rolling down his cheeks, and from time to time his body was shaken by one of those racking sobs which Mr. Teal had so grievously misunderstood. It is given to every man to enjoy just so many immortal memories and no more; and the Saint liked to enjoy them when they came.

Ten minutes later he stopped the palpitating cab in Abbot's Yard, outside the door of No. 26. Anyone else would have driven it twenty miles out of London and buried it in a field before going home, in his frantic desire to eliminate all trace of his association with it; but Simon Templar's was an inspired simplicity which amounted to genius. He knew that if the cab was found in Abbot's Yard by any prowling sleuth who could identify it, then Abbot's Yard was the last place on earth where the same sleuth would look for him and he was still smiling as he climbed down and opened the door.

"Will you come out, fair lady?" he said.

She got out, staring at him uncertainly; and he indicated the door of the house.

"This is where I live—sometimes," he explained. "Don't look so surprised. Even cab drivers can be artists. I draw voluptuous nudes with engine oil on old cylinder blocks—it's supposed to be frightfully modern."

Abbot's Yard, Chelsea, is one of those multitudinous little lanes which open off the King's

Road. To say that not twenty years ago it had been a row of slum cottages would be practising a bourgeois *suppressio veri:* it had certainly been a slum, but it still was. If anything, Simon was inclined to think that the near-artists and synthetic Bohemians who now populated it had lowered the tone of the neighbourhood; but the studio which he rented in No. 26 had often served him well as an emergency address, and in his irregular life it was sometimes an advantage to have quarters in a district where eccentric goings-on attracted far less attention than they would have in South Kensington.

He steered the girl up the dark narrow stairs with a hand on her arm and felt that she was trembling—he was not surprised. From the studio, as they drew near, came the sounds of a melancholy voice raised in inharmonious song; and the Saint grinned. He opened the door, passing the girl in and closing it again behind them, and surveyed Mr. Uniatz reprovingly.

"I see you found the whisky," he said.

"Sure," said Mr. Uniatz, rising a trifle unsteadily, but beaming an honest welcome none the less. "It was in de pantry, jus' like ya tole me, boss."

The Saint sighed.

"It'll never be there again," he said, "unless you lose your way." He was stripping off his taxi driver's overcoat and peaked cap; and as he did so, in the full light, the girl recognized him, and he saw her eyes widen. "This bloke with the skin-ful is Mr. Hoppy Uniatz, old dear—a handy man with a Roscoe but not so hot on the Higher Thought. If I knew your name I'd introduce you."

"I'm Annette Vickery," said the girl. "But I don't even know who you are."

"I'm Simon Templar," he said. "They call me the Saint."

She caught her breath for an instant; and suddenly she seemed to see him again for the first time, and the flicker of fear came and went in her brown eyes. He stood with his hands in his pockets, lean and dark and dangerous and debonair, smiling at her with a cigarette between his lips and a wisp of smoke curling past his eyes; and it is only fair to say that he enjoyed his moment. But still he smiled, at himself and her.

"Well, I'm not a cannibal," he murmured, "although you may have heard rumours. Why don't you sit down and let's finish our talk?"

She sat down slowly.

"About—pillows?" she said, with the ghost of a smile; and he began to laugh.

"Or something."

He sent Hoppy Uniatz out to the kitchen to brew coffee and gave her a cigarette. She might have been twenty-two or twenty-three, he saw—the indifferent lighting of Bond Street had had no need to be kind to her. He was more sure than ever that her red mouth would smile easily and there would be mischief in the brown eyes; but he would have to lift more than a corner of the shadow to see those things.

"I told you the Barnyard Club was no place to go," he said, drawing up a chair. "Why wouldn't you take my advice?"

"I didn't understand."

All at once he realized that she was crediting him with having known that the raid was going to take place; but he showed nothing in his face.

"You've got hold of it now?"

She shrugged helplessly.

"Some of it. But I still don't know why you should have—bothered to get me out of the mess."

"That's a long story," he said cheerfully. "You ought to ask Chief Inspector Teal about it some day—he'll be able to tell you more. Somehow, we just seem to get in each other's way. But if you're thinking that you owe me something for it, I'm afraid you're right."

He saw the glimmer of fear in her eyes again; and yet he knew that she was not afraid of him. She had no reason to be. But she was afraid.

"You—kill people—don't you?" she said after a long silence.

The question sounded so startlingly naïve that he wanted to laugh; but something told him not to. He drew at his cigarette with a perfectly straight face.

"Sometimes even fatally," he admitted, with only the veiled mockery in his eyes to show for that glint of humour. "Why—is there anyone you'd like to see taken off? Hoppy Uniatz will do it for you if I haven't time."

"What do you kill them for?"

"Our scale is rather elastic," he said, endeavouring to maintain his gravity. "Sometimes we have done it for nothing. Mostly we charge by the yard——"

"I don't mean that." She was smoking her cigarette in short nervous puffs, and her hands were still unsteady. "I mean, if a man wasn't really bad —if he'd just made a mistake and got into bad company——"

Simon nodded and stood up.

"You're rather sweet," he said humorously. "But I know what you mean. You're frightened by some of the stories you've heard about me. Well, kid—how about giving your own common sense a chance? I've just lifted you straight out of the hands of the police. They're looking for you now, and before tomorrow morning every flat-footed dick in London will be joining in the search. If I wanted to get tough with you I wouldn't need any third degree—I'd just have to promise to turn you right out into the street if you didn't come through. I haven't said a word about that, have I?" The Saint smiled; and in the quick flash of that particular smile the armour of worldlier women than she had melted like wax. "But I do want you to talk. Come on, now— what's it all about?"

She was silent for a moment, tapping her cigarette over the ashtray long after all the loose ash had flaked away; and then her hands moved in a helpless gesture.

"I don't know."

Her eyes turned to meet his when she spoke, and he knew she was not merely stalling. He waited with genuine seriousness; and presently she said: "The boy who got into bad company was my brother. Honestly, he isn't really bad. I don't know what happened to him. He didn't need to be dishonest—he was so clever. Even when he was a kid at school he could draw and paint like a professional. Everyone said he had a marvellous future. When he was nineteen he went to an art school. Even the professors said he was a genius. He used to drink a bit too much, and he was a bit wild; but that was only because he was young. I'm eighteen months older than he is, you see. I didn't like some of his friends. That man who was —arrested with me—was one of them."

"And what's his name?"

"Jarving—Kenneth Jarving. . . . I think he used to flatter Tim—make him feel he was being a man of the world. I didn't like him. He tried to make love to me. But he became Tim's best friend. . . . And then—Tim was arrested. For forgery. And it turned out that Jarving knew about it all the time. He was the head of the gang that Tim was forging the notes for. But the police didn't get him."

"Charming fellow," said the Saint thoughtfully.

Hoppy Uniatz came in with the coffee, opened his mouth to utter some cheery conversation, sensed the subtle quietness of the atmosphere, and did not utter it. He stood on one foot, leaving his mouth open for future employment, and scratched his head, frowning vaguely. Annette Vickery went on, without paying any attention to him:

"Of course, Tim went to prison. I suppose they really meant to be kind to him. They only gave him eighteen months. They said he was obviously the victim of somebody much older and more experienced. I believe he might have got off altogether if he'd put them onto Jarving, who was the man they really wanted. But Tim wouldn't do it. And he swore he'd never forgive me if I said anything. I suppose—I shouldn't have taken any notice. But he was so emphatic. I was afraid. I didn't know what the others might have done to him if he'd given them away. I—I didn't say anything. So Tim went to prison."

"How long ago was that?"

"He came out three weeks ago. He was let off some of his sentence for good conduct. I was the only one who knew when he was coming out. Jarving tried to make me tell him, but I wouldn't. I wanted to try and keep Tim out of his way. And Tim said he wouldn't go back. He got a job in a printing works at Dulwich, through the Prisoners' Aid Society; and he was going to take up drawing again in his spare time and try to make a decent living at it. I believed he would. I still believe it.

But—that pound note you changed . . . it was part of some money he gave me only yesterday, to pay back some that I'd lent him. He said he'd sold some cartoons to a magazine."

The Saint put down his cigarette and picked up the coffee pot. He nodded.

"I see. But that still doesn't tell me why you had to go to the Barnyard Club and get pinched."

"That's what I still don't understand. I'm only trying to tell you everything that happened. Jarving rang me up this evening and asked if he could see me. I made excuses—I didn't want to see him. Then he said there'd be trouble for Tim if I didn't. He told me to meet him at the Barnyard Club. I had to go."

"And what was the trouble?"

"He'd only started to tell me when the police came in. He wanted to know where he could get hold of Tim. I wouldn't tell him. He said, 'Look here, I'm not trying to get your brother in trouble again. This isn't anything to do with me. It's somebody else who wants to see him.' I still didn't believe him. Then he said he'd give me this man's name and address himself, and I could give it to Tim myself, and Tim could go there on his own. But he said Tim had got to go, somehow."

"Did he give you the name and address?"

"Yes. He wrote it down on a piece of paper, just before——"

"Have you got it?"

She opened her bag and took out a scrap of

paper torn from a wine list. Simon took it and glanced over the writing.

And in that instant all his lazy good humour, all the relaxed and patient quiet with which he had listened to her story, were swept away as if a silent bomb had annihilated them.

"Is this it?" he said aimlessly; and she found his clear blue eyes on her, for that moment absolutely without mockery, raking her face with a blaze of azure light that was the most dynamic thing she had ever seen.

"That's it," she said hesitantly. "I've never heard the name before——"

"I have."

The Saint smiled. He had been marking time since the last gorgeous climax which his reckless impetuosity had given him, feeling his way towards the next move almost like an artist waiting for renewed inspiration; but he knew now where he was going on. He looked again at the scrap of paper on which outrageous fortune had jotted down his cue. On it was written:

> *Ivar Nordsten*
> *Hawk Lodge,*
> *St. George's Hill,*
> *Weybridge.*

"I want to know why one of the richest men in Europe is so anxious to meet your brother," he said. "And I think your brother will have to keep the appointment to find out."

He saw the fear struggling back into her eyes.
"But——"

The Saint laughed and shook his head. He indicated Hoppy Uniatz, who had transferred his balance to the other foot and his scratching operations to his left ear.

"There's your brother, darling. He may not have all the artistic gifts of the real Timothy, but he's a handy man in trouble, as I told you. I'll lend him to you free of charge. What d'you say?"

"Hot diggety," said Mr. Uniatz.

IV

WHEN Annette Vickery woke up, the sun was streaming into her bedroom window, and she looked out into a wide glade of pine trees and silver birches lifting from rolling banks of heather and bracken. It was hard to believe that this was less than twenty miles from London, where so many strange things had happened in the darkness a few hours ago, and where all the forces of Scotland Yard would still be searching for her.

They had driven down over the dark glistening roads in the Saint's Hirondel—a very different proposition from the spavined taxi which he had driven before—after a telephone call which he put through to a Weybridge number; and when they arrived there were lights in the house, and a

gruff-voiced man who walked with a curious strut-
ting limp waiting to put the car away without any
indication that he was at all surprised at his
master arriving at four o'clock in the morning
with two guests. Whisky, sandwiches, and a steaming pot of coffee were set out on a table in the
living room; and the Saint grinned.

"Orace is used to me," he explained. "If I rang
up and told him I was arriving with three hungry
lions and a kidnapped bishop, he wouldn't even
blink."

It was the same man with the limp who came
in with a cup of tea in the morning.

"Nice day, miss," he said.

He put the cup down on the table beside the
bed and looked at her pugnaciously—he had a
heavy walrus moustache which made it permanently impossible for anyone to tell when he was
smiling.

"Yer barf's ready," he said, as if he were addressing a dumb recruit on a parade ground, "an'
brekfuss'll be ready narf a minnit."

It was only another curiosity in the stream of
fantastic happenings that had carried her beyond
all the horizons of ordinary life.

She was down to breakfast in twenty minutes;
but even so she found the Saint drinking coffee
and reading a newspaper, while Hoppy Uniatz
finished up the toast. Simon served her with eggs
and bacon from the chafing dish.

"You'll probably find the egg a bit tough," he remarked, "but we have to toe the line at meal times. When Orace says 'Brekfuss narf a minnit' he means breakfast in exactly thirty seconds, and you can check your stop watch by him. I hid a piece of toast for you, too; or else Hoppy would have had it. How d'you feel?"

"Fine," she told him; and, tackling succulent rashers and eggs that were not too tough to make the mouth water, she was surprised to find that a fugitive from justice could still eat breakfast with a good appetite.

She looked out of the French doors that opened from the dining room onto the same view as she had seen from her bedroom when she awoke, the sunlit glade striped with the shadows of the trees, and said: "Where am I?—isn't that what everyone's supposed to say when they wake up?"

The Saint smiled.

"Or else they call for Mother." He pushed back his chair and tapped a cigarette on his thumbnail. "This is Mr. George's hill itself, though you mightn't believe I can drive you from here to Piccadilly Circus without hurrying in half an hour. I bought this place because I don't know anywhere else like it where you can forget London so easily and get there so quickly if you have to; but it seems as if it has other uses. By the way, there's some news in the paper that may appeal to your sense of humour."

He passed her the folded sheet and marked a

place with his forefinger. It was a brief paragraph in a minor position which simply recorded that Scotland Yard detectives had entered the Barn-yard Club in Bond Street and taken away a man and a young woman "for questioning."

"Of course, the part where I butted in may have been too late for this edition," said the Saint. "But I still don't think the public will hear any more about it just now. If there's anything in the history of England which Claud Eustace Teal would perjure his immortal soul to keep out of the news, I'm willing to bet it's that little game we played last night. But it still wouldn't be fatal if the story did leak out—you've only got to see Nordsten long enough to introduce your brother, and then you push off. If he did get inquisitive afterwards, Tim wouldn't know anything—would you, Hoppy?"

"No, boss," said Mr. Uniatz, shaking his head vigorously. "I don't know nut'n about nut'n."

"But what about Jarving?" put in the girl.

"Jarving is safe in clink," said the Saint with conviction. "If the first person who found him wasn't a policeman, which it probably was at that hour of the morning, I don't think anyone who found him could get those handcuffs off without a policeman happening along. So the coast seems to be as clear as we're ever likely to have it."

She finished her breakfast and drank the coffee which he poured out for her; and then he gave her a cigarette.

"Get hold of yourself, kid," he said. "I want you to be starting soon."

For an instant her stomach felt empty as she realized that, once outside the shelter of that house, she was a fugitive again, even if the very idea of policemen seemed absurd in that peaceful place. And then she felt his blue eyes resting on her appraisingly and managed a smile.

"All right, Don Q," she said. "What is it?"

"Your share is easy. You've only got to walk up to Hawk Lodge and introduce Hoppy as your brother. I don't expect you'll be asked to stay, and I'll be waiting right round the corner to drive you back. The rest is Hoppy's funeral—or it may be if he doesn't get the lead out of his sleeve on the draw."

Looking towards Mr. Uniatz, she saw his hand move with the speed of a bullet, and stared into the muzzle of an automatic which had somehow appeared in his grasp.

"Was dat fast," he asked indignantly, "or was dat fast?"

"I think it was fast," said the girl gravely.

"Say, an' can I shoot wit' it?" proclaimed Mr. Uniatz, rewarding her with a beam that displayed all his gold fillings. "Say, I betcha never see a guy t'row two cups in de air an' bean 'em wit' one shot."

"Yes, she has," said the Saint, moving Hoppy's cup rapidly away from under his eager fingers. "And she doesn't like it. Now for heaven's sake put that Betsy away and listen. Your name's Tim Vickery—have you got that?"

"Sure. Tim Vickery—dat's my name."

"You're an artist."

"What, me?" protested Mr. Uniatz plaintively. "Say, boss, you know I can't do dat pansy stuff."

"You don't have to," said the Saint patiently. "That's just your profession. You were brought up in America—that'll account for your accent—but you're really English. About fifteen months ago you were——"

"Say, boss," suggested Mr. Uniatz pleadingly, "why can't I be a bootlegger? You know, one of de big shots. Wit' dat emerald ya gimme last night, I could do it poifect."

Simon breathed deeply.

"I tell you, you're an artist," he said relentlessly. "There aren't any bootleggers in this story. About fifteen months ago you were arrested for forgery——"

"Say, boss," said Mr. Uniatz, with his homely brow deeply wrinkled in the effort of following a train of thought that was incapable of being hurried, "what was dat crack about de pansy stuff bein' my perfession?"

The Saint sighed and got up. For a minute or two he paced up and down the room, smoking his cigarette and staring at the carpet; and then he turned abruptly.

"The hell with it," he said. "I'm going to be Tim Vickery."

"But dat's my name," complained Hoppy.

"I'll borrow it," Simon said bluntly. "I don't think it suits you." He looked at the girl. "I was going to put Hoppy in because I thought the most important part of the job would be outside, but now I'm not so sure. I don't think there's much difference—and I'm afraid the inside stand is a bit out of Hoppy's distance. Are you all set to go? I want to show you something, and I've got to make a phone call."

He led her across the hall to the study which adjoined the living room, and picked up the telephone on the desk. In a few moments he was through to London.

"Hullo, Pat," he said. "I thought you'd be back. Did you have a swell time? . . . Grand. I'm down at Weybridge. Now listen, keed—can you catch the next train down? . . . Well, we've had a certain amount of song and skylarking while you've been away, and I've got a damsel in distress down here, and now I've got to push off again. That only leaves Hoppy and Orace, so you'll have to do your celebrated chaperoning act. . . . No, nothing desperate; but Claud Eustace may be puffing and blowing a bit in the near future. . . . Good girl. Then the damsel in distress will tell you all about it when you arrive. So long, darling. Be seein' ya."

He hung up the instrument and turned back with a smile.

"You're going to meet Patricia Holm," he said.

"Which is rather a privilege. When she gets here, tell her everything—from the beginning right down to where I take up your brother's name. Do you understand? If there's any trouble—whether it's from Act of God or Chief Inspector Teal— Pat will be able to handle it better than anyone else I know."

She nodded.

"I'll be all right."

"If I didn't think so, I wouldn't be leaving you," he said and went to a bookcase beside the desk. "Now here's the next thing: If there's any trouble—and if Pat isn't here, Orace will know —this is your way out."

The entire bookcase opened like a door on well-oiled hinges, giving her a glimpse of what appeared to be a passage.

"It isn't a passage," he explained, closing the bookcase again. "It's just a space between two walls. I built it myself. But they're both solid, so it can't be found by tapping around to see if anything sounds hollow. There's an armchair and some magazines, and it's ventilated; but you'd better not smoke. This is how it works: If the door's closed, and you open this drawer of the desk till it clicks, and then pull out the second shelf . . ."

He showed her how to manipulate the series of locks which he had devised.

"There's just one other thing," he said. "I want you to ring me up tonight—or get Pat to do it and say she's you. Just talk as if you were talking to Tim, because somebody may listen on the line. But listen very carefully to what I say at the other end. If there's anything I want, I'll be able to let you know."

Mr. Uniatz, who had been nibbling the end of a black cigar and watching all these proceedings with a vacant expression, cleared his throat and gave utterance to a problem which had been puzzling him ever since he left the breakfast table. "Boss," he interrupted diffidently, "what's wrong wit' my accent?"

"Nothing at all," said the Saint. "It reminds me of a nightjar calling to its mate." He put a hand on the girl's shoulder. "If you're ready now, we'll go."

They walked down a leafy avenue over the hill. There were starlings cheeping in the undergrowth, and the air was hazy with the promise of a fine day. The world was so still, without even a whisper of distant traffic, that her adventure seemed yet more unbelievable.

"Why are you taking so much trouble?" she had to ask; and he laughed.

"You've heard that I'm an outlaw, haven't you? And an outlaw lives by the supply of boodle. I know we still haven't very much to go on; but when a bird like Ivar Nordsten is falling over himself to get in touch with a convicted forger, I kind of get inquisitive. Besides, there's another thing. If I could dump the evidence of some really full-grown ungodliness into Teal's lap, he mightn't feel quite so upset about losing you."

A quarter of an hour's walk brought them to the gates of Hawk Lodge. They went up the broad gravelled drive and came upon the house suddenly round a bend that skirted a clump of trees—a big neo-Jacobean mansion that looked out over terraced gardens to the haze that hid another range of hills far to the south.

A grey-haired saturnine butler with a slight foreign accent took their names.

"Miss Vickery and Mr. Vickery? Will you wait?"

He left them in the great bare hall and passed through a door which opened off it. In a few moments he came back.

"Mr. Nordsten does not need to see Miss Vickery today," he said. "Will Mr. Vickery come in?"

Simon nodded, and smiled at the girl.

"Okay, sister," he murmured. "Thanks for bringing me—and take care of yourself."

Quite naturally he kissed her; and she went back down the broad drive again feeling very much alone.

V

"Sit down, Mr. Vickery," said Nordsten cordially. "I'm glad we were able to find you. Would you like a cigar?"

He sat behind a wide mahogany desk in a library that was panelled out from floor to ceiling with bookcases, more like the study of a university professor than of an internationally famous financier. The illusion was heightened by his physique, which was broad-shouldered and tall in spite of a scholarly stoop, and his bald domelike skull ringed round at the level of his ears with a horseshoe of sandy grey hair. Only a trace of over-emphasis on his guttural consonants betrayed his Scandinavian upbringing; and only a certain unblinking rigidity in his pale blue eyes, a certain tense restraint in the movements of his large white hands, marked the man whose business instincts commanded millions where others played with hundreds.

"Thanks."

Simon took a cigar, sniffed it with an affectation of wisdom, and stuck it between his teeth with the band on. It was an inferior cigar; but Tim Vickery would know no better.

"You look older than I heard you were," said Nordsten, holding out a match.

The Saint shrugged sullenly.

"Prison life doesn't help you to look young," he said.

"Does it teach you any lessons?" asked Nordsten.

"I don't know what you mean," Simon answered defensively.

The financier's mouth made a fractional movement that might have been intended for a smile; but his hard unblinking gaze remained on the Saint's face.

"Only a short while ago," he explained, "you were a young man with a brilliant future. Everyone thought well of you. You might have continued your training and become a very successful artist. But you didn't. You devoted your exceptional talents to forging banknotes—doubtless, not to mince matters, because you thought the rewards would be quicker and bigger than legitimate art would pay. But they weren't. You were arrested and sent to prison. You had leisure to reflect that quick profits are not always so quick as they first appear—that is, as I was trying to find out, if you learnt your lesson."

Simon grimaced.

"Well, is that why you sent for me?"

"I take it that my diagnosis is correct," said Nordsten blandly.

"How do you know?"

"My dear boy, your conviction was mentioned quite prominently in the newspapers. I remember that it was considered remarkable that a youth of your age should have produced the cleverest forgeries that the police witness could remember. The rest is merely a matter of deduction and elementary psychology." Nordsten leaned back and rolled his match between the finger and thumb of one hand. "But I remember thinking at the time what a pity it was that so much talent should have been employed in a comparatively poor field of effort. If only you had had proper guidance—if you'd had someone behind you who could dispose of your products without the slightest possibility of detection—wouldn't it have been quite a different story?"

Simon did not answer; and Nordsten went on, as if addressing the match: "If you had another chance to use your gifts in the same way, for even greater profits, but without any risk, wouldn't you see what a marvellous opportunity it was?"

The Saint sighed quite noiselessly—a deep slow inhalation of breath that took all the rich air of adventure into his lungs.

"I don't understand," he said stubbornly; and Nordsten's hard faded stare turned to him with a sudden resolution.

"Then I'll put it more plainly. You could do some work for me, Vickery. I'll pay you magnificently. I can make you richer than you've ever been even in your dreams. Do you want the chance or not?"

Simon shook his head. It was an effort.

"It's too risky," he said; but he spoke in a way that carried no conviction.

"I've promised to eliminate the risk," said Nordsten impatiently. "Listen—would you like a hundred thousand pounds?"

The Saint was silent for a longer time. His mouth opened, and he gaped at the financier more or less as he would have expected the real Tim

Vickery to gape, in startlement and incredulity and a swelling hunger of greed; and not all of that was an effort. The same queer tingle of supernatural expectation touched his spine as had touched it when he discovered that quartet of detectives gathering in Bond Street eight hours ago; the same tiny pulse beat in his brain; but those were things that Ivar Nordsten could not see.

"What do I have to do?" he asked at last; and that humourless twitch moved the corners of the financier's thin mouth again.

"I'll show you."

Nordsten got up and opened the door. Following him out into the hall and up the broad oak staircase, the Saint's face relaxed in a fleeting smile that hardly reached beyond the corners of his eyes. It was, he reflected, only in keeping with the rest of his madcap existence that he should have been in such a situation at that moment—it was the only logical sequel to the crazy impulse which had put him into the driving seat of that prehistoric taxi such a short while ago. Adventures were still to the adventurous. One saw the tail of a wild goose whisk by in the arid deserts of the commonplace and grabbed it; and the chase led inevitably to a land flowing with ungodliness and boodle. And he would not have had his life ordered on any other lines. . . .

They went down a long corridor carpeted in rich purple; and Nordsten opened a door at the end. It gave onto a kind of small lobby, from which other doors opened on three sides. Nordsten opened the one on the left and led him in.

It was a fairly large room with windows opening onto the falling view which the Saint had seen when he approached the house. There was a good rug on the floor, and a couple of armchairs; but it was the rest of the furnishings which were unusual. Looking them over slowly, Simon grasped their purpose. The room was fitted up as a complete engraving and printing plant in miniature. There was a drawing board with a green-shaded light, a workbench at one end of which were set out orderly rows of tools and a neat stack of steel plates, an electric warming plate, bottles of printing ink of every conceivable colour, and larger containers of acid and etching ground. In one corner was a new hand press of the most modern design, and in another corner were boxes of paper of various sizes.

"I think you'll find everything you could want," Nordsten said suavely; "but if you should require anything else, it will be procured as soon as you ask for it."

Simon moistened his lips.

"What do you want me to copy?" he asked.

Nordsten went to the drawing board and picked up a small sheaf of papers which had been placed at one side of it.

"As many of these as you can manage," he said. "Some will be more difficult than others—perhaps you would do better to start on the easiest ones. You will have to work hard, but not so fast that you cannot do your best work. I will pay you one hundred thousand pounds as an indefinite retainer, and fifty thousand pounds for every plate you complete to my satisfaction. Do I take it that the proposition appeals to you?"

The Saint nodded. He held in his hands the sheaf of papers which Nordsten had given him—Italian national bonds, Norwegian national bonds, Argentine conversion bonds—a complete sample packet of international gilt-edge securities.

"All right," he said. "I'll start on Monday."

The financier shook his head.

"If you intend to accept my offer you must start at once. I have arranged your accommodation so that you can always be near your work. This is a small self-contained suite—there is a bedroom next door and a bathroom opposite. Anything you need to make yourself comfortable can be obtained in an hour or two."

"But my sister——"

"You can write to her, or telephone whenever you like—there is an extension in your bedroom. Naturally you will not tell her what you are doing; but you will doubtless be able to explain your stay easily enough."

"I shall have to match the paper."

"It is already matched." Nordsten indicated the piles of boxes in the corner. "In fact, you have here sheets of the original papers. Many of the inks, also, are those which were used in the original printings. The only things I have been unable to obtain are the original plates; but those, of course, were destroyed. That is why I sent for you. Are you ready to start?"

There was something in his voice which made Simon look at him quietly for a moment; and then he remembered again that he was supposed to be Tim Vickery and swallowed.

"Yes," he said. "I'm ready."

Ivar Nordsten smiled; but there was no more softening behind the smile than there had been behind any of the previous infinitesimal movements of his lips.

"Really, it's the only sensible decision," he said genially. "Well, Vickery, I'll leave you to make your preparations. There is a bell beside the fireplace, and it will be answered as soon as you ring. Perhaps you will have dinner with me?"

"Thank you," said the Saint.

When his host had gone, he threw his cigar into the fireplace and lighted a cigarette. Later on he lighted another. For half an hour he wandered about the workshop, stopping sometimes to examine the implements that had been provided for his use, stopping often to look at the sheaf of specimen bonds which he was asked to copy, with his brows knitted in a straight line of intense thought. And once his hand went to his hip for a reassuring feel of the weight of the automatic which he had not forgotten to put on when he dressed for the occasion; for there had been something in Ivar Nordsten's persuasive voice which told him that no Tim Vickery who refused the offer would have been allowed to take his knowledge of that strange proposition back into the open world.

Nordsten required forgeries of a round dozen government bonds of as many nationalities. Why? Not for any ordinary purpose to which such counterfeits might have been put—the very idea was absurd. What for, then?

He ran over everything he could recall about Nordsten. The name was not on the tip of every tongue, like the names of Rockefeller or Morgan, but it was a name that was no less famous in other fields of finance; and it was part of Simon Templar's business to have at least a passing knowledge of those fields where millions are dealt with which are outside the limited ken of the average man in the street. Ivar Nordsten reaped in those fields; and the Saint had heard of him.

To the few people whose interests brought them in contact with the less publicized kingdoms of industry, he was known as the Paper King. Starting from one small factory in Sweden, he had built up a chain of production units which controlled practically the whole output of Scandinavia, Germany, Belgium, France, Switzerland, and Holland, until more than half the paper which was consumed in Europe was manufactured under his management. Not long ago he had taken over the most important mills in Austria and Denmark, and penetrated the British industry with an amount of capital which completed a virtual financial monopoly of the most considerable manufacturing and consuming countries in Europe. Not even content with that, he was rumoured to be negotiating for a series of loans and amalgamations which would link up the major concerns of Canada and the United States in the gigantic organization of which he was dictator—an invulnerable world trust that would practically be able to write its own checks on every industry in which paper was used, and which would in a few years lift his already fabulous fortune into astronomical figures. This was the Ivar Nordsten of whom Annette Vickery had never heard; but it is a curious commentary on this civilization that the average man and woman hears of comparatively few of the great financial wizards until those wizards are trying to conjure themselves out of the dock in a criminal court. And this was the Ivar Nordsten who required a convicted forger to counterfeit twelve different series of foreign government bonds.

Simon Templar sat in the armchair and turned the specimen bonds over on his knee; and his second cigarette smouldered down till it scorched his fingers. There was only one possible explanation that he could see, and it made him feel giddy to think of it.

At one o'clock the saturnine butler brought him

an excellent cold lunch on a tray and asked him what he would like to drink. Simon suggested a bottle of Liebfraumilch, and it was brought at once.

"Mr. Nordsten told me to ask if you would like a letter posting to your sister," said the man when he returned with the wine.

Simon thought quickly. He would be expected to communicate with his "sister" in some way, but there were obvious reasons why he could not ring up his own house.

"I'll give you a note right away, if you'll wait a sec," he said.

He scribbled a few conventional phrases on a sheet of notepaper that was produced for him, and addressed it to Miss Annette Vickery at an entirely fictitious address in north London.

At half-past two the butler came for the tray, asked him if there was anything else he wanted, and went out again. After a while the Saint strolled over to the drawing board, pinned out one of the certificates on it, covered it with a sheet of tracing paper, and began to pick out a series of lines in the engraving. Beyond that point the mechanics of counterfeiting would stump him, but he thought it wise to produce something to show that he had made a start on his commission. The future would have to take care of itself.

He worked for two hours, and then the saturnine butler brought him tea. The Saint poured out a cup and carried it to the window with a cigarette. He had something else to think of; and that something was the sweltering spleen of Chief Inspector Teal, which by that time could scarcely be very far below the temperature at which its possessor would burst into flame if he scratched himself incautiously. Certainly the rear number plate of the taxi had been unreadable, and no one could have positively identified the eccentric driver with the Saint; but Claud Eustace Teal had seen him and spoken with him in Bond Street only a few minutes before the disastrous events which had followed, and Simon was only too familiar with the suspicious and uncharitable grooves in which Mr. Teal's mind locomoted along its orbit. That would provide an additional complication which had been ordained from the beginning, but the Saint could see no way of avoiding it.

It was rather stuffy in the workshop, and the panorama of cool greenery which he could see from the window was immensely inviting. The Saint felt an overpowering desire to stretch his legs and take his problems out for a saunter in the fresh air; and he did not see how Ivar Nordsten could object. He went to the outer door of the suite; and then, as he turned the handle, his heart stopped beating for an instant.

The door was locked; and he appreciated for the first time some of the qualities which made Ivar Nordsten such a successful man.

VI

"CURIOUSER and curiouser," said the Saint mildly and went back to the armchair to do some more thinking.

He realized that when he had surmised that Nordsten would not have let him depart easily with his knowledge if he had refused his commission, he hadn't guessed the half of it. Nordsten would not let him depart easily with his knowledge anyhow. Simon had a sudden grim foreboding that there could be only one end, in Nordsten's mind, to that strange employment. He saw the financier's point of view very clearly, but it didn't help him far with his own plans.

He lighted another cigarette in the chain that had already filled two ashtrays, and strolled back to the window. The casements were only half opened, and he flipped one of the props off its peg and flung the window wide. Leaning out with his forearms folded on the sill to admire the view and take in his fresh air as best he could, he saw a black-haired man with a scarred face walk round the corner of the house and look up. Simon restrained a prompt impulse to wave cheerily to him and watched the man saunter up underneath the window and stop there seemingly wrapped in intense contemplation of a cluster of antirrhinums. Even then he did not quite grasp the significance of the scarred stroller until the door behind him opened and he looked round to see the saturnine features of the butler.

"Did you require anything, Mr. Vickery?" he said.

Simon completed his turn and rested his elbows on the ledge behind him.

"How did you know?" he asked.

"I thought I heard you moving about, sir."

Simon nodded.

"I went to the door," he said, "and it was locked."

The butler's sallow features were expressionless.

"It was locked by Mr. Nordsten's instructions, sir. He wished to make certain that none of the staff except myself should enter these rooms. What is it you were requiring, sir?"

"I ran out of cigarettes," said the Saint casually. "Can you get me some?"

After the butler had gone, Simon examined the window again, and found the tiny electric contacts in the upper hinge which had doubtless sounded a warning somewhere in the house when he moved the casement; and he realized that no estimate he had formed of Ivar Nordsten's thoroughness was too high.

At six o'clock the butler came in again with a complete outfit of evening clothes. Simon had a bath and changed—the suit fitted him very well— and at a quarter to seven the butler returned and ushered him down to the library with all the ceremony that might have been accorded to a particularly honoured guest. Nordsten was already there, with the broad ribbon of some foreign order across his white shirtfront. He rose with a smile.

"I'm glad Trusaneff was able to judge your size," he said, glancing at the set of the Saint's coat. "Will you have a Martini, or would you prefer sherry?"

To Simon Templar it was one of the most quietly macabre evenings in his experience. In the vast panelled dining room, lighted only by clusters of candles, they sat at one end of a table which could have seated twenty without crowding. A periwigged footman stood behind each of their chairs like a guardian statue which only came to life in the act of forestalling any trivial need and returned immediately afterwards to immobility. The butler stood at the end of the room, supervising nothing but the perfection of service: sometimes he would look up and move a finger, and one of the statues would respond in silent obedience. There were six courses, each served with a different wine, each taken with the solemn ritual of a formal banquet. Without seeming to be conscious that every word which was spoken thrummed eerily through the shadowy emptiness of the room, Nordsten talked as naturally as if all the vacant places at the long table were filled; and Simon had to admit that he was a charming conversationalist. But he said nothing that gave the Saint any more information than he had already.

"I have always believed in the survival of the

fittest," was his only illuminating remark. "Business men are often criticized for using 'sharp' methods; but after all, high finance is a kind of war, and in war you use the most effective weapons you can find, without considering the feelings of the enemy."

Nevertheless, when the Saint was back in his bedroom—the butler escorted him there on the pretext of finding out whether he desired to order anything special for breakfast—he felt that he had learned something, even if that something was only a confirmation of what he had already deduced from quite a different angle. And this was that a man who was capable of putting on such a show of state for one insignificant guest, and who believed so clearly and logically in the survival of the fittest, would not find it hard to rationalize any expedient which helped him towards his unmistakable goal of power.

Abstractedly the Saint took off his shoes, his collar and tie, his stiff shirt. Whatever benefits he might have derived from it, that dinner had put the finishing touch to his feeling of being a passive calf in process of fattening for the slaughter; and it was not a feeling that fitted very easily on his temperament. He pulled off his socks, because the night was sultry, and drifted about the room in his singlet and trousers, smoking a cigarette. As if he had never thought of it before, it came to him, as he paced up and down, that his bare feet were absolutely soundless on the carpet. Almost absentmindedly he picked up the white waistcoat which he had discarded. In one pocket of it was a burglarious instrument with which he had taken the precaution of providing himself before he left his own home, with a nebulous eye to possible voyages of exploration on the Nordsten premises, and which he had thoughtfully transferred from his day suit when he changed. . . .

He watched, with the lights out, until the strip of light under the outer door of his suite turned black as the corridor lights were switched off; and then he waited half an hour longer before he set to work on the lock. He realized that it was not outside the realms of probability that the same thoroughness which had caused those minute electric contacts to be fitted to the windows might have provided some similar system of alarms on the door; but that was a risk which had to be taken, and possibly several glasses of Ivar Nordsten's excellent port on top of twelve hours' enforced passivity had made him a trifle light-headed. Every now and then he stopped, motionless, without even breathing, and listened for any whisper of sound that might betray a guard prowling around the passages; but he could hear nothing. And at last he was able to turn the handle noiselessly and slip out into the silent darkness of the house.

A tentative needle of light skimmed away from the Saint's hand, dabbed at the floor and walls, and vanished again. It came from the masked bulb

of a tiny pocket torch which was another semi-
burglarious instrument that he had brought with
him. And thereafter, with only that one brief
glimpse of the route ahead to refresh his memory,
he disappeared into the blackness like a roving
ghost.

His objective, in so far as he had an objective
at all, was the library where cocktails had been
served before dinner. If there were any intriguing
developments to be unearthed in that house, the
library seemed the obvious place to begin a search
for them; and he had always been a sublime
optimist.

He reached the head of the staircase and
stopped there to listen. A pale blue glimmer of
light came through the studio window on the
stairway and achieved little more than taking the
harsh deadness off the dark for half a flight. A
faint musty smell touched the Saint's sensitive nostrils; and he stood for a moment breathing it
silently, like a wild animal, with an invisible
frown creasing his forehead. But the associations
of it eluded him, and with a slight shrug he set
one foot stealthily on the first downward step.

As he did so he heard the scratching.

It was a queer soft noise, like some very light-
footed thing with nailed shoes pacing across a
parquet floor. It seemed to take one or two steps,
while he listened with his heart beating a shade
faster; then it stopped; then it came again. And
then the silence came down once more.

Simon remained motionless, a mere patch of shadow in the dark, so still that he could feel the blood pounding steadily in his veins. It came to him, with great clarity, that there were healthier places for him to be abroad at midnight than the house of Ivar Nordsten. He had a momentary vision of the very comfortable bed that was already turned down for him in the very comfortable bedroom to which he had been assigned, and wondered what on earth could have made him impervious to its very obvious enticement. But the scratching sound was not repeated; and at length, with a wry grin, he went on. He wouldn't stand much chance of completing his tour of investigation, he reflected ruefully, if a mouse could scare him so easily. . . .

At last he stepped down on the floor of the hall. An infinitesimal glimmer of the light from the stairway window still reached there—enough to take him to the library door without the use of his torch. Very gently he turned the handle; and as he did so he heard the scratching again.

In a flash he had whipped round and shot the pencil beam of his torch towards it. Even as he did so, he realized that his nerves had got the better of him, but the impulse was too strong for reason. And as he turned, his right hand leapt to the automatic at his hip with a grim feeling that if by any chance the scratching had a human origin it would relieve him considerably to discover it.

The dimmed beam gave too feeble a light to

show him any details. He saw nothing but a black shadow which filled one far corner, and a pair of eyes that caught the light and held it in two steady yellowish reflections as large as walnuts; and one of the happiest moments of his life began when he had got through the library door and shut it behind him.

Breathing a trifle deeply, he fished a cigarette out of his pocket and lighted it, keeping his flashlight switched on. If complete disaster had been the price, he couldn't have denied his nerves that time-honoured consolation. Whatever the black shadow with the yellow eyes might be, he felt that his system could stand a snifter of tobacco and an interval of thoughtful repose before looking at it again. Meanwhile he was on the sanctuary side of the library door, and he was stubbornly resolved to make the most of it. His torch showed him that the curtains were drawn, and with a reckless movement of his hand he switched on the lights and turned to a survey of the room.

Only the immutable law of averages can account for what followed. If a man looks for things often enough, it is reasonable to assume that at some time or other he must stumble on the right hiding place at the first attempt; and the Saint had searched for things often enough in his life, even if on that occasion he didn't know what he was looking for.

The toe of one bare foot was kicking meditatively at the edge of the carpet. The corner rolled over. His thoughts ran, more or less: "Nothing important would be left out for any inquisitive servant to get hold of. There isn't a safe. It might be a dummy bookcase, like I've got. But excavations are also possible. . . ."

Somehow he found himself looking down at a trapdoor cut in the oak planking of the floor.

It lifted easily. Underneath was a hinged stone slab with an iron ringbolt, smooth and unrusted. Without hesitation he took hold of it and lifted. It required all his strength to raise the slab, but he managed it.

He looked down into black darkness; but from the bottom of the darkness came a faint sound of shuffling movement. With a creepy tingle working across his scalp, he picked up his torch again and sent the beam down the shaft.

Ten feet below him, a face looked up with dull staring eyes that blinked painfully even in the faint ray of his flashlight. There was something hideously familiar about it, as if it were the blanched wreck of a face which he ought to know. And in another second his blood ran cold as he realized that it was the face of Ivar Nordsten.

VII

THE face was not quite the same. The nose was less dominant, the complexion had a yellow tinge which the financier's did not have, the eyes lacked the faded brightness which Nordsten's possessed; but it was recognizable. It had given the Saint such a shock that he found it difficult to speak naturally.

"Hullo, sunshine," he said at length. "And who are you?"

The man's mouth worked hungrily, like an animal's.

"All right," he said, in a curiously stiff hoarse whisper, as if he had half forgotten how to use his voice. "I'm used to it now. You can't make me suffer any more."

"Who are you?" Simon repeated.

"I'm *you*," said the man huskily. "I know now. I've thought it all out. I'm you—Nordsten!"

The Saint's nerves were steady enough now. Somehow, that last shock had been a homœopathic dose, wiping out everything else; he was left with the dizzy certainty that the trail had turned into a stranger course than anything he had dreamed of, and with a grim curiosity to find out where it led.

"I'm here to help you, you fathead," he said. "Tell uncle what it's all about."

The man below him laughed, a horrible quivering dry cackle which sent an uncanny chill down the Saint's spine, as if a spider had crawled there, in spite of the recovered steadiness of his nerves.

"Help me! Ha-ha! That's funny. Help me like you've been helping me for two years. Help me

to keep alive so that I can die at the right time!
I know. Ha-ha-ha-ha-ha-ha-ha!" Then the wild
voice fell to a whisper. *"Help,"* it breathed, with
a fearful intensity. "How long? How long?"

"Listen," said the Saint urgently. "I——"

An then, as if his command had turned back on
himself, he broke off and listened. He could hear
the scratching again. It was outside the library
door—on the door itself. . . . There was a faint
thud; and then an instant's electric silence, while
he strained his ears for he knew not what. . . .
And then, shattering the stillness of the house,
came a frightful coughing scream that rang up and
down the scale in an eldritch howl of vocal
savagery that stopped the breath in his throat.

Looking down stupidly through the trapdoor,
Simon saw the parchment face of the man who
looked like Nordsten turn whiter. The dull eyes
dilated, and the stiff unnatural voice rose in a
sobbing cry.

"No, no, no, no," it shrieked. "Not now! Not
now! I didn't mean it. I'm not ready yet! I'm
not——"

The hairs prickled on the nape of Simon's neck;
and then, with an effort that hardened his eyes to
mere slits of arctic blue, he got up from his knees
and lifted the heavy stone trapdoor again.

"I'll see you later," he said shortly and lowered
the trap much quicker than he had raised it.

In another second he had fitted the square of
dummy parquet over it, and he was rolling out

the carpet again to cover up the traces of his inspection. Whatever else his curiosity might demand to know, there was the screeching shadow with the yellow eyes to be accounted for first—everyone in the house must have been awakened by that unearthly yell, and he would achieve nothing by being discovered where he was. Whatever it might be, the Thing in the hall had to be dealt with first, and he preferred to take it on the run rather than let his nerves get the better of him again. With his automatic in his hand, he went back to the door and switched out the lights. No one would ever know what it cost him to turn the handle of the door with that screaming horror waiting for him on the other side, but he did it; and his nerves were like ice as he drew the door sharply back and waited for whatever his fate might be.

Something soft and yet heavy hissed past him and landed on the parquet beside the central rug with the same scratching noise as he had heard before, and once again his nostrils twitched to the queer musty odour which they had detected on the stairs. In the pitch darkness he heard the claws of the beast scrabbling for a turning hold on the polished oak, and kicked out instinctively with his bare foot. His toes bedded into something furry and muscular, and for the second time that fiendish worrying yell wailed through the blackness.

Simon whipped up his gun; but something like a hot iron ripped down his forearm before he could fire, and the automatic was brushed effort-lessly out of his hand. He felt hot fetid breath on his face and smashed his fist into something soft and damp; and then he went down under the clawing spitting weight of the brute with its shrill snarl of fury ringing in his ears.

More by luck than judgment he found the ani-mal's throat with his hands; and probably it was that fluke, and the reprieve of a second or two it gave him, which saved him from serious injury.

"Sheba!"

The lights had gone up in the hall, and he heard running footsteps. He had never been so breathlessly thankful to hear anything in his life. A whip lashed, and the huge black panther on top of him roared again and stepped back, turning its head with bared fangs. Simon took his chance and rolled clear—it was the fastest roll he had ever performed in his acrobatic career.

"Back!" shouted Nordsten furiously and lashed at the panther again.

It was one of the most amazing demonstrations of brutal fearlessness which Simon had ever wit-nessed. Nordsten simply advanced step by step, swinging the wire-tipped rawhide back and forth in a steady rhythm of flailing punishment; and as he went forward, the panther went back. Quite obviously it had never been tame, and no attempt had ever been made to tame it. Nordsten domi-nated it by nothing but his own savage courage. Its yellow eyes blazed with the most horrible intelligent hatred which the Saint had ever dreamed of seeing in the eyes of an animal; it clawed and bit at the slashing whip with deep growls of murderous rage; but it went back. Nordsten's face was black with anger, and he had no more pity than fear. He drove the brute right across the hall into a corner, lashed it half a dozen times more when it could retreat no farther—and then turned his back on it. It crouched there, staring after him, with a steady rumbling of frightful viciousness burring in its throat.

"You're lucky to be alive, Vickery," Nordsten said harshly, curling his whip in his big white hands.

He was in his pyjamas and dressing gown— Simon had known very few financiers who could be impressive in that costume, but Nordsten was.

The Saint nodded, dabbing his handkerchief over the deep claw-groove in his bare forearm.

"I was just coming to the same conclusion," he remarked lightly. "Have you got any more docile pets like that around the place?"

"What were you doing down here?" answered Nordsten sharply; and Simon remembered that he was still supposed to be Tim Vickery.

"I wanted a drink," he explained. "I thought all the servants would have been in bed by this time, so I didn't like to ring for it. I just came down to see if I could find anything. I was half-way down the stairs when that thing started chasing me——"

Nordsten's faded bright eyes looked away to the left, and Simon saw that the saturnine butler was standing on the stairs at a safe distance, with a revolver clutched in his hand.

"You forgot to lock the door, Trusaneff?" Nordsten said coldly.

The man licked his lips.

"No, sir——"

"It wasn't locked, anyway," said the Saint blankly.

Nordsten looked at the butler for a moment longer; then at the Saint. Simon met his gaze with an expression of honest perplexity, and Nordsten turned away abruptly and went past him into the library, switching on the lights. He saw the automatic lying in the middle of the carpet and picked it up.

"Is this yours?"

"Yes." Simon blinked and shifted his eyes with an air of mild consternation. "I—I always carry it now, and— Well, when that animal started——"

"I see." Nordsten's genial nod of understanding was very quick. He glanced at the Saint's gashed arm. "You'll need a bandage on that. Trusaneff will attend to it. Excuse me."

He spoke those few words as if with their utterance the episode was finally concluded. Somehow the Saint found himself outside the library door while Nordsten closed it from the outside.

"This way, please, Mr. Vickery," said the butler, without moving from his safe position on the lower flight of stairs.

Simon felt for his cigarette case and walked thoughtfully across the hall. Through another half-open door he caught a glimpse of the scared features of the battle-scarred warrior who had paraded under his window, peering out from an equally safe position. The black panther crouched in the corner where Nordsten had left it, lashing its tail in sullen silence. . . .

Altogether a very exciting wind-up to a pleasant social evening, reflected the Saint; if it was the wind-up. . . . He rememberd that Nordsten had carelessly omitted to give him back his automatic when ushering him so smoothly out of the library, and realized that he would have felt a lot happier if the financier had been less pointedly forgetful. He also remembered that either Annette or Patricia should have telephoned him that night, and wondered why there had been no message. Teal might have been responsible—so far as Simon knew, that persistent detective had not been aware of his latest acquisition in the way of real estate; but there had been no secrecy about the transaction, and it would have been perfectly simple for Mr. Teal to discover it after a certain amount of time. Or else they might have tried to telephone, and Nordsten or one of his servants might have been the barrier. That also was possible, since he had already been allowed to write a letter which had doubtless been read before it was posted. He was developing a profound respect for Ivar Nordsten's thoroughness——

"Vickery."

It was Nordsten's voice; and the Saint stopped, and saw the financier standing at the foot of the stairs.

"I'd like to see you again for a moment, if your arm can wait."

There was no real question of whether his arm could wait; and Simon turned with a smile.

"Of course."

He went down the stairs again. Trusaneff halted on the last flight, and Simon crossed the hall alone.

Nordsten was standing by the desk when the Saint entered the library, and the panther was crouching at his feet. Simon saw that the carpet was rolled back from the trapdoor, and the financier was holding his gun in his hand. He realized that he had been exceedingly careless; but he allowed nothing but a natural puzzlement to appear on his face.

"You tell me that Sheba started chasing you when you were on the stairs, and you tried to get in here to escape," Nordsten said, with a curious flat timbre in his voice.

"That's right," Simon answered.

"Then can you explain this?"

Nordsten pointed his whip at the floor; and Simon looked down and saw the stub of a cigarette lying beside the trapdoor—that same cigarette which his tingling nerves had forced him to light when he got inside the room, and which he had unconsciously trodden out when the demoniac snarl of the panther disturbed him in his investigations—and a few little splashes of grey ash around it.

"I don't understand," he said, with a frown of perfect bewilderment.

The financier's faded bright eyes were fixed on him steadily.

"None of my servants smoke, and I smoke only cigars."

"I still don't know why you should ask me," Simon said.

"Is your name Vickery?"

"Of course it is."

Nordsten stared at him for a few seconds longer.

"You're a liar," he said at length, with absolute calm.

Simon did not answer, and knew that there was no answer to make. He admitted nothing, continuing to gape at Nordsten with the same expression of helpless perplexity which the real Tim Vickery would have worn; but he knew that he was only carrying on mechanically with a bluff that had long since been called. It made no difference.

The thing which surprised him a little was Nordsten's complete restraint. He would have expected some show of emotion, some manifestation of nerves, fear, anger, even insensate viciousness; but there was none of those. The financier was as rock-still as if he had been contemplating an ordinary obstacle which had arisen in the course of a normal and respectable business campaign—almost as if he had already envisaged the obstacle and sketched out a rough plan of remedy, and was simply considering the remedy again in detail, to make sure that it contained no flaws. And Simon Templar, remembering the poor half-crazy wretch under the trap, had an eerie presentiment that perhaps this was only the barest truth.

Nordsten spoke only one revealing sentence.

"I didn't think it would come so soon," he said, speaking aloud but only to himself; and his voice was quiet and almost childlike.

Then he looked at the Saint again with his dispassionate and empty eyes, and the gun in his hand moved slightly.

"Lift up the trap, please . . . Vickery," he said.

Simon hesitated momentarily; but the gun was aimed on him quite adequately, and Nordsten was too far away for a surprise attack. With a slight shrug he moved the square of parquet aside and locked his hands in the ring bolt of the heavy stone door. He lifted it with a strong quiet heave and laid it back on the floor.

"This is lots of fun," he murmured. "What do we do now—wiggle our ears and pretend to be rabbits?"

The financier ignored him. He raised his voice slightly, and called:

"Erik!"

In the silence that followed, Simon listened to the sounds of stumbling movement in the cave under the floor; and presently he saw the head of the man who looked like Nordsten coming up out of the hole. The man was climbing up some sort of ladder which the Saint had not noticed, taking each rung with a shaky effort such as an old man might have made, as if his limbs had grown piti- fully feeble from long disuse. As he appeared under the full open light, Simon was even more amazed at the resemblance between the two men. There was minor differences, it was true; but most of them could be accounted for by the unimagin- ably frightful years of imprisonment which Erik had endured in that lightless pit. Even in stature they were almost identical. Simon had a moment's recollection of the man's stiff husky voice saying: *"I'm you. I know now. . . . I'm you—Nord- sten!"* And he shivered in the sudden chill of understanding.

The man had climbed out at last. His glazed eyes, tensed painfully in the brilliant light, fell on the black panther, and he swayed weakly, clutch- ing the collar of his ragged shift with a trembling hand. And then he mastered himself.

"All right," he said, with a shuddering gasp. "I'm not afraid. I didn't mean you to see me afraid. But when you opened the door just now— and the thing yelled—I forgot. But I'm not afraid any more. I'm not afraid, damn you!"

Nordsten's faded eyes, without pity, glanced at the Saint.

"So—you had opened the trap," he remarked, almost casually.

"Maybe I had," Simon responded calmly. He was not meeting Nordsten's gaze, and he only answered perfunctorily. He was looking at the man Erik; and he went on speaking to him, very clearly and steadily, trying to strike a spark of recognition from that terribly injured brain. "I was the bloke who said hullo to you just now, Erik. It wasn't Brother Ivar. It was me."

The man stared at him sightlessly; and Nordsten moved nearer to the door. The great black panther rose and stretched itself. It padded after him, watching him with its oblique malignant eyes; and Nordsten took the whip in his right hand. His voice rang out suddenly:

"Sheba!"

The whip whistled through the air and curled over the animal's sleek flanks in a terrific blow.

"*Kill!*"

The whip fell again. Growling, the panther started forward. A third and a fourth lash cracked over its body like the sound of pistol shots, and it stopped and turned its head.

Simon will never forget what followed.

It was not clear to him at the time, though the actual physical fact was as vivid as a nightmare. He knew that he faced certain death, but it had come on him so quickly that he had had no chance to grasp the idea completely. The man Erik was standing beside him, white-faced, his body rigid and quivering, his lips stubbornly compressed and the breath hissing jerkily through his nostrils. *He* knew. But the Saint, with his eyes narrowed to slits of steel and his muscles flexed for the hopeless combat, only understood the threat of death instinctively. He saw what was happening long before reason and comprehension caught up with it.

The head of the beast turned; and again the cruel whip cut across its back. And then—it could only have been that the deep-sown hate of the beast conquered its fear, and its raging blood-lust burst into the deeper channel. The twist of its magnificent rippling body was too quick for the eye to follow. It sprang, a streak of burnished ebony flying through the air—not towards the Saint or Erik, but away from them. Nordsten's gun banged once; and then the cry that broke from his lips as he went down was drowned in the rolling thunder of the panther's hate.

VIII

"SAY," pleaded Mr. Uniatz bashfully, plucking up the courage to seek illumination on a point which had been worrying him for some hours, "is a nightjar de t'ing——"

"No, it isn't," said Patricia Holm hurriedly. "It's a kind of bird."

"Oh, a boid!" Hoppy's mouth stretched horizontally in a broad grin of overwhelming relief. "I t'ought it couldn't of been what I t'ought it was."

Patricia sighed.

"Why on earth did you have to think about nightjars at all, anyway?"

"Well, it was dis way. Before de Saint scrammed, after he made me a pansy bootlegger, he said my accent reminded him of a nightjar callin' to its mate——"

"He must have been thinking of a nightingale, Hoppy," said the girl kindly.

She lighted a cigarette and strolled over to the window, watching the dusk deepening down the glade of bracken and trees. Annette Vickery gazed after her with a feeling that was oddly akin to awe. Annette herself couldn't help knowing, frankly, that she was pretty; but this slim fair girl who seemed to be the Saint's partner in outlawry had an enchanting beauty like nothing that she had ever seen before. That alone might have made her jealous, after the fashion even of the nicest women; but in Patricia Holm it was only an incidental feature. She had a repose, a quiet understanding confidence, which was the only thing that made hours of waiting tolerable.

She had come in towards midday.

"I'm Patricia," she said; and with that she was introduced.

She heard the story of the night before and the morning after, and laughed.

"I expect it seems like the end of the world to you," she said, "but it isn't very new to me. I wondered what had happened to Simon when I blew into the apartment this morning and found he hadn't been in all night. But he always has been daft—I suppose you've had plenty of time to find that out. How about a spot of sherry, kid—d'you think that would do you good?"

"You talk like a man," said Annette.

It was clearly meant for a compliment; and Patricia smiled.

"If I talk like a Saint," she said softly, "it's only natural."

She had a serene faith in the Saint which removed the last excuse for anxiety. If she had doubts, she kept them to herself. Orace served an excellent cold lunch. They bathed in the swimming pool, sunned themselves afterwards in deck chairs, had tea brought out on the terrace. The time passed; until Patricia stood at the window and watched night creeping down over the garden.

"I'll make some Old Fashioneds," she said.

In the glow of that most insidiously potent of all apéritifs, it was not so difficult to keep anxiety at bay for another hour and more. Presently Orace announced dinner. It was quite dark when they left the table and went into the study.

"I suppose we might telephone now," said Patricia at length.

She took up the telephone and gave the number calmly. It was then nearly nine o'clock. In a short while a man's voice answered.

"Can I speak to Mr. Vickery?" she asked.

"Who is that, please?"

"This is his sister speaking."

"I will inquire, madam. Will you hold on?"

She waited, and presently the man came back.

"Mr. Vickery is engaged in a very important conference with Mr. Nordsten, madam, and cannot be disturbed. Can I take a message?"

"When will the conference be over?" asked Patricia steadily.

"I don't know, madam."

"I'll call up again later," said Patricia and replaced the microphone on its bracket.

She tilted herself back in the desk chair and blew smoke at the wall in front of her. It was Hoppy Uniatz, removing his mouth temporarily from a glass of whisky, who crashed in where angels might have feared to tread.

"Well," he said cheerfully, "who's been rubbed out?"

"I can't get him just now," said Patricia evenly. "We'll call again before we go to bed. How about a game of poker?"

"I remember," said Mr. Uniatz wistfully, "one

time I played strip poker wit' a coupla broads on Toity-toid Street. De blonde one had just drawn to a bob-tailed straight an' raised me a pair of pants——"

The glances which turned in his direction would have withered any man whose hide had less in common with that of the African rhinoceros; but Hoppy's disreputable reminiscence served to relieve the strain. Somehow, the time went on. The girls smoked and talked idly; and Mr. Uniatz, finding his anecdotes disrespectfully received, relapsed into fluent silence and presently went out of the room. After a while he returned, bearing with him a fresh bottle of whisky which he had discovered somewhere and succeeded in abstracting from under Orace's vigilant eye. At half-past eleven Patricia telephoned Hawk Lodge again.

"Mr. Vickery has gone to bed, madam," said the butler suavely. "He was very tired and left orders that he was not to be awakened. He wrote you a letter which I have just posted, madam. You should receive it in the morning."

"Thank you," said Patricia slowly and rang off. She turned round serenely to the others.

"We're out of luck," she reported. "Well, there's nothing we can do about it. We'll have some news in the morning—and I'm ready for bed."

"You're very brave," said Annette, seeing more than Hoppy Uniatz would ever be capable of seeing.

Patricia laughed shortly and put an arm round her.

"My dear, if you'd known the Saint as long as I have, you'd have given up worrying. I've seen him get people out of messes that would make yours look like a flea bite. I've seen him get himself out of far worse trouble than anything I think he's in now. The man's simply made that way——"

She might have been going to say more, but she didn't; for at that moment a bell rang faintly at the back of the house. Annette looked up at her quickly, and for a second even Mr. Uniatz forgot that he was grasping a bottle of Bourbon which was as yet only half empty. But Patricia shook her head with a very tiny smile.

"Simon wouldn't ring," she said.

They listened and heard Orace's dot-and-carry footfalls crossing the hall. The front door opened, and there was a sound of other feet treading over the threshold. A voice could be heard inquiring for Mr. Templar.

"Mr. Templar ain't 'ere," Orace said brusquely.

"We'll wait for him," stated the voice imperturbably.

"Like 'ell you will," retorted Orace's most belligerent accents. "You'll wait ahtside on the bleedin' doorstep, that's wot you'll do——"

There were the sounds of a scuffle; and Mr. Uniatz, who understood one thing if there was nothing else he understood, gave a surprising demonstration of his right to his nickname. He hopped out of his chair with a leap which an athletic grasshopper might have envied, reaching for his hip. Patricia caught the other girl by the arm.

"Through the bookcase—quick!" she ordered. "Hoppy, leave the door shut, or we can't open this one."

She bundled Annette through the secret panel, saw that it was properly closed, and grabbed Hoppy's wrist as he snatched at the door handle again.

"Put that gun away, you idiot," she said. "That'll only make things worse."

Hoppy's jaw fell open aggrievedly.

"But, say——"

"Don't say," snapped Patricia, in a venomous whisper. "Get the darn thing back in your pocket and leave this to me."

She thrust him aside and opened the door herself. Outside in the hall, Orace was engaging in a heroic but one-sided wrestling match in the arms of Chief Inspector Teal and another detective. As she emerged, one of his boots landed effectively on Mr. Teal's right shin and drew a yelp of anguish in response. Patricia's cool voice cut across the brawl like a blade of honey.

"Good-evening—er—gentlemen," she said.

The struggle abated slightly; and Orace's pur-

ple face screwed round out of the tangle with its
walrus moustache whiffling.

"Sorl right, miss," he panted valiantly. "You
jus' wait till I've kicked these plurry perishers
down the thunderin' 'ill——"

"I'm afraid they'd only come back again," said
Patricia regretfully. "They're like black beetles—
once you've got them in the house, you can't get
rid of them. Take a rest, Orace, and let me talk to
them. How are you, Mr. Teal?"

Mr. Teal glared pinkly at Orace and shook him
off. He picked up his bowler hat, which had been
dislodged from his head during the mêlée and had
subsequently been somewhat trampled on, and
glared at Orace again. He appeared to have some
difficulty in controlling his voice.

"Good-evening, Miss Holm," he said at last,
breathing deeply and detaching his eyes from
Orace's stormy countenance with obvious difficulty. "I have a search warrant——"

"You must be collecting them," murmured Patricia sweetly. "Come in and tell me what it's all
about this time."

She turned and went back into the study, and
Mr. Teal and his satellite followed. Mr. Teal's
eyes discovered Mr. Uniatz and transferred their
smouldering malevolence to him. It is a regret-
table fact that Mr. Teal's soul was not at that
moment overflowing with courtesy and good will
towards men; and Mr. Uniatz had crossed his
path on another unfortunate occasion.

"I've seen you before," Teal said abruptly. "Who are you?"

"Tim Vickery," replied Hoppy promptly, with an air of triumph.

"Yes?" barked the detective. "You're the forger, eh?"

There was something so consistently unfriendly in his china-blue gaze that Hoppy reached around nervously for the whisky bottle. He had been let down. This was not what the Saint had told him. He had to think, and that always gave him a pain somewhere between his ears.

"I ain't no forger, boss," he protested. "I'm a fairy."

"You're *what?*" blared the detective.

"A bootlegger," said Mr. Uniatz, gulping hastily. "I mean, de udder business is my perfession. I got an accent like a nightingale——"

Chief Inspector Claud Eustace Teal grabbed at the scattering fragments of his temper with both hands. If only he could master the art of remaining tranquil under the goad of that peculiar form of baiting in which not only the Saint indulged, but which seemed to infect all his associates like a malignant disease, he might yet be able to score for law and order the deciding point in that ancient feud. He had missed points before by letting insult and injury get under his skin— the Saint's malicious wit had stung him, ragged him, baited him, rattled him, tied him up in a series of clove hitches and stood him on his head and rolled him over again, till he had no more chance of victory than a mad bull would have had against an agile hornet.

But this man in front of him, whose calloused throat apparently allowed whisky to flow through it like milk, was not the Saint. The style of badinage might be similar—in fact, it is interesting to record that, to Teal's overwrought imagination, the style was almost identical—but the man behind it could not conceivably be the same. In any one century, two men like the Saint could not plausibly have been born. The earth could not have survived it.

And Mr. Teal had a point to make. The man with the whisky bottle had given it to him, open-handed. It was a point which annihilated all the routine plans he had made for that raid on which he had barely started to embark—a point so free and brazen that Mr. Teal's respiratory system went haywire at the sight of it.

"Your name's Vickery, is it?" he said, in the nearest he could get to his normal sleepy voice; and Mr. Uniatz, after an appealing glance at Patricia, nodded dumbly. "Then why is it," Teal flung at him suddenly, "that when Miss Holm tried to ring you up a quarter of an hour ago, she was told that you were in bed and asleep?"

Mr. Uniatz opened his mouth, and, finding that nothing at all would come out of it, decided to put something in and hope for the best. He pushed the neck of the whisky bottle between his teeth and swallowed feverishly; and Patricia spoke for him.

"That was a mistake," she explained. "Mr. Vickery came in just a minute or two after I telephoned."

"Dat's right, boss," agreed Mr. Uniatz, grasping the point with an injudicious speed which trickled a couple of gills of good alcohol wastefully down his tie. "A minute or two after she telephones, I come in."

Mr. Teal gazed at him balefully.

"Then why is it," he rasped, "that the man I had waiting outside the front gate while I was at the telephone exchange didn't see you?"

"I come in de back door," said Hoppy brightly.

"And the man I had at the back door didn't see you either," said Chief Inspector Teal.

Hoppy Uniatz sank down into the nearest chair and tacitly retired from the competition. His brow was ploughed into furrows of honest effort, but he was out of the race. He had a resentful feeling that he was being fouled, and the referee wasn't doing anything about it. He had done his best, but that wasn't no use if a guy didn't get a break.

"It sounds even funnier," Mr. Teal said trenchantly, "when I tell you that another Tim Vickery was pulled in for questioning just before I left London, and he hasn't been let out yet." His sharp glittering eyes between the pink creases of fat went back to Patricia Holm. "I'll be interested to have a look at this third Tim Vickery who's asleep at

Hawk Lodge," he said. "But if the Saint isn't here, I can make a good guess at who *he's* going to be!"

"You do your guessing," answered Patricia, as the Saint would have answered; but her heart was thumping.

"I'll do more than that," said the detective grimly.

He turned on his heel and waddled out of the room; and his silent companion followed him. Patricia went after them to the front door. There was a police car standing on the drive, and Teal stopped beside it and called two names. After a slight interval, two large overcoated men materialized out of the dark.

"You two stay here," commanded Teal. "Inside the house. Don't let anyone out who's inside, or anyone else who comes in while I'm away—on any excuse. I'll be back shortly."

He climbed in, and his taciturn equerry took the wheel. In another moment the police car was scrunching down the drive, carrying Claud Eustace Teal on his ill-omened way.

IX

IVAR NORDSTEN was dead. He must have been dead even before Simon Templar snatched his automatic away from under the lashing tearing claws of the panther and sent two slugs through its heart at point-blank range. He lay on the shining oak close to the door, a curiously twisted and mangled shape which was not pleasant to look at. The maddened beast that had turned on him had wreaked its vengeance with fiendish speed; but it had not wrought neatly. . . .

The Saint straightened up, cold-eyed, and looked across at Erik. The man was staring motionlessly at the black glossy body of the dead panther and at the still and crumpled remains of Ivar Nordsten; and the dull glazed sightlessness had been wiped out of his eyes. His throat was working mutely, and the tears were raining down the yellow parchment of his cheeks.

Footsteps were coming across the hall; and Simon remembered the three shots which had been fired. It was not impossible that they might have been mistaken for cracks of the whip; but the end of the panther's savage snarling had begun a sudden deep silence which would demand some explanation. With a quick deliberate movement Simon opened the door and stood behind it. He raised his voice in a muffled imitation of Nordsten's:

"Trusaneff!"

The butler's footsteps entered the room. The Saint saw him come into view and stop to stare at the man Erik. Very gently he pushed the door to behind the unsuspecting man, reversed his gun, and struck crisply with the butt. . . .

Then he completed the closing of the door and took out his cigarette case. For the moment there was no reason why he shouldn't. Certainly the battle-scarred gladiator with the passionate interest in antirrhinums remained, together with heaven knew how many more of Nordsten's curious staff; but to all outward appearances Ivar Nordsten was closeted with his butler, and there was no cause for anyone else to be inquisitive. In fact, Simon had already gathered that inquisitiveness was not a vice in which Nordsten's retainers had ever been encouraged.

He lighted a cigarette and looked again at the financier's erstwhile prisoner.

"Erik," he said quietly.

The man did not move; and Simon walked across and put a hand on his shoulder.

"Erik," he repeated, and the man's tear-streaked face turned helplessly. "Was Ivar your brother?"

"Yes."

The Saint nodded silently and turned away. He went over to the desk and sat in the chair behind it, smoking thoughtfully. The demise of Ivar Nordsten meant nothing to him personally—it was all very unfortunate and must have annoyed Ivar a good deal, but Simon was dispassionately unable to feel that the amenities of the world had suffered an irreparable loss. He had it to thank for something else, which was the shock that had probably saved Erik's reason. Equally well, perhaps, it might have struck the final blow at that pitifully tottering brain; but it had not. The man who had looked at him and answered his questions just now was not the quivering half-crazed wretch who had looked up into the beam of his flashlight out of that medieval dungeon under the floor: it was a man to whom sanity was coming back, who understood death and illogical grief—who would presently talk, and answer other questions. And there would be questions enough to answer.

Simon was too sensible to try to hurry the return. When his cigarette was finished he got up and found his torch and went down into the pit. It was only a small brick-lined cellar, with no other outlet, about twelve feet square. There was a rusty iron bedstead in one corner, and a small table beside it. On the table were a couple of plates on which were the remains of some food, and the table top was spotted with blobs of candle wax. Under the table there was an earthenware jar of water and an enamel mug. A small grating high up in one wall spoke for some kind of ventilating system, a gutter along one side for some kind of drainage, but the filth and smell were indescribable. The Saint was thankful to get out again.

When he returned to the library he found that Erik had taken down one of the curtains to cover up the body of his brother. The man was sitting in a chair with his head in his hands, but he looked up quite sanely as the Saint's feet trod on the parquet.

"I'm sorry," he said. "I'm afraid I didn't understand you just now."

Simon smiled faintly and went for his cigarette-case again.

"I don't blame you, brother," he said. "If I'd spent two years in that rat hole, I guess I should have been a bit scatty myself."

The man nodded. His eyes roved involuntarily to the huddled heap under the rich curtain and returned to the Saint's face.

"He was always clever," he said, as if reciting an explanation which had been distilled through his mind so often during those dreadful years of darkness that nothing was left but the starkest essence, pruned to the barest minimum of words, to be spoken without apology or preface. "But he only counted results. They justified the means. His monopoly was built upon trickery and ruthlessness. But he was thorough. He was ready to be found out. That's why he kept me—down there. If necessary, there was to be a tragic accident. Ivar Nordsten would be killed by his panther. But I was to have been the body, and he had another identity to step into."

"Did he hate you very much?"

"I don't think so. He had no reason to. But he had a kink. I was the perfect instrument for his scheme, and so he was ready to use me. Nothing counted against his own power and success."

It was more or less a confirmation of the amazing theory which the Saint had built up in his own mind. But there was one other thing he had to know.

"What is supposed to have happened to you?" he asked.

"My sailing boat capsized in Sogne Fjord. I was supposed to be in it, but my body was never found. Ivar told me."

The Saint smoked for a minute or two, gazing at the ceiling; and then he said: "What are you going to do now?"

Erik shrugged weakly.

"How do I know? I've had no time to think. I've been dead for two years. All this——"

The gesture of his hands concluded what he could not put into words, but the Saint understood. He nodded sympathetically; but he was about to make an answer when the telephone bell rang.

Simon's eyes settled into blue pools of quiet, and he put the cigarette to his lips again rather slowly in a moment's passive hesitation. And then, with an infinitesimal reckless steadying of his lips, he stretched out a lazy arm and lifted the instrument from its rack.

"Hullo," said a girl's voice. "Can't I speak to——"

"Pat!" The Saint straightened up suddenly and smiled. "I was wondering why I hadn't heard from you."

"I tried to get through twice before, but——"

"I guessed it, old darling," said the Saint quickly. He had detected the faint tremor of strain in her voice, and his eyes had gone hard again. "Never mind that just now, lass. I've got no end of news for you, but I think you've got some for me. Let's have it."

"Teal's been here," she said. "He's on his way to Hawk Lodge right now. Are you all right, boy?"

He laughed; and his laughter held all of the hell-for-leather lilt which rustled through it most blithely when trouble was racing towards him like a charging buffalo.

"I'm fine," he said. "But after I've seen Claud Eustace, I'll be sitting on top of the world. Get the whisky away from Hoppy, sweetheart, and hide it somewhere for me. I'll be seein' ya!"

He dropped the microphone back on its perch and stood up, crushing his cigarette into an ash-tray, seventy-four inches of him, lean and dynamic and unconquerable, with a dancing light shifting across devil-may-care blue eyes.

"Listen, Erik," he said, standing in front of the man who looked so much like Nordsten, "a little while ago I tried to tell you who I was. Do you think you can take it in now?"

The man nodded.

"I'm Simon Templar. They call me the Saint. If it was only two years ago when Ivar put you away, you must have heard of me."

The other's quick gasp was sufficient answer; and the Saint swept on, with all the mad persuasion which he could command in his voice, crowding every gift of inspired personality which the gods had given him into the task of carrying away the man who looked like Nordsten on the stride of his own impetuous decision:

"I'm here because I pretended to be a man named Vickery. I pretended to be Vickery because Ivar wanted him for some mysterious job, and I wanted to find out what it was. I heard about that from Vickery's sister, because I got her away last night in London after she'd been arrested by the police. If I hadn't butted in here, Ivar wouldn't have rushed into your murder without a proper stage setting: he wouldn't have been killed, but you would. If you like to look at it that way, you're free and alive at this moment for the very same reason that the police are on their way here to arrest me now."

"I don't understand it altogether, even yet," Erik Nordsten said huskily. "But I know I must owe you more than I can ever repay."

"That's all you need to understand for the next half-hour," said the Saint. "And even then you're wrong. You can repay it—and repay yourself as well."

There was something in the quiet clear power of his voice, some quality of contagious urgency, which brought the other man stumbling up out of his chair, without knowing why. And the Saint caught him by the shoulders and swung him round.

"I'm an outlaw, Erik," he said. "You know that.

But in the end I don't do a lot of harm. You know that, too. Chief Inspector Teal, who's on his way here now, knows it—but he has his duty to do. That's what he's paid for. And he has such a nasty suspicious mind, wherever I'm around, that he couldn't come in here and see—your brother—as things are—without finding a way to want me for murder. And that would all be very troublesome."

"But I can tell him——"

"That it wasn't my fault. I know. But that wouldn't cover what I did last night. I want you to say more than that."

The man did not speak, and Simon went on: "You look like Nordsten. You *are* Nordsten— with another first name. With a bit of good food and exercise, it'd be hard for anyone to tell the difference who didn't know Ivar very well; and from the look of things I shouldn't think he encouraged very many people to know him well. You were intended to take his place eventually— why not now?"

Erik Nordsten's breath came in a jerk.

"You mean——"

"I mean—*you are Nordsten!* You've suffered for him. You've paid for anything you may get out of it a thousand times over. And you're dead. You've been dead for two years. Now you've got another life open for you to step into. You can run his business honestly, or break it up and sell out—whichever you like. I'll give you all the help I can. Nordsten got me here—thinking I was

Vickery, who's a very clever forger—to forge national bonds for him. I suppose he was going to deposit them in banks to raise the capital to take over new business. Well, I won't forge for you— I couldn't do it, anyhow—but I'll lend you money and get my dividend out of this that way. What you do in return is to swear white, black, and coloured that you met me in Bond Street at two o'clock yesterday morning and brought me straight down here, and I've been with you ever since. That's the repayment you can make, *Ivar*—and you've got about thirty seconds to make up your mind whether you care to foot the bill!"

X

STILL holding his seething wrath grimly in both hands, Chief Inspector Claud Eustace Teal tramped stolidly up the steps to the front door of Hawk Lodge and jabbed his thumb on the bell. It is not easy for any stranger to find a house on St. George's Hill, especially at night; for that aristocratic address consists of a large area of ground on which nameless roads are laid out with the haphazard abandon of a maze, connecting cunningly hidden residences which are far too exclusive to deface their gates with numbers. Sergeant Barrow had lost his way several times, and the delays had not helped Mr. Teal with his job of two-handed wrath-clutching. But during the ride he had managed it somehow; and it was very unfortunate that he had so little time to consolidate his self-control.

In a very few seconds the door was opened, and Teal pushed past the butler unceremoniously. It would not be true to say that Mr. Teal's heart was singing, but at least he had not yet plumbed the most abysmal caverns of despair.

"I want to see Mr. Vickery," he said; and the butler turned from the door.

"My name is Vickery, sir," he replied.

A spectral shade of ripe muscatel infused itself slowly into the detective's round ruddy face. His eyes protruded slowly, as if they were being gradually inflated by a very small air pump. The wobblings of his rotund body were invisible beneath his clothes, but even without those symptoms there was something about his general aspect which suggested that a piece of tinder laid on his brow would have burst instantly into flame. When at last vocal expression could no longer be denied, his voice cracked. He practically squeaked.

"*What?*"

"Vickery, sir," repeated the butler. "My name is Vickery."

Mr. Teal had been looking at him more closely.

"Your name is Trusaneff," he said. "You did three years at Parkhurst for robbery with violence."

"Yes, sir," said the butler respectfully. "Nevertheless, sir, I have changed my name to Vickery."

Teal glowered past him at a man with a scarred face who was lounging at the other end of the hall.

"And I suppose *his* name is Vickery, too?" he said scorchingly.

The butler looked round and nodded.

"Yes, sir. His name is also Vickery."

"How many more Vickerys are there in this house?" Teal howled, with his brain beginning to reel.

"Three, sir," said the butler imperturbably. "Everyone in this house is called Vickery, with the exception of Mr. Nordsten. Even the kitchen-maid," he added with a sigh, "is now known as Vickery. It is highly confusing."

Something that would have made a self-preservative rattlesnake wriggle away to hide itself down the nearest length of gas pipe welled into the detective's bulging glare. There was a strange springy sensation in his legs, as if they had been separately hitched onto two powerful steam tractors and simultaneously extended in all directions. It was, as we have already admitted, very unfortunate. It gave Mr. Teal no chance. He ploughed on doggedly; but his hold on his temper was never again the firm commanding grip of a heavyweight wrestler subduing a recalcitrant urchin—it was more akin to the frantic clutch on the pants of a man whose suspenders have come apart.

"I'll see Mr. Nordsten," he announced gratingly; and the saturnine butler bowed.

"This way, sir."

He led the simmering detective to the library; and Mr. Teal followed him in and looked the room over with a pair of eyes in which the habitual affectation of sleepiness had to be induced with a bludgeon. Two men were sitting there, smoking cigars. One of them was a pale and tired-looking Ivar Nordsten—Teal, who made it his business to have at least a sight acquaintance with every important man in the country, had no difficulty in recognizing him—the other man called for no effort of recognition.

"Good-evening, sir," Teal said curtly to Nordsten; and then he looked at the Saint. "You're also Vickery, I take it?"

The Saint smiled.

"Claud," he said penitently, "I'm afraid we've been pulling your leg."

Mr. Teal's tonsils came up into his mouth, and he gulped them back. The effort brought his complexion two or three shades closer to the tint of the sun-kissed damson.

"Pulling my leg," he repeated torridly. "Yes, I suppose you were."

"You see, Claud," Simon explained frankly, "when I heard you were on your way round here looking for a bloke named Vickery, I thought it would be rather priceless if you beetled in and found that the place was simply infested with Vickerys. I could just see your patient frog-like face——"

"Could you?" Teal's voice was thick and curdled with the frightful tension of his restraint. "Well, I'm not interested in that. What I want to hear from you is why you've been going under the name of Vickery yourself."

Nordsten cleared his throat.

"I suppose," he remarked coldly, "you consider that you have some right to come in and behave like this, Mr.—er——"

"Teal is my name, sir," said the detective tersely. "Chief Inspector Teal."

"Inspects anything," said the Saint. "Gas meters, drains, hen roosts——"

"I'm from Scotland Yard," Teal almost shouted.

"Where the Highlanders hang out their washing," Simon explained.

Mr. Teal's collar strained on its studs; and Nordsten nodded.

"That need not prevent you stating your business in a proper manner," he said stiffly. "What is all this fuss about?"

"That man," said the detective, with a sweltering glance at the Saint, "is a well-known criminal. His real name is Simon Templar; and I want to know what he's doing in this house pretending to be Vickery!"

"I can easily tell you that," answered Nordsten promptly. "Mr. Templar is an intimate friend of mine. I know his reputation, though I should hardly go so far as to call him a criminal. But he is certainly well known, and of course servants will always talk. I think he exaggerates the powers of gossip, but whenever he comes to stay with me he always insists on calling himself Vickery to save me from any embarrassment."

"And how long has he been staying with you this time, sir?" Teal inquired roughly.

"Since last night—or perhaps I should say yesterday morning."

"Can you remember the time exactly?"

"It must have been a few minutes after two o'clock. I met him in Bond Street, and he had just left the Barnyard Club. I was driving home rather late from a dinner, and I asked Mr. Templar to come down with me."

It may be confessed at once that Chief Inspector Teal had never been kicked in the stomach by a sportive mule. But if that sublime experience had ever befallen him, it is safe to affirm that the expression on his face would have been practically indistinguishable from the one which came over it as he gaped speechlessly at Nordsten. Twice he attempted to force words through his larynx, which appeared to have become clogged with glue; and at the third attempt he succeeded.

"You tell me," he said, "that you met Templar in Bond Street at two o'clock yesterday morning and brought him straight down here?"

"Of course," answered Nordsten shortly. "Why not?"

Mr. Teal took in a mouthful of air and wedged his bouncing tonsils down with it. Why not? When a taxi driver had been found that very afternoon who said that a man whom he identified from Simon Templar's photograph had paid him five hundred pounds for his taxi, his overcoat, and his cap, shortly after two o'clock. It was true that this man had said that he wanted the taxi for a museum . . .

"Did he have a taxi with him?" Teal blurted sudorifically.

"As a matter of fact, he had," said Nordsten with faint surprise. "He had just bought it because he wanted to present it to a museum. We had to take it to a garage before we drove down."

"How on earth did you guess that, Claud?" asked the Saint admiringly.

Mr. Teal's pudgy fists clenched.

"Guess it?" he yapped and cleared his obstructed throat. There were so many other things he wanted to say. How did he *guess* it? Words failed him. It was true that no one had been able to take the number of the taxi in which that particular train of trouble had begun, on account of its defective rear light; it was true that no one could positively identify the taxi, which was exactly the same as any other standard cab of pre-war vintage; it was true that no one could positively identify the man who had driven it; but there was a limit to coincidences. The Saint had met Mr. Teal outside the club and seen him go in. The Saint had bought a taxi. Mr. Teal had ridden in a taxi shortly afterwards and sustained adventures such as only the Saint's evil genius could have originated. How did he *guess* it? Mr. Teal's protruding eyes turned glassily back to the Saint; but what court in the kingdom would accept his description of Simon's smile of gentle mockery as evidence? Teal swung round on Nordsten again. "How long had he had this taxi when you met him?" he croaked.

"It can't have been many minutes," said Nordsten. "When I came down Bond Street he was standing beside it, and he pointed out the driver walking away and told me what had happened."

"Was anyone else with you?"

"My chauffeur."

"You know that your butler is a convicted criminal?"

Nordsten raised his eyebrows.

"I fail to see the connection; but of course I am familiar with his record. I happen to be interested in criminal reform—if that is any concern of yours." Erik was very tired; but the nervous tension of his voice and hands, at that moment, was very easily construed as a symptom of rising anger. "If I am to understand that you want my evidence in connection with some criminal charge, Inspector," he said with some asperity, "I shall be glad to give it in the proper place; and I think my reputation will be sufficient support of my sworn word."

Simon Templar eased a cylinder of ash off his cigar and uncoiled his lazy length from the armchair in which he had been relaxing. He stood up, lean and wicked and tantalizing in the silk dressing gown which he had thrown on over his scanty clothing, and smiled at the detective very seraphically.

"Somehow, Claud," he murmured, "I feel that you're shinning up the wrong flagpole. Now why not be a sportsman and admit that you've launched a floater? Drop in again some time, and we'll put on the whole works. There will be a trapdoor in the floor under the carpet and a sinister cellar underneath with two dead bodies in it——"

"I wish one of them could be yours," said Mr. Teal, in a tone of passionate yearning.

"Talking of bodies," said the Saint, "I believe your tummy is getting bigger. When I prod it with my finger——"

"Don't do it!" brayed the infuriated detective.

The Saint sighed.

"I'm afraid you're a bit peevish tonight, Eustace," he said reproachfully. "Never mind. We all have our off moments, and a good dose of castor oil in the morning is a great pick-me-up. . . . And so to bed."

He steered the detective affectionately towards the door; and, having no other instructions, the inarticulate Sergeant Barrow joined in the general exodus. Mr. Teal could not forbid him. Looked at from every angle that Chief Inspector Teal's overheated brain could devise, which included a few slants that Euclid never dreamed of, the situation offered no other exit. And in the depths of his soul Teal wanted nothing better than to go away. He wanted to remove himself into some un-fathomed backwater of space and sit there for centuries with a supply of spearmint in his pocket and an ice compress on his head, figuring out how it had all happened. And in his heart was some of the outraged bitterness which must have af-flicted Sisera when the stars in their courses stepped aside to biff him on the dome.

"Mind the step," said the Saint genially, at the front door.

"All right," said the detective grittily. "I'll look after myself. You'd better do the same. You can't get away with it for ever. One day I'm going to catch you short of an alibi. One day I'm going to get you in a place that you can't lie yourself out of. One day——"

"I'll be seein' ya," drawled the Saint and closed the door.

He turned round and looked at the butler, Trusaneff, who had come forward when the library door opened; and put his hands in his pockets.

"I gather that you remembered your lines, Trotzky," he said.

"Yes, sir," answered the man, with murderous eyes.

Simon smiled at him thoughtfully and moved his right hand a little in his dressing-gown pocket.

"I hope you will go on remembering them," he said, in a voice of great gentleness. "The Vickery joke is over, but the rest goes on. You can leave this place as soon as you like and take any other thugs you can find lying around along with you. But you are the only man in the world who knows that we've had a change of Ivar Nordstens, so that if it ever leaks out I shall know exactly whom to look for. You know who I am; and I have a key to eternal silence."

He went back to the library, and Erik Nordsten looked up as he came in.

"Was I all right?" he asked.

"You were magnificent," said the Saint. He stretched himself and grinned. "You must be just about all in by this time, my lad. Let's call it a day. A hot bath and a night's sleep in clean sheets'll make a new man of you. And you will be a new man. But there's just one other thing I'm going to ask you to do tomorrow."

"What is it?"

"There's a rather pretty kid named Vickery round at my house who put me into the whole thing, if you haven't forgotten what I told you. I can smuggle her out of the country easily enough, but she's still got to live. One of your offices in Sweden might find room for her, if you said the word. I seem to remember you telling Claud Eustace that you were interested in reforming criminals, and she'd be an excellent subject."

The other nodded.

"I expect it could be arranged." He stood up, shrugging himself unconsciously in the unfamiliar feeling of the smart lounge suit which Simon had found for him in Nordsten's wardrobe; and what must have been the first smile of two incredible years flickered momentarily on his tired mouth. "I suppose there's no hope of reforming you?"

"Teal has promised to try," said the Saint piously.

III

THE ART OF ALIBI

I

CHIEF INSPECTOR CLAUD EUSTACE TEAL unfolded
the paper wrapping from a leaf of chewing gum
with slow-moving pudgy fingers, and the sleepy
china-blue eyes in his pink chubby face blinked
across the table with the bland expressionlessness
of a doll.

"Of course I know your point of view," he said
flatly. "I'm not a fool. I know that you've never
done anything which I could complain about if I
were just a spectator. I know that all the men
you've robbed and"—the somnolent eyes steadied
themselves deliberately for a moment—"and
killed," he said—"they've all deserved it—in a
way. But I also know that, technically, you're the
most dangerous and persistent criminal outside of
prison. I'm a police officer, and my job is technicalities."

"Such as pulling in some wretched innkeeper
for selling a glass of beer at the wrong time, while
the man who floats a million-pound swindle gets
away on a point of law," Simon Templar suggested gently; and the detective nodded.

"That's my job," he said, "and you know it."

The Saint smiled.

"I know it, Claud," he murmured. "But it's also the reason for my own career of crime."

"That, and the money you make out of it," said the detective, with a tinge of gloomy cynicism in his voice.

"And, as you say, the boodle," Simon agreed shamelessly.

Mr. Teal sighed.

In that stolid, methodical, honest, plodding, unimaginative and uninspired mechanism which was his mind, there lingered the memory of many defeats—of the countless times when he had gone up against that blithe and bantering buccaneer, and his long-suffering tail had been mercilessly pulled, stretched, twisted, strung with a pendant of tin cans and fireworks, and finally nailed firmly down between his legs; and it was not a pleasant recollection. Also in his consciousness was the fact that the price of his dinner had undoubtedly been paid out of the boodle of some other buccaneering foray, and the additional disturbing fact that he had enjoyed his dinner immensely from the first moment to the last. It was very hard for him to reconcile those three conflicting emanations from his brain; and his heavy-lidded eyes masked themselves even deeper under their perpetual affectation of weariness as he rolled the underwear of his spearmint ration into a small pink ball and flicked it across the restaurant tablecloth. He might even have been phrasing some suitable reply which should have comprehended all the opalescent

facets of his paradox in one masterly sentence; but
at that moment a waiter came to the table.

    The chronicler, a conscientious and respectable
citizen whose income-tax payments are never more
than two years in arrears, hesitates over those last
ten words. He bounces, like an inexpert matador
on the antlers of an Andalusian bull, upon the
horns of a dilemma. All his artistic soul, all that
luminescent literary genius which has won him the
applause and reverence of the reading world, rises
in shuddering protest against that scant dismissal.
He feels that this waiter, who rejoiced in the name
of Bassanio Quinquapotti, should have more space.
He is tempted to elaborate at much greater length
the origin and obscure beginnings of this harbinger
of fate, this dickey-bird of destiny; to expatiate in
pages of elegant verbiage upon the psychological
motivations which put him into permanent evening dress, upon his feverish sex life, and upon
the atrophied talent which made him such a popular performer on the sackbut at informal Soho
soirées. For this waiter who came to the table
was the herald of five million golden pounds, the
augur of one of the Saint's most satisfactory adventures, and the outrider of yet another of the
melancholy journeys of Mr. Teal. With all these
things in mind, the sensitive psyche of the historian
revolts from that terse unceremonious description
—"a waiter came to the table." And only the
bloodthirsty impatience of editors and publishers
forces him to press on.

"Excuse me, sir," said this waiter (whose name, we insist on recording, was Bassanio Quinquapotti), "but are you Mr. Teal?"

"That's right," said the detective.

"You're wanted on the telephone, sir," said the waiter (Bassanio Quinquapotti).

Mr. Teal got up and left the table. Ulysses, at some time or another, must have got up and left a table with the same limpid innocence, undreaming of the odyssey which lay before him. . . . And the Saint lighted a cigarette and watched him go.

It was one of those rare occasions when Simon Templar's conscience carried no load; when his restless brain was inevitably plotting some fresh audacious mischief, as it always was, but there was no definite incident in the daily chronicles of London crime which could give Scotland Yard cause to inquire interestedly into his movements; and Chief Inspector Teal was enjoying a brief precarious interlude of peace. At those times the Saint could beguile Mr. Teal into sharing a meal with him, and Mr. Teal would accept it with an air of implacable suspicion; but they would both end their evening with a vague feeling of regret.

On this particular occasion, however, thanks to the egregious Mr. Quinquapotti, the feeling of regret was doomed on one side to be the reverse of vague; but this vision of the future was hidden from Claud Eustace Teal.

He wedged himself into the telephone booth in the foyer of the restaurant with the pathetic trust-

fulness of a guinea pig trotting into a vivisection-
ist's laboratory and took up the receiver.

"Teal speaking," he said.

The familiar voice of his assistant at the Yard
clacked back at him through the diaphragm. It
uttered one sentence. It uttered another.

Once upon a time there was a small non-Aryan
happily making mud pies in Palestine with a
party of pals. Looking up from his harmless play,
this urchin happened to behold the prophet Elisha
hiking up towards Bethel, and in a spirit of pure
camaraderie heaved a brick at him and encouraged him after the fashion of healthy urchins of
all time, saying, "Go up, thou baldhead." Where-
upon, to his vast and historic surprise, a brace of
she-bears came out of a wood and used him for
a quick-lunch bar, along with forty-one of his
playmates.

Chief Inspector Teal, it must be confessed, had
outgrown the instinct to heave bricks at bald-
headed prophets many years ago. In the course of
his professional career, indeed, he had even
learned to regard them with some reverence, and
had, since the supply of kind-hearted she-bears in
London is somewhat limited, been detailed at
times to protect them from similar affronts. But he
was still capable of experiencing some of the emotions that must have assailed that ancient Hebrew
guttersnipe as he felt himself, out of a clear sky,
being sucked down the gullet of a bear. The voice
of Mr. Teal's assistant went on uttering, and the

mouth of Mr. Teal opened wider as the recital
went on. The milk of human kindness, always an
unstable element in Mr. Teal's sorely tried cos-
mogony, curdled while he listened. By the time
his assistant had finished, it would, if laid aside
in a cool place, have turned itself gradually into
a piece of cheese.

"All right," he said thickly, at the end. "I'll
call you back."

He hung up the receiver and levered himself
out of the cabinet. Squeezing his way between the
tables on his way back across the restaurant, he
was grimly conscious of the Saint's face watching
his approach. It was a face that inevitably stood
out among the groups of commonplace diners, a
lean and darkly handsome face which would have
arrested any wandering glance; but it was no less
inevitably the face of an Elizabethan buccaneer,
lacking only the beard. The lean relaxed figure
struck the imagination like a sword laid down
among puddings; and for the same reason it was
indescribably dangerous. The very clear and
humorous blue eyes had a mocking recklessness
which could never have stood in awe of man or
devil; and Mr. Teal knew that that also was true.
The detective's mind went back once again over
the times when he had confronted that face, that
debonair immaculate figure, those gay piratical
blue eyes; and the remembrance was no more com-
forting than it had been before. But he went back
to the table and sat down.

"Thanks for the dinner, Saint," he said.

Simon blew a smoke ring.

"I enjoyed it, too," he remarked. "Call it a small compensation for the other times when everything hasn't been so rosy. I often feel that if only our twin souls, freed from the contagion of this detectivitis which comes over you some-times——"

"It's a pity you didn't complete the party," Teal said with a certain curious shortness.

The Saint raised his eyebrows.

"How?"

"That American gunman you've been going about with, for instance—what's his name?"

"Hoppy Uniatz? He's gone to the Ring to have a look at some wrestling. Ran into some Yankee grunter he knew over on the other side, who's doing a tour over here; so Hoppy felt he'd better go and root for him."

"Yes?" Teal was jerkily unwrapping a fresh slice of gum, although the wad in his mouth was still putting forth flavour in a brave endeavour to live up to its advertising department. "He wouldn't have gone there alone, of course."

"I think he went with this wriggler's manager and a couple of his clutching partners," said the Saint.

Mr. Teal nodded. Something was happening to his blood pressure—something which had begun its deadly work while he was listening to the voice of his assistant on the telephone. He knew all the symptoms. The movements with which he folded his wafer of naked spearmint and stuffed it into his mouth had a stupendous slothfulness which cost him a frightful effort to maintain.

"Or your girl friend, perhaps—Patricia Holm," Teal articulated slowly. "What's happened to her?"

"She came over all evening dress and went to a party—one of these Mayfair orgies. Apart from that she's quite normal."

"She'd have a good time at a party, wouldn't she?" Teal said ruminatively.

The Saint swilled liqueur brandy around in the bowl of a pear-shaped glass.

"I believe lots of young men do get trampled to death in the stampede when she turns up," he admitted.

"But there'd be enough survivors left to be able to swear she'd been dancing or sitting out with one or other of 'em from the time she arrived till well after midnight—wouldn't there?" Teal insisted.

Simon sat up. For one or two minutes past he had been aware that a change had come over the detective since he returned to the table, and there had been a sudden grittiness in the way that last question mark had been tagged on which he couldn't have missed if he had been stone deaf. He looked Teal over with thoughtful blue eyes.

"Claud!" he exclaimed accusingly. "I believe there's something on your mind!"

For a moment Teal's windpipe tied itself into a knot of indignation which threatened to strangle him. And then, with a kind of dogged resolution, he untied it and waded on.

"There's plenty on my mind," he said crunchily. "And you know what it is. I suppose you've been laughing yourself sick ever since you sat down at the table. I suppose you've been wondering if there were any limits on earth to what you could make me swallow. Well, I've bought it. I've given you your rope. And now suppose you tell me why you think it isn't going to hang you?"

"Claud!" The Saint's voice was wicked. "Are you sure you haven't had too much of this brandy? I feel that your bile is running away with you. Is this——"

"Never mind my bile!" Teal got out through his teeth. "I'm waiting for you to talk about something else. And before you start, let me tell you that I'm going to tear this alibi to pieces if it takes me the rest of my life!"

Simon raised his eyebrows.

"Alibi?" he repeated gently.

"That's what I said."

"I don't know what you're talking about."

"No?" Teal meant to be derisive, but the word plopped out of his mouth like a cork out of a bottle. "I'm talking about this precious alibi of yours which accounts for everything that fellow Uniatz and that girl Patricia Holm have been doing all the evening—and probably accounts for all your other friends as well. I mean this alibi you think you've framed me into giving *you*——"

"What on earth *are* you talking about?" asked the Saint patiently; and Teal drew another laboured breath.

"I mean," he said, and all the cumulative rancour of five years of that unequal duel was rasping through his voice like a red-hot file—"I mean that you must be thinking it was damned clever of you to get me to have dinner with you on this night of all nights, and keep me here with you from seven o'clock till now, when a dead man was picked up on the Brighton road half an hour ago *with your mark on him!*"

II

SIMON stared at him blankly. And even while he did so, he realized that he was letting the opportunity of a lifetime of Teal-baiting dawdle past him and raise its hat as it went by, without so much as lifting a hand to grab it. To be accused for once of a crime of which he was as innocent as an unborn Eskimo, and to have a made-to-measure alibi presented to him on a plate at the same time, should have presented vistas of gorgeous possibility to warm the heart. But he didn't even see them. He was too genuinely interested.

"Say that again," he suggested.

"You've heard me already," retorted the detective gratingly. "It's your turn now. Well, I'm waiting for it. I like your fairy tales. What is it this time? Did he commit suicide and tie your mark round his neck for a joke? Did the Emperor of Abyssinia do it for you, or was it arranged by the Sultan of Turkey? Whatever your story is, I'll hear it!"

It has been urged by some captious critics of these records that Chief Inspector Teal has rarely been observed in them to behave like a normal detective. This charge the scribe is forced to admit. But he points out that there are very few of these chronicles in which Chief Inspector Teal has had any chance to be a normal detective. Confronted with the slow smile and bantering blue eyes of the Saint, something went haywire inside Mr. Teal. He was not himself. He was overwrought. He gave way. He behaved, in fact, exactly as a man who had been burned many times might have been expected to behave in the presence of fire. But it wasn't his fault; and the Saint knew it.

"Now wait a minute, you prize fathead," Simon answered quite pleasantly. "I didn't kill this bloke——"

"I know you didn't," said Teal, in an ecstasy of elephantine sarcasm. "You've been sitting here talking to me all the time. This fellow just died. He drew your picture on a piece of paper and had heart failure when he looked at it."

"Your guess is as good as mine, Claud," drawled the Saint lazily. "But personally I should say that some low crook is trying to frame me."

"You would, eh? Well, if I were looking for this low crook——"

"You'd come to my address." Simon pushed his cigarette into an ashtray, finished his drink, and spread money on the table to pay the bill. "Well, here I am. You gave me the murder and you gave me the alibi. You thought of this game. Why don't you get on with it? Am I arrested?"

Teal gulped and swallowed a piece of gum.

"You'll be arrested as soon as I know some more about this murder. I know where to find you——"

The Saint smiled.

"I seem to have heard words to that effect before," he said. "But it hasn't always worked out quite that way. My movements are so erratic. Why take a chance? Let me arrest myself. My car's just round the corner, and the night is before us. Let's go and find out some more about this murder of mine."

He stood up; and for some unearthly reason Teal also rose to his feet. An exasperating little bug of uncertainty was hatching out in the detective's brain and starting to dig itself in. He had been through these scenes before, and they had lopped years off his expectation of life. He had known the Saint guilty of innumerable felonies and breaches of the peace, beyond any possible shadow of

human doubt, and had got nothing out of it—
nothing but a smile of infuriating innocence and
a glimmer of mocking amusement in the Saint's
eyes, which was not evidence. He was used to
being outwitted, but it had never occurred to him
that he might be wrong. Until that very moment,
when the smile of infuriating innocence was so
startlingly absent. . . . He didn't believe it even
then—he had reached the stage when nothing that
Simon Templar said or did could be taken at its
face value—but the germ of preposterous doubt
was brooding in his mind, and he followed the
Saint out into the street in silence, without understanding why he did it.

"Where did this news come from?" Simon inquired, as he slid in behind the wheel of the great
shining Hirondel which was parked close by.

"Horley," Teal replied curtly, and couldn't
help adding: "You ought to know."

The Saint made no retort; and that again was
unusual. The tiny maggot of incertitude in Teal's
brain laid another egg, and he chewed steadily on
his remaining sludge of spearmint in self-defensive
taciturnity while the long thrumming nose of the
car threaded its way at breath-taking speed
through the thinning traffic of south London.

Simon kindled a fresh cigarette from the lighter
on the dash and thrust the Hirondel over the
southward artery with one hand on the wheel and
the speedometer quivering around seventy, driving
automatically and thinking about other things.

Before that, he had sometimes wondered why such a notorious scapegoat as himself should have been passed over for so long by the alibi experts of the underworld, and he had only been able to surmise that the fear of attracting his own attention was what had deterred them. The man who had set a new precedent this night must either have been very confident or very rash; and the Saint wanted to know him. And there was an edge of quiet steel in the Saint's narrowed eyes as they followed the road in the blaze of his sweeping headlights which indicated that he would have an account to settle with his unauthorized substitute when they met. . . .

Perhaps it was because he was very anxious to learn something more which might help to bring that meeting nearer, or perhaps it was only because the Saint never felt really comfortable in a car unless it was using the king's highway for a race track, but it was exactly thirty-five minutes after they left the restaurant when he swung the car round the last two-wheeled corner and switched off the engine under the blue lamp of Horley police station. For the latter half of the journey Mr. Teal had actually forgotten to chew; but he released his hold on his bowler hat and climbed out phlegmatically enough. Simon followed him up the steps and heard Teal introduce himself to the night sergeant.

"They're in the inspector's office, sir," said the man.

Simon went in at Teal's shoulder and found three men drinking coffee in the bare distempered room. One of them, from his typical bulk and the chair he occupied at the desk, appeared to be the inspector; the second, a grey-haired man in pince-nez and an overcoat, was apparently the police surgeon; the third was a motorcycle patrol in uniform.

"I thought I'd better come down at once," Teal said laconically.

The inspector, who shared the dislike of all provincial inspectors for interference from Scot-land Yard, but accepted it as an unfortunate neces-sity, nodded no less briefly and indicated the motorcycle patrol.

"He can tell you all about it."

"There ain't much to tell, sir," said the patrol, putting down his cup. "Just about two mile from here, it was, on the way to Balcombe. I was on me way home when I saw a car pulled up by the side of the road an' two men beside it carryin' what looked like a body. Well, it turned out it was a body. They said they saw it lyin' in the road an' thought it was someone been knocked down by an-other car, but when I had a look I saw the man had been shot. I helped 'em put the body in their car and rode in alongside of 'em to the police station here."

"What time was this?" Teal asked him.

"About half-past ten, sir, when I first stopped.

It was exactly a quarter to eleven when we got here."

"How had this man been shot?"

It was the doctor who answered:

"He was shot through the back of the head, at close range—probably with an automatic or a revolver. Death must have been instantaneous."

Mr. Teal rolled his gum into a spindle, pushed his tongue into the middle to shape a horseshoe, and chewed it back into a ball.

"I was told you'd found the Saint's mark on the body," he said. "When was that?"

The inspector turned over the papers on his desk.

"That was when we were going through his things. It was in his outside breast pocket."

He found a scrap of paper and handed it over. Teal took it and smoothed it out. It was a leaf torn from a cheap pocket diary; and on one side of it had been drawn, in pencil, a squiggly skeleton figure whose round blank head was crowned with a slanting elliptical halo.

Teal's heavy eyes rested on the drawing for a few seconds, and then he turned and held it out to the Saint.

"And I suppose you didn't do that?" he said.

There was a sudden stillness of incomprehension over the other men in the room, who had accepted Simon without introduction as an assistant of the Scotland Yard man; and Teal glanced back at them with inscrutable stolidity.

"This is the Saint," he explained.

A rustle of astonishment stirred the local men, and Teal bit on his gum and met it with his own soured disillusion: "No, I haven't done anything clever. He's been with me all the evening. He hasn't been out of my sight from seven o'clock till now—not for five minutes."

The police surgeon blew a bubble in his coffee cup and wiped his lips on his handkerchief, gaping at him stupidly.

"But that's impossible!" he spluttered. "The body was still warm when I saw it, and the pupils contracted with atropine. He couldn't have been dead three hours at the outside!"

"I expected something like that," said the detective, with sweltering restraint. "That's all it wanted to round off the alibi."

Simon put the torn scrap of paper back on the inspector's desk. It had given him a queer feeling, looking at that crude sketch on it. He hadn't drawn it; but it was his. It had become too well known for him to be able to use it very often now, for the precise reason which Mr. Teal had overlooked—that when that little drawing was found anywhere on the scene of a crime, there was only one man to search for. But it still had its meaning. That childish haloed figure had stood for an ideal, for a justice that struck swiftly where the law could not strike, a terror which could not be turned aside by technicalities: it had never been used wantonly. . . . The three local men were staring at him inquisitively, more like morbid sightseers at a sensational trial than professional sifters of crime; but the Saint's gaze met them with an arctic calm.

"Who was this man?" he asked.

The inspector did not answer at once, until Teal's shifting glance repeated the question. Then he turned back to the things on his desk.

"He had a Spanish passport—nothing seems to have been stolen from him. The name is—here it is—Enrique. Manuel Enrique. Age thirty; domicile, Madrid."

"Occupation?"

The inspector frowned over the booklet.

"Aviator," he said.

Simon took out his cigarette case, and his eyes travelled thoughtfully back to the drawing which was not his. It was certainly rather squiggly.

"Who were these men who picked him up on the road?"

Again the inspector hesitated, and again Teal's attitude repeated the interrogation. The inspector compressed his lips. He disapproved of the proceedings entirely. If he'd had his way, the Saint would have been safely locked away in a cell in no time—not taking up a cross-examination of his own. With the air of a vegetarian being forcibly fed with human flesh, he picked up a closely written report sheet.

"Sir Hugo Renway, of March House, Betfield,

near Folkestone, and his chauffeur, John Kellard," he recited tersely.

"I suppose they didn't stay long."

The inspector leaned back so that his chair creaked.

"Do you think I ought to have arrested them?" he inquired ponderously.

The doctor smirked patronizingly and said: "Sir Hugo is a justice of the peace and a permanent official of the Treasury."

"Wearing top hat and spats?" asked the Saint dreamily.

"He was not wearing a top hat."

The Saint smiled; and it was a smile which made Mr. Teal queerly uneasy. The little beetle of dubiety in his mind laid another clutch of eggs and sat on them. In some way he felt that he was losing his depth, and the sensation lifted his temperature a degree nearer to boiling point.

"Well, Claud," the Saint was saying, "we're making progress. I arrested myself to come down here, and I'm always ready to go on doing your work for you. Shall I charge myself, search myself, and lock myself up in a cell? Or what?"

"I'll think it over and let you know," said the detective jaggedly.

"Go on a fish diet and give your brain a chance," Simon advised him.

He trod on his cigarette end and buttoned his coat; and his blue eyes went back to Mr. Teal with a level recklessness of challenge which was like a draught of wind on the embers of Teal's temper.

"I'm telling you again that I don't know a thing about this bird Manuel Enrique, beyond what I've heard here. I don't expect you to believe me, because you haven't that much intelligence; but it happens to be the truth. My conscience is as clean as your shirt was before you put it on——"

"You're a liar," brayed the detective.

"Doubtless you know your own laundry best," said the Saint equably; and then his eyes chilled again. "But that's about all you do know. You're not a detective—you're a homing pigeon. When in doubt, shove it on the Saint—that's your motto. Well, Claud, just for this once, I'm going to take the trouble to chew you up. I'm going to get your man. I've got a quarrel with anyone who takes my trade-mark in vain; and the lesson'll do you some good as well. And then you're going to come crawling to me on your great fat belly——"

In a kind of hysteria, Teal squirmed away from the sinewy brown forefinger which stabbed at his proudest possession.

"Don't do it!" he blared.

"—and apologize," said the Saint; and in spite of himself, in spite of every obdurately logical belief he held, Chief Inspector Teal thought for a moment that he would not have liked to stand in the shoes of the man who ventured to impersonate the owner of that quiet satirical voice.

III

MARCH HOUSE, from one of the large-scale ord-
nance maps of which Simon Templar kept a complete and up-to-date library, appeared to be an
estate of some thirty acres lying between the village of Betfield and the sea. Part of the southern
boundary was formed by the cliffs themselves, and
a secondary road from Betfield to the main Folkestone highway skirted it on the northwest. The
Saint sat over his maps with a glass of sherry for
half an hour before dinner the following evening,
memorizing the topography—he had always been
a firm believer in direct action, and, wanting to
know more about a man, nothing appealed to him
with such seductive simplicity as the obvious
course of going to his house and taking an opti-
mistic gander at the scenery.

"But whatever makes you think Renway had
anything to do with it?" asked Patricia Holm.

"The top hat and spats," Simon told her gravely.
He smiled. "I'm afraid I haven't got the childlike
faith of a policeman, lass, and that's all there is to
it. Claud Eustace would take the costume as a
badge of respectability, but to my sad and worldly
mind it's just the reverse. From what I could
gather, Hugo wasn't actually sporting the top hat
at the time, but he seems to have been that kind of
man. And the picture they found on the body *was*
rather squiggly—as it might have been if a bloke

had drawn it in a car, traveling along. . . . I know it's only one chance in a hundred, but it's a chance. And we haven't any other clue in the whole wide world."

Hoppy Uniatz had no natural gift of subtlety, but he did understand direct action. Out of the entire panorama of human endeavour, it was about the only thing which really penetrated through all the layers of bullet-proof ivory which protected his brain. Detaching his mouth momentarily from a tumbler of gin nominally diluted with ginger ale, he said: "I'll come wit' ya, boss."

"Is it in your line?" asked the Saint.

"I dunno," Hoppy confessed frankly. "I ain't never done no boiglary. Whadda we have to wear dis costume for?"

Patricia looked at him blankly.

"What costume?"

"De top hat an' spats," said Hoppy Uniatz.

The Saint covered his eyes.

Six hours later, braking the Hirondel to a smooth standstill under an overarching elm where the road touched the northwest boundary of March House, Simon felt more practically cautious about accepting Hoppy's offer of assistance. On such an expedition as he had undertaken, a sportive elephant would certainly have been less use; but not much less. All the same, he had no wish to offend Mr. Uniatz, whose proud spirit was perhaps unduly sensitive on such points. He swung himself out into the road, detached the spare wheel, and opened up the tool kit, while Hoppy stared at him puzzledly.

"This is where you come in," the Saint told him flatteringly. "You're going to be an unfortunate motorist with a puncture, toiling over the wheel."

Mr. Uniatz blinked at him dimly.

"Is dat part of de boiglary?" he asked.

"Of course it is," said the Saint unscrupulously. "It's probably the most important part. You never know when some village slop may come paddling around these parts, and if he saw a car standing by the road with nobody in it he'd naturally be suspicious."

Hoppy reached round for his hip flask and nodded.

"Okay, boss," he said. "I get it. If de cop comes while you're gone, I give him de woiks."

"You don't do anything of the sort," said the Saint wearily. "They don't allow you to kill policemen in this country. What you do is to give your very best imitation of a guy fixing a flat. You might possibly get into conversation with him. Talk sentimentally about the little woman at home, waiting for her man. Make him feel homesick and encourage him to push on. But you don't give him de woiks."

"Okay, boss," repeated Hoppy accommodatingly. "I'll fix it."

"God help you if you don't," said the Saint harrowingly and left him to it.

The frontier of the March House estate at that

point consisted of a strong board fence about eight
feet high topped with three lines of barbed wire
carried on spiked iron brackets beetling outwards
at an angle: the arrangement was effective enough
to have checked any less experienced and determined trespasser than the Saint, and even
Simon might have wasted some time over it if it
had not been for the overhanging elm under which
he had thoughtfully stopped his car. But by
balancing himself precariously on the side of the
tonneau and leaping upwards, he was able to get
a fingerhold on one of the lower branches; and he
swung himself up onto it as if Tarzan had been
his grandfather.

Finding his way through the tree, in the dark,
was not quite so easy; but he managed it more or
less silently, and dropped from another branch
onto a mat of short undergrowth on the inside of
the fence.

From there, while the muffled mutterings of
Hoppy Uniatz wrestling with a wheel drifted
faintly to his ears, he surveyed the lay of the land
ahead of him. He was in a spinney of young trees
and brushwood; barred here and there with the
boles of older trees similar to the one by which he
had made his entrance; a half-moon, peeping fit-
fully between squadrons of cirrus cloud, gave his
night-hunter's eyes enough light to make out that
broad impression and at the same time suggested
an open space some distance farther on beyond
the coppice. The house itself stood roughly in the

same direction, according to his map-reading; and
with a fleeting smile for the complete craziness of
his intentions he began to pick his way through
the scrub towards it.

A small bird let out a startled squeak at his feet
and went whirring away into the dark, and from
time to time he heard the rustlings of diminutive
animal life scurrying away from his approach;
but he encountered no pitfalls or trip wires or
other unpleasant accidents. The clear space ahead
was farther away than he had thought at first, and
as he went on he seemed to make very little progress towards it. Presently he understood why,
when he broke out through a patch of thinner
shrubbery into what seemed to be a long narrow
field laid out broadside to his route: twenty yards
away, on the other side, was a single rank of taller
trees linked by what appeared to be another fence
—it was this wall of shadow and line of lifting
tree trunks which he had never seemed to come
any nearer to as he threaded his way through the
spinney.

As he crossed the field and came close to this
inner boundary, he saw that it was not a fence, but
a loosely grown hedge about six feet high. He was
able to see this without any difficulty because when
he was still a couple of yards away the pattern of
it was suddenly thrown up in silhouette by the
kindling of a light behind it.

At first his only impression was that the moon
had chosen that moment for one of its periodical

peeps from behind the drifting flotillas of cloud.
Then, very quickly, the light flared up brighter.
He saw the patchwork shadow of the hedge
printed on his own clothes, and instinctively
ducked behind the sheltering blackness of the
nearest tree. And as he did so he became aware
that the humming noise he had been hearing had
grown much louder.

It was a noise which had been going on, very
faintly, for some time; but he had thought nothing of it. A car passing on another road half a
mile away might have caused it, and a subconscious suggestion of the same car drawing nearer
had prevented him paying much attention to the
first increase in its volume. But at this moment it
had swelled into a steady drone that was too
powerful and unvarying for any ordinary car to
make, rising to the indefinable borderline of as-
sertiveness at which his sense of hearing was
jolted into sitting up and taking notice. He listened to it, frowning, while it grew to sharp roar
—and then stopped altogether.

The Saint remained as still as the tree beside
which he stood, as if he had been an integral part
of it, and looked out over the hedge at the field
where the light was. Rising a little on his toes, he
was able to get a clear view of it and see the cause
of the light.

A double row of flares was being kindled in the
field, like a file of tiny brilliant bonfires—with a
sudden jerk of understanding, he remembered

other days in his life, and knew what they were. Mounds of cotton waste soaked in petrol or paraffin. Even while he watched, the last of them was lighted: a reddish glow danced in the dark, licked up into a tentative flame, and spring suddenly into blazing luminance. The shadow of the man who had lit it stretched out in a sudden long bar of blackness into the surrounding gloom where the light exhausted itself. The twin rank of flares was complete, forming a broad lane of light from northwest to southeast, six flares to each side, two hundred yards long at a rough guess. The dimension of the field beyond that was lost in the darkness which lapped the light.

Over his hear there was a rush of air and a dying hiss of wind as though a monstrous bird sighed across the sky. Looking upwards, he saw a shadow like a great black cross diving against the hazy luminousness of the clouds, barely skimming the tree tops: it plunged into the lane of light, gathering shape and detail—flattened out, bumped once, and landed.

Almost at the same moment the nearer flares began to flicker and die down. One of them went out; then another. . . .

"Never again, so long as I live, will I be rude to luck," the Saint said to Patricia Holm, much later. "For every dozen minor troubles the little lady gives us, somehow or other she manages to let you draw three to a straight flush and fill your hand—once or twice in a lifetime."

He stood, fascinated, and watched the flares going out. Fifteen minutes earlier, he might have run into no end of trouble, without profit to himself or anybody else; fifteen minutes later, there might have been nothing whatever to see; only the blind gods of chance had permitted him to arrive at the exact moment when things were happening. In the outer glow of the farthest flare he saw a man attaching himself to the tail of the aëroplane and beginning to push it farther into the darkness; in a few seconds he was joined by the pilot, unidentifiable in helmet and goggles and leather coat. The engine had been switched off as the ship touched the deck, and the last scene of the drama was played out in utter silence. The two men wheeled the machine away, presumably into some invisible hangar: the last flare wavered and blinked, and the fitful gloom of the night came down once again upon the scene.

Simon Templar drew a long deep breath and stepped back out of the shadow of his tree. Of all the sins which he might have accused the top hat and spats of Sir Hugo Renway of camouflaging, ordinary smuggling was the last; but he was always accessible to new ideas.

In this case the most obvious course which presented itself was a further and yet more sleuthlike investigation into the topography and individual peculiarities of March House; and with the sublime abandon of the congenitally insane he proposed to pursue the said course without delay. The

last flare was finally extinguished, and the peaceful darkness settled once more upon the field. As
far as anyone outside the estate could have told,
the aëroplane had flown on across the Channel—
if any reflected glow of light had been visible beyond the belt of woodland through which he had
passed, and the high fence beside the road, it could
hardly have attracted any ordinary citizen's attention, and it had lasted such a short time that there
would have been nothing particularly remarkable
about it anyway. But to anyone who had been
privileged to witness the performance from the
inside, the whole thing was highly furtive and irregular, especially at the country house of a justice of the peace and permanent Treasury official;
and the Saint could see nothing for it but to in-
trude.

And it was at that psychological moment that
the moon, to whose coy tactics we have already
had occasion to refer, elected once again to say
peekaboo to the slumbering world.

Simon Templar had owed his life to many
queer things, from opening a window to dropping
a cigarette, but he had never owed it before to
such a rustic combination of items as a flirtatious
moon and a rabbit. The rabbit appeared about
one second after the moon, by lolloping out of a
bush into the pool of twilight which the moon
provided between two trees. The Saint had been
so absolutely immobile in his observation post by
the tree trunk that it could never even have noticed

him: it had simply been attracted by the lighting effects provided in the adjoining field, and, being a bunny of scientific appetites and an inquisitive turn of mind, it had suspended its foraging for a space to explore this curious phenomenon. Simon saw the moving blur of it out of the corner of his eye before he realized what it was—and froze instinctively back into motionlessness almost before he had begun to move. Then he saw the rabbit clearly and moved again. A dry leaf rustled under his foot, and the rabbit twitched its nose and decided to abandon its cosmic investigations for that evening.

But it didn't lollop back into the bush from which it had emerged. Perhaps it had a date with some loose-moraled doe in the next parish and had merely paused to admire the wonders of nature on its way to more serious business or perhaps it had only heard news of some fresh young lettuces sprouting in the kitchen gardens of March House; only its reincarnation in the shape of a theosophist will ever tell. But at all events, it pushed on instead of turning back. It made a rapid hopping dive for the nearest gap in the hedge through which Simon himself had been preparing to pass.

And it died.

There was a momentary flash of blue flame, and the rabbit kicked over backwards in a dreadful leap and lay twitching in the patch of moonlight.

IV

SIMON turned it over with his foot: it was in-dubitably one of the deadest rabbits in the county of Kent. Then he took a tiny flashlight from his pocket and examined the hedge with great cau-tion. There were lines of gleaming copper wire strung through it at intervals of about six inches and rising to a height of six feet above the ground —if he had not stopped to watch the rabbit he could not have helped touching one of them.

The Saint pushed a hand somewhat unsteadily across his forehead and turned his attention to the tree. But there was no chance there of repeating his Tarzan impersonation, for there were similar copper wires coiled round the trunk to a greater height than he could reach. Without rubber gloves and insulated wire cutters he could go no farther; and he had no doubt that the same high-voltage circuit continued all the way round the landing field and enclosed everything else that might be interesting to look at.

Twenty minutes later he dropped out of another tree into the road beside his car and found Hoppy Uniatz sitting on the running board and gazing disconsolately at an inadequate hip flask which had long since run as dry as a Saharan water hole.

"Hi, boss," said Mr. Uniatz, rising stiffly from his unprofitable meditations. "Dijja get de dough?"

Simon shook his head, lighting a cigarette in his cupped hands.

"I didn't get to first base," he said. "A rabbit stopped me." He saw a vacuous expression of perplexity appear on Mr. Uniatz's homely dial and extinguished his lighter with a faint grin. "Never mind, Hoppy. Pass it up. I'll tell you all about it next year. Let's get back to London."

He slid into the driving seat; and Mr. Uniatz put his flask away and followed him more slowly, glancing back doubtfully over his shoulder with a preoccupied air. As Simon pressed the starter, he coughed.

"Boss," said Mr. Uniatz diffidently, "is it oke leavin' de cop here?"

"Leaving the which?" ejaculated the Saint limply.

"De cop," said Mr. Uniatz.

Simon pushed the gear lever back into neutral and gazed at him.

"What are you talking about?" he inquired.

"Ya see, boss," said Mr. Uniatz, with the manner of Einstein solving a problem in elementary arithmetic, "de tire wasn't flat."

"What tire?" asked the Saint heroically.

"De tire you told me to change," explained Hoppy. "Ya told me to fix de flat, but it wasn't."

The Saint struggled with his vocabulary in an anguished silence, seeking words in which he might deal suitably with the situation; but before he had counted all the syllables in the phrases he

proposed to use, Mr. Uniatz was ploughing on,
as if determined, now that he had started, to make
a clean breast of the matter.

"Well, boss, I put back de wheel an' sat down
to wait for de cop. After a bit he rides up on a
bicycle. 'Hi-yah, guy,' he says, 'whaddaya doin'
here?' So I tells him I was fixin' a flat, but it
wasn't. 'Well, whaddaya waitin' for?' he says. So I
remembers what ya tells me, boss, an' I says: 'I'm
t'inkin' of de little woman back home, waitin' for
her man.' 'Ya big bum,' he says, 'ya drunk.' "

"I'll bet he didn't," said the Saint.

"Well, it was sump'n like dat," said Hoppy,
dismissing the quibble, "only he talked wit' an accent."

"I see what you mean," said the Saint. "And
what did you do?"

"Well, boss, I hauls off an' gives him a poke in
de jaw."

"And what does he say to that?"

"He don't say nut'n, boss." Mr. Uniatz jerked a
nicotine-stained thumb backwards at an undistin-
guishable quarter of the night. "I tucks him up in
de bushes an' leaves him. Dat's what I mean, is it
oke leavin' him here," said Hoppy, harking back
to his original problem.

Simon Templar fought with his soul for a short
time without speaking. If he had followed his
most primitive instincts, there would probably
have been a late lamented Mr. Uniatz tucked up
in the bushes alongside the sleeping rural con-

stable; but the Saint's sense of civic responsibility was improving.

"I guess we'll leave him," he said at length. "It can't make things any worse."

He drove back to London in a thoughtful frame of mind. It was one of those times when the hundredth chance turned up in magnificent vindication of all harebrained enterprise; and when the established villain was a man in the position of Sir Hugo Renway, the Saint was inclined to have a few things to think about. There were only two forms of smuggling in which the rewards were high and the penalties heavy enough to justify such extreme measures as the murdered airman on the Brighton road and that lethally electrified wire fence at March House—it is curious that the Saint was still far from reading the real interpretation into the facts he knew.

The wandering policeman whom Hoppy Uniatz had poked in de jaw was a complication which had not been allowed for in his plan of campaign as seriously as it might; and he was not expecting the repercussions of it to reach him quite so quickly as they did.

He put the Hirondel back in its garage at about a quarter to four and walked round to his apartment on Piccadilly. A sleepy night porter took them up in the lift: he was a new employee of the building whom the Saint had not seen before, and Simon made a mental note to learn more about him at an early date—he had found it a very sound

principle to enlist the sympathies of the employees
in any such building where he lived, for there
were other detectives besides Mr. Teal who had
visualized a cast-iron arrest of the Saint as a signpost to promotion. But he was not thinking of
doing anything about it at that hour, and his mind
was too much occupied with other matters to
notice that the man looked at him with more than
ordinary curiosity as he got in.

His apartment lay at the end of a short corridor.
He strolled innocently towards it, taking out his
key, with Hoppy following him; and he was on the
point of putting his key in the lock when a voice
that was only too familiar spoke behind him:

"Do you mind if we come in?"

The Saint turned rather slowly on his heel and
looked at the two men who had appeared from
somewhere to bar the way back along the corridor
—there was something rather solid and purpose-
ful about the way they stood shoulder to shoulder
so as to fill the passage, something which put the
glint of steel back in his eyes and set his heart
ticking a fraction faster. Hoppy's hand was leaping automatically to his hip; but Simon caught it
by the wrist and smiled.

"You know you're always welcome, Claud,"
he murmured. "But you do choose the most
Bohemian hours for your visits."

He turned back to the door and unlocked it and
led the way into the living room, spinning his hat
onto a peg in the hall as he passed through. He

took a cigarette from the box on the table and lighted it, facing round with one hand in his pocket and that thoughtful smile still on his lips.

"Well, what's the fun, boys?" he inquired genially. "Has somebody pinched the north side of Oxford Street and do you think I did it, or have you just dropped in to sing carols?"

"Where have you been tonight?" asked Mr. Teal.

His manner was not the manner of a man who had dropped in to sing carols. Even in his wildest flights of whimsy, the Saint had never thought of Chief Inspector Teal as the Skylark of Scotland Yard, but he had known him to look more like an embryonic warbler than he did just then. Simon smiled even more genially and even more thoughtfully and trickled out a lungful of blue smoke.

"We've been on a pub-crawl with Andrew Volstead and Lady Astor, and Hoppy came along to carry the bromo-seltzer."

Teal did not smile.

"If you've got another alibi," he said, "I'd like to hear it. But it had better be a good one."

The Saint pondered for a moment.

"You are getting particular," he said. "A story like that would always have kept you amused for hours in the old days. I suppose you've been taking a correspondence course in this detective business. All right. We haven't been on a pub-crawl. We've been splitting hairs on the dome of St. Paul's and looking for needles in the Haymarket."

Mr. Teal's hands remained in his pockets, but his whole attitude suggested that they were grasping something as heavy as a steam roller.

"Is that all you've got to say?" he demanded hoarsely.

"It'll do for the time being," said the Saint calmly. "That's what I say we've been doing; and what the hell does it matter to you?"

The detective appeared, somehow, in spite of his mountainous immobility, to approach the verge of gibbering. It may seem unkind of the chronicler to mention this, but he is conscientiously concerned to deal only with the bare facts, without apology or decoration. And yet he must admit that Mr. Teal had lately suffered much.

"Now listen," Mr. Teal got out through his teeth. "About half-past eleven tonight the watchman at Hawker's factory, down at Brooklands, was knocked on the head by someone he found prowling around the sheds. When he woke up and raised the alarm, one of the hangars had been forced open and an aëroplane had been stolen!"

Simon tapped his cigarette on the edge of an ashtray. His brain was starting to turn over like an electric motor responding to the touch of a switch, but no hint of that sudden mental commotion could have been seen in his face. His gaze went back to the detective from under quizzically slanting eyebrows.

"It sounds pretty ambitious," he remarked. "But what makes you think I'd be interested?"

"I don't have to think——"

"I know, Claud. You just chew a thistle and your ears flap."

"I don't have to think," Teal said grimly, "when you leave your mark behind you."

The Saint raised one eyebrow a little further.

"Meaning?"

"When the watchman woke up, there was a piece of paper pinned to his coat. There was a drawing on it. It was the same drawing that was found in the pocket of that dead airman last night —Manuel Enrique. It was your mark!"

"Dear me!" said the Saint.

The detective's china-blue eyes were as hard and bright as porcelain. His mouth had disappeared altogether—it was a mere slit in the hardened round chubbiness of his face.

"I suppose you can explain that away," he snapped.

"Of course I can," said the Saint easily. "The same low criminal who was taking my name in vain on the Brighton road last night——"

"Is that all the alibi you've got this time?" Teal asked, with a kind of saw-edged note in his voice.

"More or less," said the Saint. He watched the detective take a second grip on himself, watched a glimmer of tentative relief and triumph creep hesitantly into the angry baby-blue eyes, watched the thinned mouth begin to open for an answer— and added, with a seraphically apologetic smile, at the very last and most devastating instant: "Oh, yes, there was something I forgot to mention. On the way from St. Paul's to the Haymarket I did stop at the Lex Garage off Piccadilly to collect my car; and now I come to think of it, Claud, it must have been exactly half-past eleven."

Mr. Teal blinked. It was not the nervous bashful blink of a gentle botanist being rudely confronted with the facts of mammalian reproduction: it was the dizzy blink of a bather who has made unwary contact with an electric eel. His chest appeared to deflate; then it swelled up again to a point where his coat was straining on its seams.

"You expect me to believe that?" he blared.

"Of course not," said the Saint. "You haven't enough intelligence to save yourself that much time. But you can verify it. Go to the garage and find out. Their records'll show what time I checked out. The night staff'll remember me. Go and ask 'em. Push off and amuse yourself. But if that's all that's on your mind tonight, I'm going to bed."

"You can wait a little longer," retorted Teal. "Half-past eleven isn't the only time I want you to account for."

The Saint sighed.

"What's the rest of it?"

"You seemed rather interested in Sir Hugo Renway last night," Teal said waspily, "so I asked the police down there to keep an eye on his place. I know your methods pretty well by now, and I had an idea you might go there. At half-past one this morning the constable was cycling round the estate when he saw your car—and him!"

"What, Brother Uniatz?" drawled Simon. "Did you see a cop, Hoppy?"

Mr. Uniatz, who had been trying to unlock the cellaret with a piece of bent wire, turned round vacantly.

"Yes, boss," he said.

"Ha!" barked Mr. Teal. It may sound improbable, but that is a close approximation to the noise he made.

"I see one only yesterday," Hoppy elaborated hastily, with the Saint's blue stare scorching through him. "In de Haymarket."

Chief Inspector Teal did not burst. Perhaps it is not actually possible for the human organism to become so inflated with spleen that it explodes into small fragments—the chronicler is inclined to take this as the only plausible reason why his favourite detective did not stand there and pop. But there was something about him which suggested that even the point of a joke might have punctured him into the power of performing that impossible disintegration. He glared at the Saint again with reddening eyes.

"This constable was also knocked on the head," he went on, getting the words out somehow through his contracting larynx; "and when he woke up——"

"The garden gate had been forced open and

March House had been stolen," murmured Simon. "I know. The bloke flew off with it in the aëroplane."

"He reported to the local station, and they telephoned me. The other thing I want to know is what you were doing at *that* time."

"We were driving round and round Regent's Park; and I'll give you half a million pounds if you can prove we weren't!"

The detective bit on his long-forgotten chewing gum with a force that almost fractured his jaw.

"Do you think you can make a monkey out of me?" he roared.

Simon shook his head.

"Certainly not," he replied solemnly. "I wouldn't try to improve on God's creation."

The chronicler has already submitted, perhaps somewhat rashly, his opinion that the human organism is not capable of literally expanding into small and separate pieces under no other influence than the dilation of its own wrath. But he has, fortunately, offered the suggestion that some outside prod might succeed in procuring this phenomenal disruption.

Mr. Teal did not burst, physically. But he performed the psychological equivalent. Moved by a cosmic passion which stronger men than he might have failed lamentably to control, he grasped destiny in both his quivering hands. He did something which he had never in all his life contrived to do before.

"All right," he said throatily. "I've heard all I want to hear tonight. You can tell the rest of it to a jury. I'm arresting you on charges of common assault, burglary, and wilful murder."

V

SIMON extinguished his cigarette in an ashtray. The ticking of his heart was going faster, but not so very much faster. It was curious how Teal's ultimate explosion surprised him; curious also that it did not find him unprepared. Perhaps, in his heart of hearts, he had always known that something of the kind must happen, some day. The gay career of Teal-baiting could not go on for ever: it had gone on for a long time, but Mr. Teal was human. There was no more concrete evidence now than there had ever been; but the Saint had a good deal of belated psychological understanding. In Teal's place, he would probably have done the same.

The detective was still speaking, with the same rather frantic restraint and rather frantic consciousness of the awful temerity of what he was going to do:

"I caution you that anything you say now will be taken down and may be used in evidence at your trial."

The Saint smiled. He understood. He deeply

sympathized. In Teal's place, he would probably have done the same. But he was not in Teal's place.

"If you want to make a fool of yourself, Claud, I can't stop you," he said; and his left fist leapt out and crashed like a cannon ball into the furrow between Chief Inspector Teal's first and second chins.

The expression of compressed wrathfulness vanished startlingly from the detective's face. For a moment it was superseded by a register of grotesque surprise; and then every other visible emotion was smudged out by a vast blank sleepiness which for once was entirely innocent of pose. Mr. Teal's legs folded up not ungracefully beneath him; he lay down on the floor and went to sleep.

Mr. Teal's mute equerry was starting forward, and his mouth was opening: it is possible that at any moment some human sound might have emerged from that preternaturally silent man, but Simon gave it no chance. The man was grabbing for his wrists, and the Saint obligingly permitted him to get his hold. Then he planted his left foot firmly in the detective's stomach and rolled over backwards, pushing his foot vimfully upwards as he pulled his wrists down. The man sailed over his head in an adagio flying somersault and hit the carpet with an explosive *"wuff!"* which any medium-sized dog could have vocalized much better; and Simon somersaulted after him more gently and sat astride his chest. He grasped the man's coat collar in his hands and twisted his knuckles scientifically into the carotid arteries—unconsciousness can be produced in two or three seconds by that method, when employed by a skilful exponent, and Sergeant Barrow's resistance had been considerably impaired already by the force with which his shoulder blades had landed on the floor. It was all over in far less time than it takes to describe; and Simon looked up at Mr. Uniatz, who was prancing about like a puppy with his revolver reversed in his hand.

"Fetch me a towel from the bathroom, Hoppy," he ordered. "And for heaven's sake put that blasted cannon away. How many more times have I got to tell you that this is the closed season for policemen?"

While he was waiting, he handcuffed the two detectives with their own bracelets; and when the towel arrived he tore it into two strips and gagged them.

"Get your hat," he said, when the job was finished. "We're going to travel."

Mr. Uniatz followed him obediently. It may be true, as we have acknowledged, that the higher flights of philosophy and metaphysics were for ever beyond the range of Mr. Uniatz's bovine intellect; but he had an incomparable grip on the fundamentals of self-preservation. Experience had taught him that after an active encounter with the police the advantages of expeditious travelling could be taken for granted—a fact which relieved his brain of much potentially painful exertion.

As they turned into Berkeley Square, he followed a little more hesitantly; and eventually he plucked at the Saint's sleeve.

"Where ya goin', boss?" he asked. "Dis ain't de way to de garage."

"It's the way to the garage we're going to," answered the Saint.

He had automatically ruled out the Hirondel as a conveyance for that getaway—the great red-and-cream speedster was far too conspicuous and far too well known, and it was the car whose description would be immediately broadcast by Mr. Teal as soon as that hapless sleuth had worked the gag out of his mouth and reached the telephone. Simon had another and more commonplace car in reserve, in another garage and another name, which he had laid up some weeks ago with a far-sighted eye to just such a complication as this; and he was inclined to flatter himself on his forethought without undertaking the Herculean labour of hammering the idea into Hoppy's armour-plated skull.

Whether any net was actually spread out for him in time to cross his path, he never knew; certainly he slipped through London without incident, making excellent time over the almost deserted roads in spite of several detours at strategic points where he might have been stopped. He abandoned the car outside the entrance of the Vickers factory on the Byfleet road, where there would soon be a score of other cars parked around it, and one more modest saloon might easily pass unnoticed for days; and walked through the woods to his house as the dawn was breaking. There was no hope that Teal would fail to draw that covert as soon as he had reorganized his forces; but it was a temporary haven, and the Saint had a few items of personal equipment there which he wanted to pick up.

There were sounds of movement in the kitchen when he let himself in at the front door, and in another moment the belligerent walrus-moustached visage of Orace appeared on the opposite side of the hall. Simon threw his hat at him and smiled.

"What's our chance of breakfast, Orace?" he asked.

"Narf a minnit," said Orace expressionlessly and vanished again.

Over the bacon and eggs, golden brown toast and steaming coffee which Orace produced necromantically in very little more than the time he had promised, the Saint's brain was working overtime. For the time being, Teal had been dealt with; but the past tense had no more permanent stability than the haven in which Simon Templar was eating his breakfast. Ahead of those transient satisfactions lay the alternatives of penal servitude or a completed getaway; and he had no spontaneous leaning towards either. He turned them over in his mind like small beetles discovered under a log and decided that he liked them even less. But there was a third solution which took him longer to think over—which, in fact, kept him wrapped in silent concentration until his plate was pushed away and he was smoking a cigarette over a second cup of coffee and Mr. Uniatz intruded his bashful personality again.

Hoppy's brain had not been working overtime, because the hours between one breakfast and the following bedtime were rarely long enough to let it do much more than catch up with where it had left off the previous night. Nevertheless the wheels, immersed in the species of thick soup in which nature had asked them to whizz round, had been doggedly trying to revolve.

"Boss," said Hoppy Uniatz, articulating with some indistinctness through a slice of toast, two ounces of butter, a rasher of bacon, and half an egg, "de cops knows you got dis house."

Simon harked back over some leagues of his own cerebrations and recognized the landmark which Hoppy had contrived to reach.

"That's perfectly true," he remarked admiringly. "Now don't go doing any more of that high-pressure thinking—give your brain a minute to cool off, because I want you to listen to me."

He rang the bell and smoked quietly until Orace answered. Mr. Uniatz, happily absolved from further brainwork, engulfed the rest of the food within his reach and cast longing eyes at a decanter of whisky on the sideboard.

"Orace," said the Saint, "I'm afraid Claud Eustace is after us again."

"Yessir," said Orace phlegmatically.

"You might sound more sympathetic about it," Simon complained. "One of the charges is wilful murder."

"Well, it's yer own thunderin' fault, ain't it?" retorted Orace, unmoved.

The Saint sighed.

"I suppose you're right," he admitted. "Anyway, Hoppy's idea is that we ought to pull an Insull."

"Dat means to take it on de lam," explained Hoppy, clarifying the point.

Orace's faded eyes lost none of their ferocity, but his overhanging moustache twitched.

"If yer can wite 'arf a minnit, sir," he said, "I'll go wiv yer."

The Saint laughed softly and stood up. His hand fell on Orace's shoulder.

"Thanks a lot, you old humbug; but it isn't necessary. You see, Hoppy's wrong. And you ought to know it, after all the years you've been around with me." He leaned back against the mantelpiece, one hand in his pocket, and looked at the two men with eyes that were beginning to twinkle again. "Hoppy reminds me that Teal knows all about this house, but he's forgotten that Teal also knows I know it. Hoppy thinks we ought to pack our keisters and take it on the lam, but he's forgotten that that's the very thing Teal is expecting

us to do. After all, Claud Eustace has seen me
hang it on the limb before. . . . Are you there,
Hoppy?"

"Yes, boss," said Mr. Uniatz, after glancing
around to reassure himself of the fact.

"It's quite true that you'll probably see some
cops skating up the drive before long; but somehow I don't think Claud Eustace will be with
them. It'll be almost a formality. They may browse
around looking for incriminating relics, but they
won't be seriously looking for me—or Hoppy.
And that's why none of 'em will ever be great
detectives, because this is exactly where Hoppy is
going to be—lying snug and low in the secret room
off the study, which is one of the things they still
don't know about this house."

"Chees!" said Mr. Uniatz, in pardonable awe.
"Didja t'ink of all dat while ya was eatin' breakfast?"

The Saint smiled.

"That and some more; but I guess that's enough
for your head to hold at one time." He looked at
his watch. "You'd better move into your new quarters now—Orace will bring you food and drink
from time to time, and I'll know where to find
you when I want you."

He steered Hoppy across the hall and into the
study, slid back the bookcase beside the desk, and
pushed him through the gap in the wall behind it.
Framed in the narrow opening, Mr. Uniatz
blinked out at him pleadingly.

"Boss," he said, "it's gonna be toisty waitin'."

"Hoppy," said the Saint, "if I think you're going to have to wait long, I'll tell Orace to have a pipeline laid from a distillery right into the room. Then you can just lie down under the tap and keep your mouth open—and it'll be cheaper than buying it in bottles."

He slammed the bookcase into place again and turned round on the last puff of his cigarette as Orace came in.

"You've got to be an Orpen of the Storm, and draw the fire," he said. "But it shouldn't be very dangerous. They've nothing against you. The one thing you must do is get in touch with Miss Holm —let her know all the latest news and tell her to keep in contact. There may be fun and games for all before this party's over."

"Addencha better 'ide in there yerself, sir?" asked Orace threateningly. "I can look after everythink for yer."

The Saint shook his head.

"You can't look after what I'm going to look after," he said gently. "But I can tell you some more. It won't mean much to you, but you can pass it on to Miss Holm in case she's curious, and remember it yourself in case anything goes wrong." He caught Orace by the shoulders and swung him round. The mocking blue eyes were reckless and wicked; the Saintly smile was as blithe and tranquil as if he had been setting out on a picnic—

which, according to his own scapegrace philosophy, he was.

"Down at Betfield, near Folkestone," he said, "there's a place called March House, where a guy called Sir Hugo Renway lives. The night before last, this guy murdered a Spanish airman named Manuel Enrique, on the Brighton road—and left my mark on him. Last night, this same guy pinched an aëroplane out of the Hawker factory over the road—and left my mark on the night watchman. And in the small hours of this morning, an aëroplane which may or may not have been the one that was pinched landed in the grounds of March House. I was there, and I saw it. A few hours back, Claud Eustace Teal tried to run me in for both those efforts.

"I wasn't responsible for either of 'em, but Teal doesn't believe it. Taking things by and large, you can't exactly blame him. But *I* know better, even if he doesn't; and I'm just naturally curious. I want to know what all this jolly carnival is about that Renway's trying to tack onto me. And there's one thing you'll notice, Orace, with that greased-lightning brain of yours, which ties all these exciting goings-on together. What is it, Orace?"

The war-like moustache of his manservant bristled.

"Hairyplanes," said Orace brilliantly; and Simon smote him on the back.

"You said it, Horatio. With that sizzling brain of yours, you biff the ailnay on the okobay. Hairy-

planes it is. We've got to get to the bottom of
this, as the bishop said to the actress; and it strikes
me that if I were to fetch out the old Gillette and
go hairyplaning—if I blundered into March
House as a blooming aviator waiting to be
pruned——"

The peremptory *zing* of the front doorbell interrupted him, and he looked up with the mischief
hardening on his lips. Then he chuckled again.

"I expect this is the deputation. Give them my
love, Orace—and some of those exploding cigarettes. I'll be seein' ya!"

He reached the window in a couple of strides
and swung himself nimbly through. Orace
watched him disappear into the dell of bracken at
the other end of the lawn and strutted off, glowering, to answer the front door.

VI

THERE is believed to exist a happy band of half-
wits whose fondest faith it is that the life of a
government official, the superman to whom they
entrust their national destiny, is one long tread-
mill of selfless toil from dawn to dusk. They picture the devoted genius labouring endlessly over
reports and figures, the massive brain steaming,
the massive stomach scarcely daring even to call a
halt for food. They picture him returning home

at the close of the long day, his shoulders still bowed beneath the cares of state, to fret and moil over their problems through the night watches. They are, we began by explaining, a happy band of half-wits.

The life of a government official is very far from that; particularly if he is of the species known as "permanent," which means that he is relieved even of the sordid obligation of being heckled from time to time by audiences of weary electors. His job is safe. Only death, the Great Harvester, can remove him; and even when he dies, the event may pass unnoticed until the body begins to fall apart. Until then, his programme is roughly as follows.

10:30 a.m.	Arrive at office in Whitehall. Read newspaper. Discuss night before with fellow officials. Talk to secretary. Pick up correspondence tray. Put down again.
11:30 a.m.	Go out for refreshment.
12:30 p.m.	Return to office. Practise putting on H. M. carpet.
1:00 p.m.	Go out to lunch.
3:00 p.m.	Back from lunch. Pick up correspondence tray. Refer to other department.
3:30 p.m.	Sleep in armchair.
4:00 p.m.	Tea.
4:30 p.m.	Adjourn to club. Go home.

As a matter of fact, Sir Hugo Renway was not thinking of his office at all at half-past nine that morning. He was discussing the ravages of the incorrigible green fly with his gardener; but he was not really thinking of that, either.

He was a biggish thin-lipped man, with glossily brushed grey hair and a slight squint. The squint did not make him look sinister: it made him look smug. He was physically handicapped against looking anyone squarely in the face; but the impression he managed to convey was, not that he couldn't, but that he didn't think it worth while. He was looking at the gardener in just that way while they talked, but his air of well-fed smugness was illusory. He was well-fed, but he was troubled. Under that smooth supercilious exterior, his nerves were on edge; and the swelling drone of an aëroplane coming up from the Channel harmonized curiously well with the rasp of his thoughts.

"I don't think none of them new-fangled washes is any good, zir, if you aarsk me," the man was reiterating in his grumbling brogue; and Renway nodded and noticed that the steady drone had suddenly broken up into an erratic popping noise.

The man went on grumbling, and Renway went on pretending to listen, in his bored way. Inwardly he was cursing—cursing the stupidity of a man who was dead, whose death had transformed the steady drone of his own determination into the erratic popping which was going through his own nerves.

The aëroplane swept suddenly over the house. It was rather low, wobbling indecisively; and his convergent stare hardened on it with an awakening of professional interest. The popping of the engine had slackened away to nothing. Then, as if the pilot had seen sanctuary at that moment, the machine seemed to pull itself together. Its nose dipped, and it rushed downwards in a long glide, with no other accompaniment of sound than the whining thrum of the propeller running free. Instinctively Renway ducked; but the plane side-slipped thirty feet over his head and fishtailed down to a perfect three-point landing in the flat open field beyond the rose garden.

Renway turned round and watched it come to a standstill. He knew at once that the helmeted figure in the cockpit had nothing left to learn about the mastery of an aëroplane. That field was a devil to get into, he had learned from experience; but the unknown pilot had dumped his ship in it with a dead stick as neatly as if he had had a whole prairie to choose from. Enrique had been the same—a swarthy daredevil who could land on a playing card and make an aëroplane do anything short of balancing billiard balls on its tail, whose nerveless brilliance had been so maddeningly beyond the class of all Renway's own taut-strung effort. . . . Renway's hands tensed involuntarily at his sides for a moment while he went on thinking; and then he turned away and began minutely examining some buds of rose-crimson

Papa Gontiers as the pilot walked under a rustic arch and came towards him.

"I'm terribly sorry," said the aviator, "but I'm afraid I've had a forced landing in your grounds."

Renway looked at him for a moment. He had a dangerous devil-may-care sort of mouth, which showed very white teeth when he smiled. Enrique had had a smile very much like that.

"So I see," said Renway and returned to his study of rosebuds.

His voice was an epitome of all the mincing rudeness which the English lower classes have been so successfully trained to regard as a symbol of superiority. The Saint would have liked to hit him with a spanner; but he restrained himself.

"I'm terribly sorry," he repeated. "My oil pressure started to drop rather quickly, and I had to come down where I could. I don't think I've done any damage. If you can direct me to the village, I'll arrange to get the machine moved as quickly as possible."

"One of the servants will show you the way."

Renway looked up with his complacent squint and glanced at the gardener, who put away his pruning knife and dusted his hands.

"It's very good of you," said the Saint; and then an unfortunate accident happened.

He was carrying a valise in one hand, which he had taken out of the machine and brought with him. It could not have been very securely fastened, for at that moment it fell open.

A cascade of shirts, socks, pyjamas, shaving tackle, and similar impedimenta might not have distracted Renway for more than a couple of seconds from his horticultural absorption; but nothing of the kind fell out. Instead, the valise emptied itself of a heavy load of small square tins such as cough lozenges are sold in. The tins did, in fact, carry printed labels proclaiming their contents to be cough lozenges; but one of them burst open in its fall and scattered a small snowfall of white powder over the path.

Simon dropped on his knees and shoveled the tins back with rather unsteady hands, forcing them into the attaché case with more haste than efficiency. He scraped the white powder clumsily back into the one which had burst open; and when Renway touched him on the shoulder he jumped.

"Pardon my curiosity," said Renway, with unexpected suaveness, "but you have the most unusual luggage."

Simon laughed somewhat shortly.

"Yes, I suppose it is. I'm the Continental traveller for—er—some patent-medicine manufacturers——"

"I see."

Renway looked back at the aëroplane again; and again his hands tensed involuntarily at his sides. And then, once more, he looked at the Saint. Simon forced the last tin into his case, crammed the locks together, and straightened up.

"I'm awfully sorry to give you so much trouble," he said.

"Not at all." Renway's voice was dry, unnatural. He was aghast at himself, sweating coldly under the arms at the realization of what he was doing; but he spoke without any conscious volition. The jangling of his nerves forced him on, provided the motive power for the fantastic inspiration which had seized him. "In fact, my chauffeur can drive into Folkestone himself and make the necessary arrangements, while you stay here. You can give him instructions; and it's sure to mean a good deal of waiting about. I suppose the authorities will have to be notified . . ."

He was watching the pilot closely when he uttered that last sentence, although the cast in his eye made him appear to be staring past him; and he did not miss the slight instantaneous tightening of the dangerous mouth.

"Oh, I couldn't possibly let you do that," Simon protested. "I've given you quite enough trouble as it is——"

"Not a bit of it," insisted Renway, still watching him.

He was quite sure now. The pilot stiffened almost imperceptibly—Renway saw the shift of his eyes and the whitening of his knuckles on the hand which clutched the valise, and went on with more pronounced assurance: "It's no trouble at all to me, and my chauffeur has far too little to do. Besides, that landing must have given you one or two bad moments; and I'm sure you wouldn't refuse a drink. Come along up to the house, my dear fellow, and let me see what I can find for you."

He took the Saint's arm and led him away with a grim cordiality which it would have been difficult to resist—even if Simon had wanted to. They went through a small rockery up to the tennis lawn, across the lawn to a paved terrace, through open French windows into a rather stuffy library.

"Will you have a cigarette—or is it too early for a cigar?"

Simon took a cigarette and lighted it while Renway rang the bell.

"Sit down, Mr.—er——"

"Tombs."

"Sit down, Mr. Tombs."

The Saint sat on the edge of a plush armchair and smoked in silence until the butler answered the bell. Renway ordered drinks, and the butler went out again. The silence went on. Renway went over to a window and stood there, humming unmusically to himself.

"Awkward thing to have happen to you," ventured the Saint.

Renway half turned his head.

"I beg your pardon?"

"I said, it's an awkward thing to have happened to you—oil pressure going down."

"Quite," said Renway and went on humming.

The butler came in with a tray, put it down,

and departed. Renway crossed over to it and poured whisky into two glasses.

"Soda?"

"Thanks."

Renway worked the siphon and handed over the drink. Then he took up his own glass; and abruptly, as if he were blurting out something which he had been mustering his determination to say for several minutes, he snapped: "I suppose you don't think I believe that story of yours about being a patent-medicine salesman?"

"Don't you?" said the Saint evasively.

"Of course not. I know cocaine when I see it."

Simon, who had carefully filled all his tins with boracic, wanted to smile. But he glanced apprehensively at the valise, which he had put down beside his chair, and then hardened his face into an ineffective mask.

"But don't worry," said Renway. "I'm not going to tell the police. It's none of my business. I'm only wondering why a fellow like you—clever, daring, a good pilot—why you should waste your time over small stuff like that."

Simon licked his lips.

"It isn't so very small. And what else is there for me to do? There aren't so many jobs going these days for an out-of-work ace. You know yourself that war heroes are two a penny nowadays. I'm desperate enough to take the risk; and I want the money."

"You'll never make a million out of it."

"If you know anything that I can make a million out of, I'll do it."

Renway swallowed another gulp of whisky and put down his glass. In the last few moments the jangling of his nerves seemed to have risen to a pitch at which anything might crack. And yet it was without the tense wearing raggedness that he had felt before—he had a crazy breathless presentiment of success, waiting for him to grasp if he risked the movement. It had come miraculously, incredibly, literally out of the blue; and it was all personified in the broad-shouldered blue-eyed shape of the dangerous young man whose leather coat filled his armchair. Renway wiped his mouth on a silk handkerchief and tucked it away.

"Tomorrow morning," he said, "an aëroplane will leave Croydon for Paris with about ten tons of gold on board—as a matter of fact, the value will be exactly three million pounds. It is going to be shot down over the Channel, and the gold is going to be stolen. If you were desperate enough, you would be the man to do it."

VII

SIMON TEMPLAR did not need to act. The peculiar stillness that settled over him called for no simulation. It was as starkly genuine as any expression his face had ever worn.

And far back in the dim detached recesses of

consciousness he was bowing down before the ever-lasting generosity of fortune. He had taken that wide sweep out over the sea and choked his engine over the cliffs at the southern boundary of March House, staged his whole subsequent demonstration of guilt and truculence, rolled the dice down the board from beginning to end with nothing more substantial behind the play than a vast open-minded optimism; but the little he knew and the little he had guessed, the entire nebulous theory which had given him the idea of establishing him-self as a disreputable airman, was revealed to be so grotesquely inadequate that he was temporarily speechless. His puerile stratagem ought to have gained him nothing more than a glimpse of March House from the inside and a quick passage to the nearest police station; instead of which, it had flung doors wide open into something which even now he could scarcely believe in cold blood.

"It couldn't be done," he said at length.

"It can be done by a few men with the courage to take big chances for a share in three million pounds," said Renway. "I have all the necessary information. I have everything organized. The only thing I need to make it certain is the perfect pilot."

Simon tapped his cigarette.

"I should have thought that was the first thing."

"It was the first thing." Renway drank again. He was speaking with more steadiness now, with a conviction that was strengthening through every sentence; his faded stare weaved endlessly over the Saint's face, changing from one eye to the other. "I had the ideal man; but he—met with an accident. There wasn't time to find anyone else. I was going to try it myself, but I'm not an expert pilot. I have no fighting experience. I might have bungled it. You wouldn't."

Meeting the gaze of those unequally staring eyes, Simon had an eerie intuition that Renway was mad. He had to make a deliberate effort to separate a part of his mind from that precognition while he pieced his scanty facts together again in the light of what Renway had said.

There had been a pilot. That would have been Manuel Enrique, who died on the Brighton road. A new pilot swooped down out of the sky, and within twenty minutes was being offered the vacant post. With all due deference to the gods of luck, it seemed as if that new aviator were having a remarkable red carpet laid out for him.

"You don't only need a pilot," said the Saint mechanically. "You need a proper fighting ship, with geared machine guns and all the rest of it."

"There is one," said Renway. "I took it from Hawker's factory last night. It's one of a new flight they're building for the Moravian government. The one I took had been out on range tests, and the guns were still fitted. I also took three spare drums of ammunition. I flew it over here myself—it was the first night landing I've ever made."

It had not been a particularly clean one, Simon remembered; and then he saw the continual tensing and twitching of Renway's hands and suddenly understood much more.

There had been a pilot; but he had—met with an accident. And yet the plot in which he had a vital rôle could not be given up. Therefore it had grown in Renway's mind to the dimensions of an obsession, until the point had been reached where it loomed up as the needle's eye of an insanely conceived salvation. Although Enrique was dead, the aëroplane had still been stolen: Renway had flown it himself, and the ordeal of that untutored night flight had cut into the marrow of his nerves. Still the goal could not be given up. The new pilot arrived at the crisis of an eight-hour sleepless nightmare of strain—a solution, an escape, a straw which he could grapple even while preserving the delusion that he was a superman irresistibly turning a chance tool to his need. Simon recalled Renway's abrupt defiant plunge into the subject after that long awkward silence, and hypothesis merged into certainty. It was queer, he reflected, how that superman complex, that delusion of being able to enslave human instruments body and soul by the power of a hypnotic personality which usually existed only in the paranoiac's own grandiose imagination, had been the downfall of so many promising criminals.

"You did that?" said the Saint, in a tone which

contained exactly the right blend of incredulous admiration and sober awe.

"Of course."

Simon put out his cigarette and helped himself to a second.

"That's a beginning," he said. "But the pilots will be armed—they're in touch with the shore by radio all the way——"

"What is the good of that?" asked Renway calmly. "The conditions aren't the same as they would be in war time. They aren't really expecting to be attacked. They see another aëroplane overtaking them, that's all—there's always plenty of traffic on that route, and they wouldn't think anything of it. Then you dive. With your experience, they'd be an easy target. It ought to be finished in a couple of bursts—long before they could wireless any alarm to the shore. And as soon as their wireless stops, I shall carry on with their report. I have a short-wave transmitter installed in this house, and I have a record of every signal that's been sent out by cross-Channel aircraft for the last month. I know all the codes. The shore stations will never know what's happened until the aëroplane fails to arrive."

The Saint blew out a flick of smoke and kept his eyes on Renway's pale complacent face. It was dawning on him that if Renway was a lunatic, he was the victim of a very thorough and methodical kind of madness.

"There isn't only traffic in the air," he said.

"There's also shipping. Suppose a ship sees what happens?"

Renway made a gesture of impatience.

"My good fellow, you're going over ground that I covered two months ago. I could raise more objections than you know yourself. For instance, all the time the aëroplane is over the Channel, there will be special motorboats cruising off the French and English coasts. One or more of them may possibly reach the scene. It will be part of your job to keep them at a distance by machine-gun fire from the air until all the gold has been secured."

"How do you propose to do that?" persisted the Saint. "You can't lift ten tons of gold out of a wrecked aëroplane in five minutes."

A sudden sly look hooded Renway's eyes.

"That has also been arranged," he said.

He refilled his glass and drank again, sucking in his lips after the drink. As if wondering whether he had betrayed too much already, he said: "You need only be concerned with your own share in the proceedings. Do you feel like taking a part?"

Simon thought for a moment and nodded.

"I'm your man," he said.

Renway remained looking at him for a while longer, and the Saint fancied he could almost see the man's nerves relaxing in the sedative glow of conquest.

"In that case, I shall not need to send for my chauffeur."

"What about my machine?" asked the Saint.

"You can keep it here until you require it again. I have plenty of accommodation, and one of my mechanics can find out the cause of your trouble and put it right."

For a second the Saint's eyes chilled, for no mechanic would take long to discover that there was nothing whatever the matter with the machine in which he had landed. But he answered easily enough:

"That's very good of you."

Renway picked up his valise and took it to a big built-in safe at one end of the room, into which he locked it. He came back blandly, rubbing his hands.

"Your—er—samples will be quite safe there until you need them. Shall we go and attend to your aëroplane?"

They walked out again in the strengthening sunshine, down through the rose garden and across the small field where the Saint had made his landing. Simon felt the dead weight of the automatic in his pocket bumping his hip as he walked, and felt unexpectedly glad of its familiar comfort: the nervous twitching of Renway's hands had finished altogether now, and there was an uncanny inert calm about his sauntering bulk which was frightful to study—the unnatural porcine opaqueness of a man whose mind has ceased to work like other men's minds. . . .

Renway went on talking, in the same simpering

monotone, as if he had been describing the layout of an asparagus bed: "I shall know the number of the transport plane and the time it leaves Croydon five minutes after it takes off—you'll have plenty of time to be waiting for it in the air."

On the other side of the field there was a big tithe barn with the hedge laid up to one wall. Renway knocked on a small door, and it opened three inches to show a narrow strip of the grimy face and figure of a man in overalls. After the first pause of identification it opened wider, and they went in.

The interior was cool and spacious, dimly lit in contrast with the sunlight outside by a couple of naked bulbs hung from the high ridge. Simon's first glance round was arrested by the grey bull-nosed shape of the Hawker pursuit plane at the far end of the shed. In another two or three hours he would have found it less easy to recognize, except by the long gleaming spouts of the machine guns braced forward from the pilot's cockpit, for an-other overalled man mounted on a folding ladder was even then engaged in painting out the wing cocardes with a layer of neutral grey dope. But the national markings on the empennage were still untouched—if the Saint had ever been tempted to wonder whether he had lost himself in a fantastic dream, the sight of those shining strips of colour was the last thing that was needed to show him that he was in touch with nothing more fantastic than astounding reality.

He fished out his case and selected another cigarette while he surveyed the other details of his surroundings. While he was in the air he had guessed that the field adjoining the one in which he had landed was the one where he had watched the Hawker ship land some hours ago, and a glimpse of other and wider doors outlined in cracks of light on the opposite wall of the barn was his confirmation. There was a stack of petrol cans in one corner, and a workbench and lathe in another. He saw the spare drums of ammunition which Renway had referred to under the workbench, and some curious pear-shaped objects stacked in a wooden rack beside it—in another moment he realized that they were bombs.

He indicated them with a slight movement of his thumb.

"For use on the rescue boats?" he queried; and Renway nodded.

Simon left the cigarette between his lips, but thoughtfully refrained from lighting it.

"Isn't it a bit risky?" he suggested. "I mean, having everything here where anybody might get in and see it?"

Renway's mouth widened slightly. If another muscle of his face had moved it might have been a smile, but the effect of the surrounding deadness of flesh was curiously horrible.

"I have two kinds of servants—those who are in my confidence, and those who are merely menials. With the first kind, there is no risk—

although it was a pity that Enrique met with an accident. . . ." He paused for a moment, with his faded eyes wandering inharmoniously over the Saint; and then he pointed to a big humming engine bedded down in the concrete floor on his right. "To the second kind, this is simply the building which houses our private electric light plant. The doors are kept locked, and there is no reason for them to pry further. And all of them are having a special holiday tomorrow."

He continued to watch the Saint satirically, as if aware that there was another risk which might have been mentioned; but Simon knew the answer to that one. The case of "samples" which his host had locked up in the library safe, so long as they remained there, must have constituted a reasonably sound security for the adventitious aviator's faithful service—from Renway's point of view. The Saint was acquiring a wholesome respect for the Treasury Pooh-ba's criminal efficiency; and his blue eyes were rather quiet and metallic as he watched the two mechanics wheel his machine through a gate in the hedge and bring it through the broad sliding doors into the barn.

As they strolled back to the house again, Renway pulled out his watch.

"I shall have to attend to some business now," he said. "You'll be able to spend your time making the acquaintance of the other men who are helping me."

They entered the house by another door and

went down a long dark low-ceilinged corridor which led into a large panelled room lighted by small leaded windows. Simon ducked his head automatically, but found that he could just stand upright under the black oak beams which crossed the ceiling. There was a billiard table in the centre with a strip of carpet laid round it, and an open brick fireplace at one side; but the room had the musty dampness of disuse.

"March House is rather an architectural scrap-heap," Renway explained impersonally. "You're in the oldest part of it now, which goes back to the fifteenth century. I discovered this quite by accident——"

"This" was a section of panelling, about five and a half feet by three, which sprang open on invisible hinges—Simon could not see exactly what the other did to open it. Renway fumbled in the dark aperture and switched on a light.

"I don't know where the passage originally went to," he said, as they groped their way down a flight of rickety wooden stairs. "At present it leads into the cellars. There used to be an ordinary entrance from a more modern part of the house, where the kitchen is now, but I had that bricked up."

At the foot of the stairway there was a narrow stone-flagged tunnel. Renway switched on another light and they went on, bent almost double in the cramped space. At intervals there was a rough wooden buttress to carry a weak section of the roof, but for the most part the upper curve of the burrow consisted of nothing but the natural chalk.

Simon Templar, who had seen the inner workings of more secret doors, rooms, and passages than any other living man, had never managed to lose the first primitive schoolboy thrill of such subterranean accessories of adventure. He followed Renway with whole-hearted enthusiasm; but there was an equally whole-hearted vigilance about him nevertheless, for the thought had crossed his mind that Sir Hugo Renway might be even more clever and efficient than he had yet begun to believe, and he had no overpowering ambition to be suddenly pushed down a well and left there to contemplate the follies of over-optimism until hunger and thirst put an end to contemplation.

After about fifteen yards Renway turned a right-angled corner and disappeared; and Simon crept up in his tracks with that knife-bladed vigilance honed to a razor edge. Rounding the corner, he found himself stepping out into a fairly large stone chamber illuminated by several electric bulbs. At the distant end there was a row of beds; a cheap square of carpet was laid out on the floor, and the room was sketchily furnished with a bare wooden table in the centre, a couple of washstands, and a heterogeneous selection of chairs. Four of the men in the room were congregated at one end of the table over a game of cards; the fifth was stitching a button on his coat; the sixth was reading a newspaper. They were all turned rigidly towards the end of the tunnel; and the Saint carefully set his hands on his hips—where one of them would be within handy diving range of his gun.

"Gentlemen," Renway's high-pitched B. B. C. voice was saying, "this is Mr.—er—Tombs, who is taking Enrique's place."

None of the flat fishlike eyes acknowledged the introduction by so much as a flicker.

Renway turned to the Saint.

"You must meet Mr. Petrowitz," he said; "Mr. Jeddy . . . Mr. Pargo . . ,"

He ran through a list of names, indicating their owners with curt movements of his head; and Simon, looking them over, decided that they were the ugliest gang of cutthroats that even the most rabid Bolshevik could ever hope to find gathered together in a strategic position under the house of an English aristocrat.

His decision embodied something more than pure artistic comment. The sight of those staring immobile men added the last touch to his grim understanding that if Sir Hugo Renway was mad, he was a maniac with the cold logical resolution that was needed to carry out his insane scheme.

His glance fell on the newspaper which the sixth man had put down. The black-type banner line across the top of the page leapt to his eye:

SAINT STEALS ARMED AËROPLANE

It reminded him that he had not yet inquired the name of his new employer.

"Are you the Saint?" he asked.

Renway's lids drooped.

"Yes," he said.

VIII

ACCORDING to his watch, Simon Templar stayed in that secret cellar for about eighteen hours: without that evidence, he could have been fairly easily persuaded that it was about eighteen days.

It was so completely removed from the sense of reality, as well as from the ordinary change of lights and movements of the outer world, that time had very little meaning. At intervals, one of the men would go to a cupboard in the corner and dig out a loaf of bread and a slab of cheese, a tin of beans, or a bottle of beer: those who felt inclined would join him in a sketchy meal or a drink. One of the card players got up from the table, lay down on one of the beds, and went to sleep, snoring. Another man shuffled the cards and looked flat-eyed at the Saint.

"Want a game?"

Simon took the vacant chair and a stack of chips. Purely as an antidote to boredom, he played blackjack for two hours and finished five chips down.

"That's five hundred pounds," said Pargo, writing figures with a half-inch stub of pencil on a soiled scrap of paper.

"I haven't got five hundred pounds on me," said the Saint.

The man grinned like a rat.

"Nor have any of us," he said. "But you will have after tomorrow."

Simon was impressed without being pleased. He had watched Jeddy rake up a stack of chips that must have represented about three thousand pounds at that rate of exchange, without any sign of emotion; and Mr. Jeddy was a man whose spiritual niche in the Buddy-can-you-spare-a-dime class was as obvious as the fact that he had not shaved for three days.

The others were not vastly different. Their physical aspects ranged from the bearded and faintly odorous burliness of Mr. Petrowitz to the rat-faced and yellow-toothed scrawniness of Mr. Pargo; but all of them had the same dominant characteristic in common. It was a characteristic with which the Saint had become most familiar on the west side of the Atlantic, although it was confined to no single race or nationality; a characteristic which Hoppy Uniatz, who couldn't have spelt the word to save his life, would have been the first to recognize: the peculiar cold lifelessness of the eye which brands the natural killer. But there are grades in killers, just as there are in singers; and the men in that cellar were not in the grand-opera class, the class that collects diamonds and expensive limousines. They were men who did their stuff at street corners and in dingy alleys, for a chance coin or two; the crude hacks of their profession. And they were the men whom Renway had inspired with so much confidence in the certainty of his scheme that they were calmly gambling their hypothetical profits in hundred-pound units.

God alone knew how Renway had gathered them together—neither the Saint nor Teal ever found out. But they constituted six more amazing eye-openers for the Saint to add to his phenomenally growing collection—six stony-faced witnesses to the fact that Sir Hugo Renway, whom Simon Templar would never have credited with the ability to lead anything more piratical than a pompous secession from the Conservative Party, had found the trick of organizing what might have been one of the most astounding robberies in the history of crime.

The men took him for granted. Their conversation, when they spoke at all, was grumbling, low-voiced, monosyllabic. They asked Simon no questions, and he had a sure intuition that they would have been surprised and hostile if he had asked them any. The business for which they were collected there was never mentioned—either it had already been discussed so much that there was nothing left to say on the subject, or they were too fettered by habitual suspicion for any discussion to have a chance of getting under way. Simon decided that in addition to being the ugliest, they were also the dullest assortment of thugs he had ever come across.

The man who had been reading the newspaper put it down and added himself to the increasing company of sleepers, and Simon reached out for the opportunity of getting acquainted with the latest lurid accounts of his own entirely mythical activities. They were more or less what he would have expected; but there was a subheading with the words "SCOTLAND YARD ACTIVE" which made him smile. Scotland Yard was certainly active— by that hour, it must have been hopping about like a young and healthy flea—but he would have given much to see their faces if they could have been miraculously enabled to find him at that moment.

As it turned out, that pleasure, or a representative part of it, was not to cost him anything.

"Put those damn lights out," a voice from one of the beds growled at last; and Simon stretched himself out on a hard mattress and continued his meditations in the dark, while the choral symphony of snores gained new and individual artistes around him. After a while he fell asleep himself.

When he woke up the lights were on again, and men were pulling on their coats and gulping cups of hot tea. One by one they began to slouch off into the tunnel; and Simon splashed cold water on his face from a basin and joined in the general move with a reawakening of vitality. A glance at his

watch showed him that it was half-past four, but
it might have been morning or afternoon for all
the sense of time he had left. When he came up
the creaking stairladder into the billiard room,
however, he saw that it was still dark. Renway, in
a light overcoat, was standing close to the panel
watching the men as they emerged: he beckoned
the Saint with a slight backward tilt of his head.

"How are you getting on?" he asked.

Simon glanced at the last two men as they stum-
bled through the panel and followed their com-
panions across the room and out by the more
conventional door.

"I have been in more hilarious company," he
murmured.

Renway did not appear to hear his answer—the
impression was that his interest in Mr. Tombs's
social progress was merely formal. He did something to the woodwork at the level of his shoulder,
and the secret panel closed with a slight click.

"You'd better know some more about our arrangements," he said.

They went out of the house by the same route as
they had finally come in the previous morning.
The file of men who had preceded them was already trudging southwards over the rough grass
as if on a journey that had become familiar by
routine—the Saint saw the little dabs of light
thrown by their electric torches bobbing over the
turf. A pale strip of silver in the east promised
an early dawn, and the cool sweetness of the air

was indescribably delicious after the acrid frowstiness of the cellar. Renway produced a flashlight of his own and walked in flat-footed taciturnity. They reached the edge of the cliffs and started down a narrow zigzag path. Halfway down it, the Saint suddenly missed the dancing patches of torchlight ahead: he was wondering whether to make any comment when Renway touched his arm and halted.

"This way."

The oval imprint of Renway's flashlight flickered over the dark spludge of a shrub growing in a cleft beside the path: suddenly Renway's own silhouette appeared in the shrinking circle of light, and Simon realized that the Treasury official was going down on all fours and beginning to wriggle into the bush, presenting a well-rounded posterior which might have proved an irresistible and fatal temptation to an aggrieved ex-service civil servant. The Saint, however, having suffered no especial unkindness from the government, followed him dutifully in the same manner and discovered that he could stand upright again on the other side of the opening in the cliff. At the same time he saw the torches of the other men again, heading downwards into the dark as if on a long stairway.

Thirty feet lower down the steps levelled off into an uneven floor. Simon saw the gleam of dark waters in the light of Renway's torch and realized that he was at the foot of a huge natural cave. The lights of the other men were clustered a few yards away—Simon heard a clunk of wood and metal and the soft plash of an oar.

"The only other way to the sea is under water," Renway explained, his thin voice echoing hollowly. "You can see it at low neap tides, but at this time of year it's always covered."

It was on the tip of the Saint's tongue to make some facetious remark about submarines when Renway lifted his torch a little, and Simon saw a shining black whaleback of steel curving out of the water a couple of dozen feet from where they stood, and knew that his flippancy could only have seemed ridiculous beside the truth.

"Did you catch that with a rod and line?" he asked, after a considerable silence.

"It was ostensibly purchased by a French film company six months ago," Renway said prosaically.

"And who's going to run it?"

"Petrowitz—he was a U-boat officer during the war. The rest of the crew had to be trained. It was more difficult to obtain torpedoes—in case anything should come to the rescue which was too big for you to drive off, you understand. But we succeeded."

The Saint put his hands in his pockets. His face was chiselled bronze masked by the dark.

"I get it," he said softly. "The gold is taken on board that little beauty. And then you go down to the bottom and nobody ever sees you any more.

And then when you turn up again somewhere in South America——"

"We come back here," said Renway. "There are certain reasons why this is one of the last places where anyone would ever expect to find us."

Simon admitted it. From Renway's point of view, it must have loomed out as one of the most cunning certainties of crime. And the Saint was quite cold-bloodedly aware that if he failed to separate himself from the picnic in time, it would still be true.

The party of men in the rowboat had reached the submarine and were climbing out.

"My information is that the gold will be leaving Croydon about eight o'clock," Renway said in a matter-of-fact tone. "Perhaps you'd like to check over your aëroplane—there are one or two things I want to talk over with Petrowitz."

The Saint did not want to check over any aëroplane, but there was something else he very much wanted to do. He found his way back up the stairway with Renway's torch and wriggled out again through the hole in the cliff—the last glimpse he had of that strange scene was the lights glinting on the water far below him and the shadows moving over the dull sheen of the submarine's arched back. Renway had certainly spared no effort or expense to provide all the most modern and sensational accessories of melodrama, he reflected as he retraced his tracks to the house, what with electrified wire fences, stolen aëroplanes landing by night, bombs, secret panels, caves, submarines, and unshaven desperadoes; but he found the actuality less humorous than he would have found the same recital in a book. Simon had long had a theory that the most dangerous criminal would be a man who helped himself to some of the vast fund of daring ingenuity expended upon his problems by hordes of detective-story writers; and Sir Hugo Renway's establishment looked more like a detective story come to life than anything the Saint had ever seen.

The dawn was lightening as he found his way into the library and went directly to the safe. He knelt down in front of it and unrolled a neat leather wallet which he took from a pocket in his voluminous flying coat—the instruments in that wallet were the latest and most ingenious in the world, and would in themselves have been sufficient to earn him a long term of imprisonment, without any other evidence, if Mr. Teal had caught him with them. The safe was also one of the latest and most useful models, but it was at a grave disadvantage. Being an inanimate object, it couldn't change its methods of defense so nimbly as the Saint could vary his attack. Besides which, the Saint was prepared to boast that he could make any professional peterman look like a two-year-old infant playing with a rubber crowbar when it came to safe-opening. He worked with unhurried speed and had the door open in twenty minutes; and then he carefully rolled up his kit and put it away again before he turned to an examination of the interior.

He had already charted out enough evidence within the thirty-acre confines of March House to have hanged a regiment, but there were still one or two important items missing. He found one useful article very quickly, in a small heap of correspondence on one of the shelves—it was a letter which in itself was no evidence of anything, but it was addressed to Sir Hugo Renway and signed by Manuel Enrique. Simon put it away in his pocket and went on with his search. He opened a japanned deed box and found it crammed with bank notes and bearer bonds: that was not evidence at all, but it was the sort of thing which Simon Templar was always pleased to find, and he was just tipping it out when he heard the rattle of the door handle behind him.

The Saint moved like a cat touched with a high-voltage wire. In what seemed like one connected movement, he scooped the bundle of currency and bonds into his pocket, shoved the deed box back on its shelf, swung the door of the safe, and leapt behind the nearest set of curtains; and then Renway came into the room.

He walked straight across to the safe, fishing out the key from his waistcoat pocket; but the door opened as soon as he touched the handle, and he froze into an instant's dreadful immobility. Then he fell on his knees and dragged out the empty deed box. . . .

Simon stepped quietly out from behind the curtains, so that he was between Renway and the door.

"Don't cry, Mother Hubbard," he said.

IX

RENWAY got to his feet and looked down the barrel of the Saint's gun. His face was pasty, but the lipless gash of a mouth was almost inhumanly steady.

"Oh, it's you," he whispered.

"It is I," said the Saint, with impeccable grammar. "Come here, Hugo—I want to see what you've got on you."

He plunged his left hand swiftly and dexterously into the other's inner breast pocket and found the second thing he had been looking for. It was a cheap pocket diary, and he knew without examining it that it was the one on which his forged trade-marks had been drawn. Renway must have been insanely confident of his immunity from suspicion to keep it on him.

"What ho," drawled Simon contentedly. "Stand back again, Hugo, while I see if you've been compromising yourself."

He stepped back himself and barely had time

to feel the foot of the man behind him under his heel before a brawny arm shot over his shoulder and grasped his gun wrist in a grip like a twisting clamp of iron. Simon started to turn, but in the next split second another brawny arm whipped round his neck and pinned him.

The wrenching hand on his wrist forced him to drop his gun—it had begun to twist too long before he began resisting. Then he let himself go completely limp, while his left hand felt for the knees of the man behind him. His arm locked round them and he heaved himself backwards with a sudden jerk of his thighs. They fell heavily together, and the grips on his wrist and neck were broken. Simon squirmed over, put a knee in the man's stomach, and sprang up and away; and then he saw that Renway had snatched up the automatic and was covering him.

Simon Templar, who knew the difference between certain death and a sporting chance, put up his hands quickly.

"Okay, boys," he said. "Now you think of a game."

Renway's forefinger weighed on the trigger.

"You fool!" he said almost peevishly.

"Admitted," said the Saint. "Nobody ought to walk backwards without eyes in the back of his head."

Renway had also picked up the diary, which Simon had dropped in the struggle. He put it back in his pocket.

The Saint's brain was turning over so fast that he could almost hear it hum. He still had Enrique's letter—and the bundle of cash. There was still no reason for Renway to suspect him of anything more than ordinary stealing: his taking of the diary was not necessarily suspicious. And Simon understood very clearly that if Renway suspected him of anything more than ordinary stealing, he could, barring outrageous luck, only leave March House in one position. Which would be depressingly and irrevocably horizontal.

Even then, there might be no alternative attitude; but it was worth trying. Simon had a stubborn desire to hang onto that incriminating letter as long as possible. He took out the sheaf of bonds and banknotes and threw them on the desk.

"There's the rest of it," he said cynically. "Shall we call it quits?"

Renway's squinting eyes wandered over him.

"Do you always expect to clear yourself so easily?" he asked, like a schoolmaster.

"Not always," said the Saint. "But you can't very well hand me over to the police this time, can you? I know too much about you."

In the next moment he knew he had made a mistake. Renway's convergent gaze turned to Petrowitz, who was massaging his stomach tenderly.

"He knows too much," Renway repeated.

"I suppose there's no chance of letting bygones

be bygones and still letting me fly that aëroplane?"
Simon asked shrewdly.

The nervous twitch which he had seen before
went over Renway's body, but the thin mouth only
tightened with it.

"None at all, Mr. Tombs."

"I was afraid so," said the Saint.

"Let me take him," Petrowitz broke in with his
thick gruff voice. "I will tie iron bars to his legs
and fire him through one of the torpedo tubes.
He will not talk after that."

Renway considered the suggestion and shook his
head.

"None of the others must know. Any doubt or
fear in their minds may be dangerous. He can go
back into the cellar. Afterwards, he can take the
same journey as Enrique."

Probably for much the same offense, Simon
thought grimly; but he smiled.

"That's very sweet of you, Hugo," he remarked;
and the other looked at him.

"I hope you will continue to be satisfied."

He might have been going to say more, but at
that moment the telephone began to ring. Renway
sat down at the desk.

"Hullo. . . . Yes. . . . Yes, speaking." He
drew a memorandum block towards him and took
up a pencil from a glass tray. With the gun close
to his hand, he jotted down letters and figures.
"Yes. G-EZQX. At seven. . . . Yes. . . . Thank
you." He sat for a little while staring at the pad,

as if memorizing his note and rearranging his plans. Then he pressed the switch of a microphone which stood on the desk beside the ordinary post-office instrument. "Kellard?" he said. "There is a change of time. Have the Hawker outside and warmed up by seven o'clock."

He picked up the automatic again and rose from the desk.

"They're leaving an hour earlier," he said, speaking to Petrowitz. "We haven't any time to waste."

The other man rubbed his beard.

"You will be flying yourself?"

"Yes," said Renway, as if defying contradiction. He motioned with his gun towards the door. "Petrowitz will lead the way, Mr. Tombs."

Simon felt that he was getting quite familiar with the billiard room, and almost suggested that the three of them should put aside their differences and stop for a game; but Renway had the secret panel open as soon as the Saint reached it. With the two men watching him, Simon went down the shaky wooden stair and heard the spring door close behind him.

He sat down on the bottom step, took out his cigarette case, and computed that if all the cellars in which he had been imprisoned as an adjunct or preliminary to murder had been dug one underneath the other, they would have provided the shaft of a diametric subway between England and the Antipodes. But his jailers had not always been

so generous as to push him into the intestines of the
earth without searching him; and his blue eyes
were thoughtful as he took out his portable bur-
gling kit again. Renway must have been going to
pieces rapidly, to have overlooked such an obvious
precaution as that; but that meant, if anything,
that for a few mad hours he would be more dangerous than before. The attack on the gold plane
would still be made, Simon realized, unless he got
out in time to stop it. It was not until some
minutes after he had started work on the door
that he discovered that the panel which concealed
it was backed by a solid plate of case-hardened
steel. . . .

It was a quarter past six by his wrist watch when
he started work; it was five minutes past seven
when he got out. He had to dig his way through
twelve inches of solid brick with a small screw-
driver before he could get the claw of his tele-
scopic jemmy behind the steel panel and break the
lock inwards. Anyone who had come that way
must have heard him; but in that respect his luck
held flawlessly. Probably neither Renway nor
Petrowitz had a doubt in their minds that the tem-
pered steel plate would be enough to hold him.

He was tired and sweating when he got out, and
his knuckles were raw in several places from ac-
cidental blows against the brickwork which they
had suffered unnoticed in his desperate haste; but
he could not stop. He raced down the long
corridor and found his way through the house to

the library. Nobody crossed his path. Renway had said that the regular servants would all be away, and the gang were probably busy at their appointed stations; but if anyone had attempted to hinder him, Simon with his bare hands would have had something fast and savage to say to the interference. He burst recklessly into the library and looked out of the French windows in time to see the grey shape of the Hawker pursuit plane skimming across the far field like a bullet and lofting airily over the trees at the end.

Simon lighted another cigarette very quietly and watched the grey ship climbing swiftly into the clear morning sky. If there was something cold clutching at his heart, if he was tasting the sourest narrowness of defeat, no sign of it could have been read on the tanned outline of his face.

After a second or two he sat down at the desk and picked up the telephone.

"Croydon 2720," he called, remembering the number of the aërodrome.

The reply came back very quickly:

"I'm sorry—the line is out of order."

"Then get me Croydon police station."

"I'm afraid we can't get through to Croydon at all. All the lines seem to have gone wrong."

Simon bit his lip.

"Can you get me Scotland Yard?"

He knew the answer to that inquiry also, even before he heard it, and realized that even at that stage of the proceedings he had underestimated Sir Hugo Renway. There would be no means of establishing rapid communication with any vital spot for some hours—that was because something might have gone wrong with the duplicate wireless arrangements, or one of the possible rescue ships might have managed to transmit a message.

The Saint blew perfect smoke rings at the ceiling and stared at the opposite wall. There was only one other wild solution. He had no time to try any other avenues. There would first be the business of establishing his *bona fides,* then of convincing an impenetrably skeptical audience, then of getting word through by personal messenger to a suitable headquarters—and the transport plane would be over the Channel long before that. But he remembered Renway's final decision—*"None of the others must know"*—and touched the switch of the table microphone.

"Kellard?" he said. "This is Tombs. Get my machine out and warmed up right away."

"Yessir," said the mechanic, without audible surprise; and Simon Templar felt as if a great load had been lifted from his shoulders.

Probably he still had no chance, probably he was still taking a path to death as certain as that which he would have trodden if he had stayed in the cellar; but it was something to attempt—something to do.

Of course, there was a radio station on the premises. Renway had said so. But undoubtedly it was well hidden. He might spend half an hour and more looking for it. . . .

No—he had taken the only way. And if it was a form of spectacular suicide, it ought to have its diverting moments before the end.

It was only natural that in those last few moments he should think of Patricia. He took up the telephone again and called his own number at St. George's Hill. In ten seconds the voice of Orace, who never seemed to sleep, answered him. "They've gorn," Orace informed him, with a slight sinister emphasis on the pronoun. "Miss 'Olm says she's sleepin' at Cornwall 'Ouse. Nobody's worried 'er."

Simon called another number.

"Hullo, sweetheart," he said; and the Saintly voice had never been more gentle, more easy and light-hearted, more bubbling over with the eager promise of an infinite and adventurous future. "Why, I'm fine. . . . No, there hasn't been any trouble. Just an odd spot of spontaneous combustion in the withered brain cells of Claud Eustace Teal—but we've had that before. I've got it all fixed. . . . Never mind how, darling. You know your Simon. This is much more important. Now listen carefully. D'you remember a guy named George Wynnis, that I've talked about soaking sometime? . . . Well, he lives at 366 South Audley Street. He never gets up before ten in the morning, and he never has less than two thousand quid in his pockets. Phone Hoppy to join you, and go get that dough—now! And listen. *Leave my mark behind!*"

"You're crazy," she said; and he laughed.

"I am and I'm not," he said. "But this time I have the perfect alibi; and I want to get you every cent I can lay hold of before I cash in my chips." The lilt in his voice made it impossible to take him literally. "God bless you, keed," he said. "Be seein' ya!"

He hung up the handpiece and leaned back in his chair, inhaling the last puffs of his cigarette. Surely, this time, he had the perfect and immutable alibi. A dry sardonic smile touched his lips; but the fine-cut sapphires in his eyes were twinkling. It would give Claud Eustace something more to think about, anyway. . . . He looked out of the windows, down the long gentle slope that was just being gilded by the sun, and saw his own Tiger Moth standing beside the old tithe barn, the propeller lost in a swirling circle of light, the mechanic's hair fluttering in the cockpit, a thin plume of haze drifting back from the exhaust. The sky was a pale crystalline eggshell blue, clear and still as a dream, a sky that could give a man pleasant memories to carry with him into the long dark. . . .

Without conscious thought, he hauled out his helmet from a side pocket, pulled it over his head, buckled the strap, and adjusted the goggles on his forehead. And he was doing that when a shadow fell across the desk, and he looked up.

A broad-shouldered portly form, with a round cherubic pink face and small baby-blue eyes, crowned with an incongruous black bowler hat of old-fashioned elevation, was filling the open French doors. It was Chief Inspector Teal.

X

SIMON sprang up impetuously.

"Claud!" he cried. "I never thought I should be glad to see your huge stomach——"

"I thought you might be here," said the detective stiffly.

He came on into the room, but only far enough to allow Sergeant Barrow to follow him through the window. With that end accomplished, he kept his distance. There was still a puffy tenderness in his jaw to remind him of a fist like a chunk of stone driven by a bolt of lightning, which had reached him once already when he came too near.

"It must be this deductive business that Scotland Yard is taking up," Simon remarked more slowly.

Teal nodded without relaxing.

"I knew you were interested in Renway, and I knew you'd been here once before—when Uniatz knocked out the policeman. It occurred to me that it'd be just like you to come back, in spite of everything."

"In spite of hell and high water," Simon murmured with a faint smile, "we keep on doing our stuff. Well, it's not a bad reputation to have. . . . But this time I've got something more important to say to you."

"I've got the same thing to say to you as I had last time," said the detective, iron-jawed. "I want you, Saint."

Simon started round the desk.

"But this is serious!"

"So is this," said Teal implacably. He took his right hand out of his pocket, and there was a gun in it. "I don't want to have to use it, but I'm going to take you back this time if it's the last thing I do."

The Saint's eyes narrowed to shreds of flint.

"You're damn right it'll be the last thing you do!" he shot back. And then his tensed lips moved into the thinnest of thin smiles. "Now listen to me, you great oaf. You want me for being mixed up with a guy named Hoppy Uniatz who smacked a cop on the button outside here the other night. Guilty. But you also want me for the murder of Manuel Enrique and the knocking off of an aëroplane from Hawker's. Not guilty and not guilty. That's what I wanted to see you for. That's the only reason on earth why I couldn't have been more glad to see anything else walk in here than your fatuous red face. I want to tell you whom you really do want!"

"I know whom I want," answered Teal stonily.

"Yeah?" The Saint's voice was one vicious upward swoop of derision. "Then did you know you were standing inside his house right now?"

Mr. Teal blinked. His eyes began a fractional widening; his mouth began an infinitesimal opening.

"Renway?" he said. And then the baleful skepticism came back into his face with a tinge of colour. "Is that your new alibi?" he jeered.

"That's my new alibi," said the Saint, rather quickly and quietly; "and you'd better listen to it. Did you know that Renway was the man who stole that aëroplane from Hawker's?"

"I didn't. And I don't know it yet."

"He brought it here and landed it here, and I watched him. Go down to that field out there and have a look at the scars in the grass where he had his flares, if you're too dumb to believe me. Did you know that he had a submarine in a cave in the cliffs, with live torpedoes on board?"

"Did I know——"

"Did you know that the crew of the submarine have been sleeping in a secret room under this house for months? Did you know they were the toughest bunch of hoodlums I've seen in England for years?"

"Did I——"

"Did you know," asked the Saint, in a final

rasp, "that three million pounds in gold is on its
way flying from Croydon to Paris right now while
you're getting in my hair with your blathering
imitation of a bum detective—and Renway has got
everything set to shoot it down and set up a crime
record that'll make Scotland Yard look more half-
witted than it's ever looked since I started taking
it apart?"

The detective swallowed. There was an edge of
savage sincerity in the Saint's voice which bit into
the leathery hide of his incredulity. He suffered a
wild fantastic temptation to begin to listen, to take
in the preposterous story that the Saint was putting up, to consider the items of it soberly and
seriously. And he was sure he was making a fool
of himself. He gulped down the ridiculous impulse and plunged into defensive sarcasm.

"Of course I didn't know all that," he almost
purred. "Is Einstein going to prove it for you, or
will Renway admit it himself?"

"Renway will admit it himself," said the Saint
grimly. "But even that won't be necessary. Did
you know that these ten tons of gold were being
shipped on aëroplane G-EZQX, which took off
from Croydon at seven?" He ripped the top sheet
off the memorandum block on the desk and thrust
it out. "Do you know that that's his handwriting,
or will you want his bank manager to tell you?"

Teal looked at the sheet.

"It doesn't matter much whether it's his writing
or your version of it," he said, with an almost im-

perceptible break in the smoothness of his studied purr. "As a Treasury official, Renway has a perfect right to know anything like that."

"Yeah?" Simon's voice was suddenly so soft that it made Teal's laboured suaveness sound like the screech of a circular saw. "And I suppose he had a perfect right to know Manuel Enrique, and not say anything about it when he brought him into the police station at Horley?".

"Who says he knew Enrique?"

The Saint smiled.

"Not me, Claud. If I tell you he did, it'll just make you quite sure he didn't. This is what says so."

He put his hand in his pocket and took out the letter which he had found in the safe. "Or maybe I faked this, too?" he suggested mildly.

"You may have done," said Teal dispassionately; but his baby-blue eyes rested with a rather queer intensity on Simon's face.

"Come for a walk, Claud," said the Saint gently, "and tell me I faked this."

He turned aside quite calmly under the muzzle of Teal's gun and walked to the door. For no earthly reason that he could have given in logical terms, Mr. Teal followed him. And all the time he had a hot gnawing fear that he was making a fool of himself.

Sergeant Barrow followed Mr. Teal because that was his job. He was a fool anyway, and he knew it. Mr. Teal had often told him so.

In the billiard room, Simon pointed to the panel sagging loose on its hinges as he had torn it off— the hole he had chipped through the wall, the wooden stairway going steeply down into the chalk.

"That's where those six men have been living, so that the ordinary servants never knew there was anything going on. You'll find their beds and everything. That's where I was shut up when they got wise to who I was; and that's where I've just got out of."

Teal said nothing for several seconds. And then the most significant thing was, not what he said, but what he did.

He put his gun back in his pocket and looked at the Saint almost helplessly. No one will ever know what it cost him to be as natural as that. But whatever his other failings may have been, Chief Inspector Teal was a kind of sportsman. He could take it, even when it hurt.

"What else do you know?" he asked.

"That the submarine is out in the Channel now, waiting for the aëroplane to come down. That Renway's up over here in that Hawker ship, with loaded machine guns to shoot down the gold transport, and a packet of bombs to drop on any boat that tries to go to the rescue. That all the telephone lines to Croydon Aërodrome, and between the coast and London, have been cut. That there's a radio transmitter somewhere in this place—I haven't found it yet—which is just waiting to carry on signalling when the transport plane stops. That there isn't a hope in hell of getting a warning through to anywhere in time to stop the raid."

Teal's pink face had gone curiously pale.

"Isn't there anything we can do?" he said.

"There's only one thing," answered the Saint. "Down on the landing field you probably saw a Tiger Moth warming up. It's mine. It's the ship I came here in—but that's another story. With your permission, I can go up in it and try to keep Renway off. Don't tell me it's suicide, because I know all that. But it's murder for the crew of that transport plane if I don't try."

The detective did not answer for a moment. He stared at the floor, avoiding the Saint's straight blue gaze.

"I can't stop you," he said at last; and Simon smiled.

"You can forget about Hoppy hitting that policeman, if you're satisfied with the other evidence," he said. He had a sudden absurd thought of what would shortly be happening to a certain George Wynnis, and a shaft of the old mockery touched his smile like sunlight. "And next time I tell you that some low criminal is putting his stuff onto me, Claud," he said, "you mayn't be so nasty and disbelieving."

His forefinger prodded Mr. Teal's stomach in the old maddening way; but his smile was only reminiscent. And without another word he went out of the billiard room, down the long dark corridor to the open air.

As he climbed into the cockpit of his ship he looked back towards the house and saw Mr. Teal standing on the terrace, watching him. He waved a gay arm, while the mechanic dragged away the chocks from under the wheels; and then he settled down and opened the throttle. The stick slid forward between his knees, the tail lifted, and he went roaring down the field to curve upwards in a steep climbing turn over the trees.

He had left it late enough; and if the wind had been in the north instead of in the south he might have been too late. Winding up the sky in smoothly controlled spirals, he saw the single wide span of a big monoplane coming up from the northern horizon, and knew that it must be the transport plane for which Renway was waiting—no other ship of that build would have been flying south at that hour. He looked for Renway and saw a shape like a big square-tipped seagull swinging round in a wide circle over the Channel, six thousand feet up in the cloudless blue. . . .

Renway! The Saint's steady fingers moved on the stick, steepening the angle of climb by a fraction; and his lips settled in a grim reckless line at the remainder that those fingers had no Bowden trips under them, as Renway's had. He looked ahead through the propeller between a double rank of dancing valve springs instead of between the foreshortened blued jackets of a pair of guns. He was taking on a duel in which nothing but his own skill of hand and eye could be matched against the spitting muzzles of Renway's guns— and whatever skill Renway could bring to the handling of them. And suddenly the Saint laughed —a devilish buccaneering laugh that bared his teeth and edged the chilled steel in his eyes, and was drowned to soundlessness in the smashing howl of his engine and whipped away in the tearing sting of the wind.

Renway! The man who had taken his name in vain. The man who had murdered Enrique and put the Saint's mark on him. The man who had stolen the very aëroplane which he was now going up to fight—and had put the Saint's mark on the theft. The overfed, mincing, nerve-ridden, gaschoked, splay-footed, priggish, yellow-bellied, pompous great official sausage who had had the everlasting gall to say that he himself—he—was the Saint!

Simon Templar glanced at the altimeter and edged the stick forward again along his right thigh. Five thousand feet. . . . A gentle pressure of his right foot on the rudder, and the Tiger Moth swung round and levelled off. The country beneath him was flattened out like a painted map, the light green of fields, the darker green of woods, white ribbons of road, and a white ribbon of surf along the edge of the grey-green sea. The transport plane was slipping across the map half

a mile under him, cruising at ninety miles an hour
air-speed—a lumbering slow-motion cargo boat of
the skies. His eagle's eyesight picked out the letters painted across the upper fabric of the wing:
G-EZQX. His own air-speed indicator showed a
hundred and eighty. It went through his mind
that Renway must have watched him coming up.
Renway must have seen the Tiger Moth warming
up outside the barn and seen it take off. Renway
must have guessed that something had gone wrong
—must, even then, have been staring down with
glazed eyes and twitching fingers, realizing that
there was an obstacle in his path that must be
blotted out.

Simon wondered when the attack would come.

And at that moment it came.

His machine quivered slightly, and he saw an
irregular line of punctures sewing itself diag-
onally across his left wing. Even above the roar of
his own engine he heard the Hawker's guns
cackling their fierce challenge down the sky. He
kicked the rudder and hauled the stick back into
his groin, and grinned mirthlessly at the downward drag of his bowels as the nose of the Moth
surged upwards, skew-eyed, like the prow of a
ship in a terrific sea, and whipped over in a flick
roll that twisted into the downward half of a
tight loop.

XI

RENWAY came about in a skidding turn and plunged after him. Screwed round to watch him over the tail, Simon led him down in a shallow dive, weaving deftly from side to side against the efforts of the Hawker's nose to follow him. Little hiccoughs of orange flame danced on the muzzles of Renway's guns; gleaming squirts of tracer went rocketing past the Moth, now wide on the right, now wide on the left. The Saint went on smiling. Aiming an aëroplane is a fine art, and Renway hadn't had the practice—it was the only factor which Simon could count on his side.

A chance swerve of the Hawker sprayed another line of pockmarks across the fuselage; and Simon drew back on the stick and went over in a sudden loop. Renway shot past under his tail and began to pull round in a belated vertical bank. The Saint put a curve in the fall of his loop and went to meet him. They raced head-on for a collision. Simon held his course till the last split second, lifted his nose slightly for a hint, and zoomed over the Hawker's prop on the upturn of a switchback that carried him clear of death by shaved inches.

He looked down on the swing-over of the stalling turn that ended his zoom, and saw Renway's ship sloping down, wobbling erratically. And his fine-drawn hell-for-leather smile opened out wick-

edly as he opened out the throttle and went down
on the Hawker again in a shrieking power dive.

Down . . . down . . . The engine howling
and the wires moaning shriller and shriller as the
air-speed indicator climbed over three hundred
and twenty miles an hour. His whole body tensed
and waiting fearfully for the first vibration, the
first shiver of the wing tips, that would spell the
break-up of the machine. The Tiger Moth wasn't
built for that sort of work. It was the latest, strongest, fastest thing of its kind in the air; but it
wasn't designed for fighting aërobatics. He saw the
Hawker dodging in hesitant clumsy efforts to
escape; saw Renway's white goggled face staring
back over the empennage, leaping up towards him
at incredible speed. He set his teeth and pulled
back the stick. . . . Now! The Moth seemed to
squat down in the air, momentarily blinding him
as the frightful centrifugal force sucked the blood
down from his head; but the wings held. He
peered over the side and saw the Hawker diving
again, veering wildly in the trembling control of
its pilot.

Simon looped off the top of his zoom and went
down again.

That was the only thing he could do, the only
hope he had of beating the Hawker's guns. Dive
and zoom, loop and dive again. Wipe the Moth's
undercarriage across the Hawker's upper wing
every time. Split-arch and dive again. Ride the
Hawker down by sheer reckless flying. Wing-over

and dive again, wires screaming and engine thundering. Smash down on Renway from every angle of the sky, pitting nerve against nerve, judgment against judgment; make him duck and push the stick forward a little more, every time, with the wheels practically rolling over his head with every hairbreadth miss. Beat him down five hundred feet, a thousand, fifteen hundred. Loop and dive again. . . .

The Saint flew as he had never flown before. He did things that couldn't be done, took chances that could never come off, tore his machine through the air under strains that no ship of its class could possibly survive—and kept on flying. If Renway had been able to fly half as well, it couldn't have gone on.

But Renway couldn't fly half as well. For minutes at a time, his guns never had a target within forty-five degrees of them; and when he brought them round, the target had gone. And each time, a little more of his nerve went with it. He was losing height faster and faster, losing it foot by foot to that nerveless demon of the sky who seemed to have made up his mind to lock their machines together and send them crashing to earth in a single shroud of flame. . . . The Saint smiled with merciless blue eyes like chips of frozen sea water; and dived again. . . . He was going to win. He knew it. He could see the Hawker wobbling more wildly at every moment, plunging more panickily downwards at every effort to escape, sprawling more clumsily on every amateurish manœuvre. He saw Renway's white face looking round again, saw a gloved fist impotently shaken at him, saw the mouth open and heard in his imagination the scream of fury that was ripped to fragments in the wind; and he laughed. He could divine what was in Renway's mind—divine the trembling twitching fear that was shuddering through his flabby limbs, the clammy sweat that must have been breaking out on the soft body—and he laughed through a mask of merciless bronze and swept the Moth screeching down again to whisk its wheels six inches over Renway's helmet. Renway, the snivelling jelly who had called himself the Saint!

Then, for the first time in a long while, he looked down to see what else was happening, and saw that the dogfight had carried them about a mile out over the sea, and the transport plane was just passing over the cliffs.

Renway must have seen it, too. Suddenly, in a frantic vertical bank which almost went into a power spin, he turned and dived on it, his guns rattling.

Simon pushed the stick into the dash, flung the throttle wide, and went down like a plummet.

The sobbing growl of the motor wailed up to an eldritch shriek as the ship slashed through the air. Down and down; with a wind greater than anything in nature slapping his face and plucking at his goggles, while the transport plane curled away in a startled bank and Renway twisted after it. Down and down, in the maddest plunge of that fantastic combat. Fingers cool and steady on the stick, feet as gentle on the rudder bar as the hands of a horseman on the reins, every coördinated nerve and muscle holding the ship together like a living creature. Bleak eyes following every movement of his quarry. Lips parted and frozen in a deadly smile. Down and down, till he saw the bulk of the Imperial Airways monoplane leap upwards past the tail of his eye, and realized that Renway had shot down past his mark without scoring a hit. Downwards still, while Renway flattened out in a slow turn and began to climb again.

Finish it now—before Renway got in another burst which might be lucky enough to score.

Down . . . But there wasn't a civil aëroplane built which could squat down out of a dive like that without leaving its wings behind. It would have to be fairly gentle—and that would be bad enough. As coolly as if he had been driving a car at twenty miles an hour, the Saint judged his margin and felt the resistance on the stick. For one absurd instant he realized that Renway's cockpit was coming stone-cold into the place where the sights would have been if the Moth had been armed. . . .

Crash!

The Moth shuddered under him in an impact like the explosion of a big gun. The painted map whirled across his vision while he fought to get the ship under control. He glanced out to right and left—both wings were still there, apparently intact. The nose of the machine began to lift again, steadily, across the flat blue water and the patchwork carpet, until at last it reached the horizon.

Simon looked down.

The Hawker was going down, five hundred feet below him, in a slow helpless spin. Its tail section was shattered as if a giant club had hit it, and tangled up with it were some splintered spars which looked as if they had belonged to his own landing gear. He had glimpses of Renway struggling wildly in the cockpit, wrestling with the useless controls, and felt a momentary twinge of pity which did not show in his face. After all, the man must have been mad. . . . And even if he had killed and tried to kill, he was not going to the most pleasant of all deaths.

Then Simon remembered the bombs which the Hawker was supposed to carry, and realized that the end might be quick.

He watched the Hawker with a stony fascination. If it fell in the sea, the bombs might not go off. But it was very near the cliffs, bobbing and fluttering like a broken grey leaf. . . . For several seconds he thought it would miss the land.

And then, in one of those queer freaks of aërodynamics which every airman knows, it steadied up. For an instant of time it seemed to hang poised in the air. And then, with the straight clean swoop of a paper dart it dived into the very rim

of the surf which was creaming along the foot of
the white cliffs. There was a split second of horrible suspense; and then the wreckage seemed to
lift open under the thrust of a great tongue of
orange-violent flame. . . .

Simon Templar tasted his sherry and lighted a
cigarette.

"It was fairly easy after that," he said. "I did a
very neat pancake on the water about fifty yards
offshore, and a motorboat brought me in. I met
Teal halfway up the cliff and showed him the
entrance of the cave. We took a peek inside, and
damn if Petrowitz and his crew weren't coming
up the steps. Renway had crashed right on top of
the underwater exit and blown it in—and the sub
was bottled up inside. Apparently the crew had
seen our scrap and guessed that something had
gone wrong, and scuttled back for home. They
were heading for the last round-up with all sail
set, and since they could only get out one at a time
we didn't lose any weight helping them on their
way."

Patricia Holm was silent for a moment.

"You didn't deserve to come out of it with a
whole skin," she said.

"I came out of it with more than that, old darling," said the Saint, with impenitent eyes. "I
opened the safe again before I left, and collected
Hugo's cash box again. It's outside in the car
now."

Hoppy Uniatz was silent somewhat longer. It is doubtful whether he had any clear idea of what all the excitement had ever been about; but he was able to grasp one point in which he seemed to be involved.

"Boss," he said tentatively, "does it mean I ain't gotta take no rap for smackin' de cop?"

The Saint smiled.

"I guess you can put your shirt on it, Hoppy."

"Chees," said Mr. Uniatz, reaching for the whisky with a visible revival of interest, "dat's great! Howja fix it?"

Simon caught Patricia's eye and sighed. And then he began to laugh.

"I got Claud to forget it for the sake of his mother," he said. "Now suppose you tell your story. Did you catch Wynnis?"

The front doorbell rang on the interrogation, and they listened in a pause of silence, while Hoppy poured himself out half a pint of undiluted Scotch. They heard Orace's limping tread crossing the hall, and the sounds of someone being admitted; and then the study door was opened and Simon saw who the visitor was.

He jumped up.

"Claud!" he cried. "The very devil we were talking about! I was just telling Hoppy about your mother."

Mr. Teal came just inside the room and settled his thumbs in the belt of his superfluous overcoat. His china-blue eyes looked as if they were just

about to close in the sleep of unspeakable boredom; but that was an old affectation. It had
nothing to do with the slight heliotrope flush in
his round face or the slight compression of his
mouth. In the ensuing hiatus, an atmosphere radiated from him which was nothing like the sort of
atmosphere which should have radiated from a
man who was thinking kindly of his mother.

"Oh, you were, were you?" he said, and his
voice broke on the words in a kind of hysterical
bark. "Well, I didn't come down from London to
hear about my mother. I want to hear what you
know about a man called Wynnis, who was held
up in his flat at half-past eight this morning . . ."

(BE SEEIN' YA!)

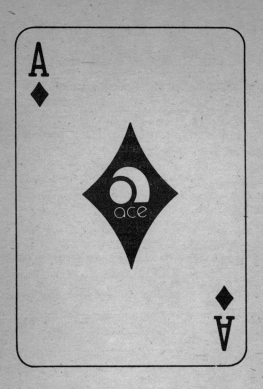

There are a lot more
where this one came from!

ORDER your FREE catalog of ACE paper-backs here. We have hundreds of inexpensive books where this one came from priced from 75¢ to $2.50. Now you can read all the books you have always wanted to at tremendous savings. Order your *free* catalog of ACE paperbacks now.

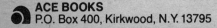

ACE BOOKS
P.O. Box 400, Kirkwood, N.Y. 13795

NICK CARTER

Page-turning Suspense from
CHARTER BOOKS